Love Put Me In, Love Got Me Out

James Blurton

ISBN 978-1-68570-154-3 (paperback)
ISBN 978-1-68570-155-0 (digital)

Christian Faith Publishing
832 Park Avenue
Meadville, PA 16335
www.christianfaithpublishing.com

Printed in the United States of America

CONTENTS

PROLOGUE

It was a hot Friday morning in southern Georgia. Billy was in ankle-deep swamp water, leaning against a cypress tree to catch a moment's rest from being chased by the prison hounds and guards. He watched as the sun's rays filtered through the trees draped in Spanish moss and danced around him. At the age of twenty-one, he thought about how his life had changed over the past couple of years. He started wondering where he would be at the age of fifty or sixty. Would he be on the run for the rest of his life? Would he ever find out who killed Luke Hampton?

Then he heard ole Red's loud howl. He shook his head to clear these thoughts and wiped the sweat from his forehead. From the edge of the swamp, he looked back across the open field he had just ran across, then started to run deeper into the Georgia swamp in hopes of hiding his scent from the hounds.

CHAPTER 1

⚬

Billy's Early Years in Hardwood; Sarah's Murder

It was late summer; the Georgia sun was sometimes shaded by the passing of large grayish rain clouds. Billy, Sam, and his little sister, Bobbie Jo, stood at the end of the railroad platform to watch the passengers disembark from the train that had just pulled in. After a few minutes, they got bored and headed for the road leading out of town. They had gone only a few steps when Billy heard Sam say, "Hey, would you look at that."

Billy turned around, and a boy, around Billy and Sam's age, stepped off the train onto the wooden platform, followed by a young girl. Billy's eyes locked on the girl. She wore a bright floral dress, white shoes, and clutched a small green suitcase. Her hair, golden in color, was lifted slightly from her shoulders by a small gust of wind. Billy couldn't move. He had never seen anyone so beautiful.

Sam, too, was stunned but managed to squeak out, "She'd make a rabbit hug a hound." Billy stood there motionless, saying nothing until Sam pushed him and said, "Did you hear me?"

"Yeah, I heard ya."

"Do you think she's the one that's movin' here?" Sam questioned.

Billy replied in a slow even tone, "I don't know, but I sure hope so. She is the prettiest thing this town has ever seen."

Bobbie Jo could not help but notice the way Billy looked at her. Bobbie Jo was about six years younger than Billy and she knew that Billy thought of her as a tomboy, but she still adored him, even though he did not pay much attention to her. Sam had taught her how to hunt and fish, and she followed Sam and Billy everywhere. She knew she could not compete with this new girl; she was beautiful. Bobbie Jo was shorter, had short dark-brown hair, bright-green eyes, and an average body shape, but she thought, *I am thirteen and still growing*. A tall man pushed his way between Sam and Billy and spoke loudly to the young boy and girl several feet away.

"Sarah Lou, Matt, over here, here I am." The girl turned, clutching her small suitcase as she ran to him.

"Father, I am so glad to see you." She dropped her bag and wrapped her arms around his waist.

"Sweetie, I am so glad you're finally here. Where is your mother?" As he questioned her, he saw his wife stepping off the train. She was a slender woman of average height, with sharp features and golden hair like her daughter's. She would make any man take a second look. As she started toward her husband, Sam and Billy noticed a slight coldness between the husband and wife when they met. The man gave his wife a quick kiss on the cheek, picked up his daughter's luggage, and the four of them headed toward downtown. On the walk home, Billy could not stop thinking about her. For once, he was looking forward to getting back in school.

William Benson had arrived in Hardwood about six months earlier. His banking firm had bought the only bank in town as well as a few banks in the small towns surrounding Hardwood. The Hampton Lumber Company, owned by Tom Hampton, had its headquarters in Hardwood, and being the bank's largest depositor, this was where the Bensons would live. The Bensons had two children: Sarah Lou and her older brother, Matt, who was Billy's and Sam's age. Whereas the Hamptons had two sons: Luke, who was he same age as Billy and Sam, and a younger son, Danny Paul, who was several years younger than Luke and idolized his older brother. Most people around town got to know him as Danny.

Billy, Sam, Luke Hampton, and Matt Benson were all starting their last year in high school. Sara Lou Benson was starting her junior year, and Danny Paul Hampton was still in grade school. Hardwood's high school wasn't large, it only had twenty-five students in the senior class. After the Bensons had lived in Hardwood a few months, everyone in town and school figured that Luke Hampton and Sarah Benson would be together since Luke's dad owned the lumber mill and Sarah's dad owned the bank. They were the wealthiest families in the county. For the first few weeks of school, Billy never spoke to Sarah other than to say hello. As weeks went on, Sarah started talking to Billy more and more, and they both knew there was an attraction igniting between them. Luke and Matt noticed this as well, and word got back to Sarah's parents. She was told not to associate with Billy or any kids of the people who worked for the lumber mill. This did not stop Billy and Sarah from seeing each other when they could, and by the end of the school year, they were in love. Sarah told her parents how she felt about Billy and was going to marry him as soon as she graduated from high school and would not have anything to do with Luke Hampton. Matt Benson, Sarah's older brother, was Luke's lookout. He told Luke each time Sarah and Billy met or talked, making it difficult for them to see each other.

After graduation, Billy and Sam, like most young boys that stayed in Hardwood, went to work at the sawmill. Billy saved as much as he could during Sarah's last year in high school. He wanted to buy a small piece of land and build a house for himself and Sarah. Sarah and Billy saw each other when they could, even though her parents and Luke's family disapproved. A few weeks after Sarah graduated, Sam borrowed his dad's pickup and Bobbie Jo, Sarah, Billy, and Sam drove to the county seat where Sarah and Billy got married. Bobbie Jo tried to show how happy she was for them, but inside, she was heartbroken. She had a crush on Billy the first time she saw him. Sarah's parents were so angry they disowned their daughter. They told her they would never have anything to do with her again, and she should never ask for money. She would now have to live on the wages of a sawmill-hired hand. Billy and Sarah did not have a place to live, so they moved in with Billy's parents, which was uncomfortable. This also made it hard on Billy's dad because he worked for the Hampton Lumber Company, owned by Luke's father, Tom Hampton, who did not like it that Billy's dad was helping his son and Sarah. The Benson and Hampton family had plans for Sarah and Luke to go off to college, come back home, get married, and live happily ever after, but Billy ruined those plans. Luke and his dad were not going to let it be.

Luke did go to college for a year, then came back and became a foreman at the sawmill. At work, Luke made it as difficult as possible for Billy and his dad. Both worked longer hours at harder jobs than most of the other employees. Luke made sure Billy got the lowest-paying jobs at the sawmill, making it difficult for him to save money for the land. Everyone in town thought that Billy's dad had worked himself to death because a little over a year after Sarah and Billy got married, Billy's dad died of a heart attack, and shortly after that, his mother died. Billy's grandparents thought she died of loneliness over the death of her husband, as well as blaming herself for her youngest son's crib death, and she just gave up living. With the death of both of his parents, Billy knew he could not make the mortgage payments to the Hardwood National Bank, owned by the Bensons. After a few months, the bank took the house. With no place to live, Sarah's parents hoped she would leave Billy, move back in with them, marry Luke Hampton, and all would be as planned. However, Sarah told her parents she had no intention of leaving Billy, moving back home, and, most of all, no plans of marrying Luke Hampton. Shortly after Billy's father and mother passed away, Sarah found out she was pregnant. Sarah had decided to get a job to help with the mortgage and bills even though she was pregnant, but Billy disagreed.

After the bank took the house and Sarah being pregnant, Billy's granddad and grandmother made them an offer. They had a twenty-acre tract of land outside of town that they had bought and paid for over the years. Billy's granddad told him and Sarah that since they were their only heirs, they could have the land and build a home on it if they named their first son after him, William Bruce Bersha. It didn't seem to be a hard decision, so Billy agreed. Billy's granddad had been storing up lumber to build a cabin on the land, he gave it to them as well so they could start building a home. They lived with Billy's grandparents for over a year, and with the help of Billy's granddad, Sam, and his dad, they got the little house built. It had one large room in front—the main room with the kitchen on one side—two small bedrooms toward the back, and a bathroom. There was a small room that could be entered from the back of the house that Billy used to get out of his work or hunting clothes so as not to mess up the rest of the house. When Luke Hampton found out that Billy's granddad had given them the land and lumber, Billy was put on swing shifts at the sawmill, and anytime the workload got behind, Billy and Sam had to stay and work until it was caught up. This made it hard for Billy to help with the house, and he hated being away from Sarah.

While they were living with Billy's grandparents, Sarah had Sally Ann. Billy's granddad was a little disappointed that it wasn't a boy, but Sarah named her after Billy's grandmother, whose first name was Sally. Granddad and Grandma Bersha loved Sally Ann as if she was their daughter. They would take care of her a couple of times a month so Billy and Sarah could have some time alone, go to town to eat, or be with Sam and his girlfriend. The townspeople would stare and talk about them behind their backs. They would whisper to one another; a sawmill boy marrying a rich girl, she should have married that Hampton boy, she would be much better off and wouldn't have to live in that little shack outside town, and now the baby has to live there as well. It seemed as though Billy and Sarah's only friends were Sam, his little sister, Bobbie Jo, and their parents.

Billy, Sarah, and little Sally Ann were happy; they just didn't get out much. When Sarah would go to town while Billy was at work, her brother, Matt, would tell Luke, and they both would find her and tell her how much better off she would be if she left Billy. Luke even told her he would take Sally Ann as his own if she would leave Billy. Sarah told Luke she would never leave Billy. On one occasion, Matt and Luke cornered her, and Matt told her, Billy works at a dangerous place, there is always the possibility of an accident, then where would she go, what would she do? Sarah knew Luke and Matt were capable of causing an accident, but she would never marry Luke Hampton.

When Billy got in that evening, she told him what Matt and Luke had said and that he needed to be extra careful.

Tensions were growing at work between Luke and Billy. Billy knew he had to control his anger so he could keep his job. He had a wife and a new baby to think of. They thought about moving to another town but did not have the money to move, and his grandparents were getting older and depended on him more and more to help around their home. One Friday afternoon, Matt, who oversaw the loading of the rail cars and shipments going out of the sawmill, told Billy and Sam they had to come in early that Saturday morning. Enough timber needed to be sawed to size and loaded onto flatcars to be shipped out first thing Monday morning. Sam had to work the extra day because he was Billy's friend. It was a way Luke had of punishing Sam. Billy and Sam both knew there was enough lumber to ship out Monday morning, and they both knew if they didn't go on Saturday, it would simply cause more trouble in the future.

Sam came by the following morning to pick Billy up so Sarah would have their truck if she needed to go to town. Billy kissed Sarah and the baby and headed out the door to Sam's truck, knowing he would probably be late getting back. Just after lunch, Luke and Matt went to the mill and checked on Sam and Billy's progress. Luke wanted them to know how important it was for them to get the flatcars loaded and ready to ship Monday morning. Even if it took all night, it had to get done. Again, Billy and Sam knew it was just to keep them working so Billy would have as little time with his family as possible. Billy had a feeling Luke was up to something, so he and Sam took no breaks. About midafternoon, Sam's dad stopped by to check on them and saw the boys might be working till after dark, so he pitched in; and with his help, by late afternoon, the timber was cut and loaded on the flatcars and chained down. With the flatcars loaded, they got in Sam's truck and headed for Billy's house, which was a couple of miles outside of Hardwood.

Billy got out of the truck and started walking down the dirt drive to his house. The little frame house sat at the front of the twenty acres, a couple of hundred feet from the county road. It was surrounded in back and on both sides by a thick forest, with vines and Spanish moss hanging from the trees. There was a path along the side of the house that made a fork at the back of the house, one path went into the woods while the other path led to the entrance at the back of the house. Billy used this one that led to the small room where he took off his work clothes.

As he passed by the front porch, he heard Sarah scream, "Stop, get out of here!"

He ran onto the porch, shoved open the front door, and saw Sarah lying on the floor with no clothes on and Luke standing over her. It looked like blood was coming from the corner of her mouth.

Luke turned, grabbed the pistol he had just tucked in his pants, and pointed it at Billy. Sarah screamed, and with her foot, kicked Luke's leg. This made Luke pull the trigger; the bullet hit the doorframe just to the left of Billy's head. Small splinters of wood went flying. This gave Billy enough time to dive at Luke; grabbing him around the waist, they both fell to the floor, knocking the pistol from Luke's hand. With Billy on top of him, Luke managed to crawl to the pistol and grab it. Billy grabbed Luke's hand with the pistol, and they wrestled on the floor, trying to land hits with their free hands. In the struggle, the gun fired. They rolled back and forth on the floor until Billy was able to pull his leg up between them and gave Luke a hard shove to the stomach. This separated the two, and the pistol came free and slid just out of reach of both of them. Billy rolled over and grabbed the pistol then looked over to see Luke get to his feet and head for the door. Billy aimed and pulled the trigger but missed, and Luke kept running. Billy turned to Sarah lying on the floor; blood was pooling under her. He knelt down and held her head in his hands, and he could see the life leaving her eyes.

She looked up at him and said softly, "I will always love you." She let out a slow soft breath of air. He told her to try and hang on but knew that was her last breath. Billy screamed out her name, knowing she was gone.

Anger raced through his body. Clutching the pistol, he jumped up and ran out the front door looking for Luke. He looked up the dirt drive leading to the county road but didn't see Luke. He ran around to the side of the cabin and saw Luke running along the trail leading into the woods and started after him. In the excitement, Luke had taken the path going into the woods instead of the one leading to the county road, hoping to lose Billy in the woods. The trail twisted and curved, and at a point where the path straightened out, Billy caught a glimpse of him and pulled the trigger. Billy continued to run, but because of the twisting and curving of the trail, Luke never came into sight again. Billy thought maybe he had hit him with his wild shot. As Billy rounded a sharp curve in the path, there he was, lying in the middle of the dirt path with a large knife in his chest. Billy froze and looked around, but saw no one. Who had done this? He heard Luke take a deep breath, then saw Luke's chest sink in. He did not move again. Billy dropped the pistol and ran back to the cabin, hoping he was wrong about Sarah and that she was alive. When Billy went through the front door, she was still lying on the floor, no life in her. He sat down beside her and held her head on his lap for a long time. He was jolted out of his thoughts by the crying of Sally Ann. He prayed that she was okay; he picked her up, and she stopped crying and seemed to be all right.

He put a sheet over Sarah, and with Sally Ann in one arm, drove to his grandparents' house and told them what had happened. Billy and his granddad drove to the sheriff's office. At the sheriff's office, Billy told them exactly what had happened. Sheriff Smith told two of his deputies to drive to the house and take a look to confirm what he had been told. The sheriff sat back in his chair and looked at Billy. He knew that Luke Hampton and Billy did not get along. The sheriff felt the same as most people in Hardwood, Sarah Lou should have married Luke Hampton. Billy sat there, remembering the times his dad and the sheriff did not see eye to eye on the corruption that went on in Hardwood. Billy wondered how much influence that would have on the story he told about finding Luke with a knife in his chest. Billy started to worry about what was going to happen. The sheriff took Billy and his granddad to a little room off to the side of his office and told them to wait until his deputies returned.

After an hour, the sheriff came in and told Billy he would have to stay in jail until the bodies were brought to town and the doctor could look at them. Billy's granddad asked if Billy was being charged with murder. The sheriff said the county district attorney would decide that. Until he knew more, Billy would stay there. His grand-dad gave him a hug and said it would all be okay, but Billy had his doubts. The Benson and Hampton families ran the town and, as far as he knew, most of the officials, which included the sheriff.

Throughout the next day, sitting in his cell, Billy could hear faint conversations between the sheriff and some of the townspeople he had called in. Billy heard the doctor say Sarah Lou had been raped and died from a gunshot. Luke was killed with a knife about one hundred yards in the woods behind the cabin. The people that the sheriff interviewed knew very little about what had happened. Sam and his little sister, Bobbie Jo, came to see Billy and said that most of the town believed Billy had killed Luke but didn't know who shot Sarah Lou. They guessed that Billy's story about fighting with Luke caused the gun to go off, hitting Sarah and killing her. As he sat in his cell, listening to what conversations he could hear, Billy knew without witnesses, he would probably go to prison and probably get the death penalty.

CHAPTER 2

❧

The Trial and Prison Time

Billy spent a week in jail, and with what little evidence there was, the county district attorney charged him with the killing of Luke Hampton, but not Sarah Lou. He thought her death was an apparent accident. The trial was set for the next court session, which would be in thirty days. Neither Billy nor his grandparents had the money for an attorney, so the county appointed one. There were only two attorneys in Hardwood: one was the county district attorney, and the other was Jack Taylor, who was appointed to be Billy's attorney. Jack Taylor had been practicing in Hardwood for only a couple of years and mainly handled small lawsuits—family matters, wills, divorces, and minor offenses. In their first meeting, he told Billy that he was not a criminal attorney but would do what he could. Billy knew he was going to prison; too many people in town had already convicted him of Luke's murder. Some were even saying he had gotten Sarah pregnant, so she would marry him instead of Luke. This could not be true; Sally Ann was born over a year and a half after they were married, but that was not considered in small-town gossip. Sam and Bobbie Jo came to visit as often as they could. Bobbie Jo always left with tears in her eyes and always told Billy she knew he could not have killed Luke. Billy began to feel sorry for her, knowing she wanted to help, but she nor Sam could do anything. Billy's grandparents would bring Sally Ann so he could see her and they were glared at by most of the townspeople when they did, Billy asked them not to come anymore. He did not want to cause any more problems than they already had, especially taking care of a new baby at their age.

It seemed to take forever for the first day of the trial to arrive. Billy was so nervous the first day of the trial his attorney kept asking if he was sick. No, he wasn't sick, he just knew there was no chance as he looked at the people that sat in the jurors' seats. Billy knew they had already convicted him. Billy knew his attorney would do the best job he could, but he had no chance of going up against the county attorney, who probably had represented most of the jurors at one time or another.

The first day of the trial only a few character witnesses were called revealing very little except that Luke and Billy did not get along. At the end of the day, the judge told the court the trial would continue first thing in the morning with closing arguments. Billy's attorney objected and said since there were no more witnesses, he wanted to call his client the first thing the next morning to tell his version of what happened. The judge agreed and told Billy's attorney he would have his chance in the morning. Billy and his attorney were led back to his cell, where Billy asked what his chances were. His attorney explained he would call him to the stand in the morning. He thought they had a 50-50 chance. The attorney and Billy both knew he would probably be charged with the death of Luke Hampton and sentenced to death.

The following day, the judge asked the district attorney if he had any more witnesses to call to the stand. The district attorney said no. Billy's attorney had called Sam and his dad the day before. Sam had testified that he and Billy had been told to work that Saturday to cut lumber and load it on flatcars, which they did, and with the help of Sam's dad had finished around 5:00 p.m. Then Sam told the court he drove Billy home, dropped him off, and after stopping by a little store, he went straight home. He did not see or hear anything while dropping Billy off. Sam's dad testified that he had finished his work and checked on the boys and knew they would be working until after dark, so he helped them, and around 5:00 p.m. they completed the loading. He said Sam got home around 5:30 p.m. after dropping Billy off at his house, and Sam was at home the rest of Saturday evening. The judge then asked Billy's attorney if he still wanted to call his client to the stand, and he said yes.

"I call William Billy Bersha." Billy's attorney asked him to tell the court exactly what happened after Sam had dropped him off at his house.

Billy told the court he had worked all day, and Sam dropped him off around 5:00 p.m., and when he walked by the front porch of his house, he heard Sarah screaming, "Get out of here." He pushed open the front door and saw Sarah lying naked on the floor, with Luke standing over her. It looked like blood was coming from her mouth. Billy said Luke pulled out a pistol and shot at him, and the bullet hit the doorframe. This gave him time to jump at Luke, and they wrestled around on the floor, and the pistol fired again. Billy said he somehow was able to push Luke away, and in doing so, the pistol fell to the floor, and he crawled over and grabbed it. Luke was running out the door, and Billy shot at him but missed. Billy said he then went to Sarah, and she died in his arms. He jumped up and ran after Luke, who had taken the path that led into the woods. The path had bends and curves in it, and when he saw Luke running on one of the straighter parts of the path, he shot at Luke again. Billy said he did not see Luke fall, but when he rounded a curve in the path, he found Luke lying on the ground with a knife in his chest. Billy said he looked around for anyone that might have done the stabbing but saw no one. He then told the court he went back to the house, covered Sarah with a sheet, got his daughter, Sally Ann, drove to his grandfather's house, and told him what had happened. His grandfather drove him to the sheriff's office, and he told the sheriff what had happened.

When Billy was through, the judge asked the district attorney if he had any further questions; he said, "yes, only one." The district attorney asked Billy if he was angry when he walked in and saw what was going on. Billy knew the only answer he could give was yes, which would seal his fate of guilt, even though he didn't kill Luke Hampton.

Billy wanted to yell out to the courtroom, "Wouldn't you be mad, too, if you saw your naked wife lying on the floor, with Luke Hampton standing over her?" He knew it would make no difference.

The judge gave his orders to the jurors, and they filed out to the side room to discuss the verdict.

Billy and his attorney, along with Sam and Bobbie Jo, sat in a small room across the hall from the courtroom, waiting for the decision. In about three hours, they were called back to the courtroom for the verdict. Billy did not look at the jurors. He just looked down at the tabletop, listening. The judge told Billy to stand, and he asked the juror foreman to read the verdict. All Billy heard was guilty, and immediately thought of hanging or an electric chair.

During the trial, his attorney stressed the fact the Luke was killed with a knife, and not shot. The gun that Luke and Billy had fought over had been fired four times. One bullet was fired, hitting the doorframe; the second while Luke and Billy were wrestling on the floor, probably hitting Sarah Lou, causing her death; and the other two were the ones Billy fired at Luke going out the door and then running down the path. The gun was a revolver that held six rounds, and there were two bullets left in the cylinder. He had argued, why would Billy have used a knife instead of the gun to kill Luke? This question did puzzle a couple of the jurors, but the district attorney had said he probably dropped the gun while running, and a knife was all he had. Billy's attorney reminded the jurors that the sheriff's deputies had found the gun beside Luke's body and not dropped along the path. If he had the gun, why would he use a knife? Because it was brought out that Sarah Lou's death was considered an accident, and it had not been proven why Billy used a knife instead of the gun, the jurors had a choice—death or life without parole. They decided on a sentence of ninety-nine years to life, without parole, instead of the death penalty. It was still a death sentence to Billy.

After the trial, Billy was placed back in the local jail cell and told he would be driven to the prison in South Georgia that coming Friday. That gave him two days to figure out what to do with Sally Ann. His grandparents were too old to look after her, and he did not want her going to an orphanage. Most of the town thought she should go to the Bensons so she could have a good secure life. Billy did not want that for her, as they had disowned their own daughter. What would they tell their granddaughter about her mother and father? That her dad killed her mother and a man and was put in prison? Sam and Bobbie Jo had talked to their parents, and they had agreed to take her since her biological grandparents wanted nothing to do with her. It was decided the Williamsons would take her, and they would bring her to the prison for visits when they could. Billy was hesitant about them bringing her to prison and told them to simply tell her that her mother had died and her father had left town, and they had taken her in. He was sure she would eventually find out the truth about her mother and him on her own. He didn't want to see her, which wasn't the truth. He simply thought it was best. Billy's granddad did not agree, and he had always told Billy, telling the truth is always the best. Even though he was in prison, he was still her father, and she needed to know that he loved her.

Friday morning came. With tears in all their eyes, Billy said his goodbyes to everyone and gave everyone a long hug, stepped onto the prison bus, and never looked back as it pulled away from the sheriff's office.

It was an all-day drive to the prison, and it was dark when the bus pulled through the gate at the prison. Billy tried to sleep on the bus ride, but with all that was filling his mind, he only took short naps. When the bus finally stopped, he was abruptly slapped on the shoulder with a stick. A tall man with a rough face told him naptime is over, and he had to get up and follow the others. There were thirteen prisoners on the bus. They unloaded and were told to form a line in front of a long building and not to move. They stood there for what seemed like forever. The boy standing beside Billy said he had to pee. Billy told him he needed to go as well, but both were afraid to ask. Finally, a guard came out of a door from the building in front of them. The guard walked forward slowly, stopped, and slightly spread his legs apart.

He told them, "You're mine now, so listen up."

He told them as he pointed to the building behind him, "This building is your new home from now on, and you better take care of it." There were poles at each corner of the fenced-in prison yard with dim lights on them. The lights gave off only a little light, but it was enough for the guard to see that the boy standing next to Billy had peed his pants. The guard walked up to him and drove his nightstick into his stomach, and he fell to his knees in pain. Billy knew this was going to be a hard place to spend the rest of his life, especially for something he didn't do. The guard told them to get in their new home, sort out the bedding, lights out in five minutes.

The prisoners stood there for a second, and another guard snapped a whip and said, "Get moving, now!" With this command, everyone started to run toward the door.

There were dim lights at each end of the long room, small iron beds along the walls with rolled-up mattresses, and small pillows on top. There were two beds at the far end of the long room, with someone in each bed with their backs turned toward them.

One of the men in the back said, "You have four minutes to get the beds sorted out, then it's lights out."

Billy stopped at the second bed from the door and started unrolling the thin mattress with a pillow on top. There was one sheet and a thin blanket rolled inside the mattress. He finished unrolling the mattress, put the sheet and blanket on top and wondered where he could go to pee. At the far end of the room, there was a dim light coming from under a doorway. Billy hoped that it was a bathroom. He went toward the door, but the lights in the main room went out but he could still see the dim light coming from the crack at the bottom of the door. He got to the door and slowly opened it. There were four wooden toilets on one side of the small room and four showerheads on the other. It was such a relief to pee; he had been holding it till he thought his bladder would burst.

As he stood there, he heard men in the main room arguing over the beds. Then he heard a loud noise that sounded like two pieces of metal being slammed together. Billy buttoned up his pants just as the two men came tumbling through the small doorway into the bathroom and were wrestling on the floor, both trying to land blows on the face of the other without much luck. The lights in the barracks came on, and standing in the bathroom doorway was a tall man.

In a deep loud voice, he yelled out, "Take it outside or get to bed. If you go outside, don't come back in, you're sleeping outside tonight." He turned and walked away.

The two men got up, mumbling to each other, and walked to the beds they had knocked together during their wrestling. They pulled them apart and settled into them without saying another word. Billy slowly walked out of the bathroom to his bunk. It had been slid away from the wall, but it was still empty, so he settled in as best he could for the night as the lights went out. Deep sleep was tough to accomplish. He only took short naps, which were interrupted by someone snoring or crying out. As the night slowly passed by, Billy lay there thinking of the people he had lost in his short life and blamed himself for their lost lives.

The next morning, everyone in the barracks was called outside and told to form a line. One by one, each man's name was called and taken to see the warden. Billy stood scared in front of the warden, who sat behind a wooden desk in a high-back swivel chair that creaked under his weight every time he moved. This was Billy's first time in front of any kind of authority that had total control over his life. He had been called to the office at school for minor things that boys do—getting too rough on the playground, not being at class on time—but nothing like this. This man could make his life a living hell if he did not follow every rule.

The warden, in a deep and powerful voice, said as he looked at a piece of paper, "Billy Bersha, looks like you're here till ya die, you won't last ninety-nine years. There ain't no second chances here, if you break a rule, in the box you go. So, you ain't gonna break no rules, are ya, boy?"

In a shaky voice, Billy said, "No."

The warden slammed his big fat fist down on the top of the desk with a thud, and shouted, "That's 'no, sir, boss.' Now say it."

Billy gathered himself as best he could and said, "No, sir, boss," in a way that he hoped the warden would accept.

"Guard," the warden hollered. A tall thin man appeared. He had a pistol in his holster on one side of his hip, and on the other hip was a small club hanging from a clip. He led Billy back outside where other prisoners were still standing. Everyone stood outside while each prisoner had his meeting with the warden, which took most of the morning.

There was no breakfast or lunch that day, and after everyone had their meeting, they were told to go back to the bunkhouse and wait for supper. Most of them just laid on their beds without talking.

Billy thought to himself, *how did I get here?* It was almost dark when one of the two men, who slept at the back of the barracks, came through the door and told everyone supper was in the bags, and he tossed two large bags on the floor. There were dried slices of bread in one bag, and in the other was what looked like jerky. Billy was one of the last to get his turn, and there wasn't much left, but he ate what he found. After eating, he got a drink of water out of a community drinking bucket that was by the entrance of the barracks.

Shortly after the small meal, the lights went out. Billy lay on his bunk, trying to sleep, again, it did not come easy; finally, he drifted off. That was his first full day of prison life.

Billy lay in bed the next morning watching the dust particles float round in the breeze and thought, *I will be here for the rest of my life. How will I survive?* A door opened from the small room at the far end of the barracks, and the same tall man from the night before stepped through it. Billy had not noticed this door the night before. He only saw the open doorway leading to the bathroom. The man stood there, slapping a short round wooden club into the palm of his open hand. He told everyone he is the top boss and that he rules this barracks and everyone in it. There were four barracks, and this one was his. They would obey him and his rules, no matter what the bosses of the other barracks did.

The barrack's boss walked slowly down the middle of the long room, looking at each one of them, and when he reached the double screen doors leading to the outside, he turned and said something Billy would never forget.

"There's one main rule—do as I say, and you will have it a lot easier during your stay here. Break my rules, and you will spend time in the hot box, and time will be added to your enjoyable stay here at camp happy."

Billy thought, *What's happy about this place?* The boss turned and waved his arm in a gesture for them to follow. All the prisoners hurried outside and watched him draw a long straight line in the dirt and pointed at it. Most everyone ran to it, not knowing if that was what he wanted, and turned to face him. The other inmates moved a little slower now, knowing this was what he wanted them to do. There were fifteen prisoners in our barracks and about the same in the other two barracks. There were four barracks in total: number 1, 2, and our barrack was number 3. Number 4 barrack was not occupied. Another group of prisoners from another prison was expected to arrive in a week or two.

They stood there for some time, waiting as the sun slowly rose higher in the sky and beat down on them, while half a dozen guards and the barracks bosses waited in the shade of the porch. Everyone was told to turn around, the overweight warden came out of the door of his building, across the prison yard from the barracks. He walked slowly toward them and pushed his way between the groups of prisoners and walked onto the barracks' porch. He told everyone that as long as he had been here, no one had ever escaped. They might be gone for a day, maybe two, but they had always been caught and paid dearly for it. Some even died in the hot box, so the prisoners better think twice before trying to escape. His guards were good, but what he had that was better than any other prison in the state were his tracking hounds. They were the best in the south. They could even track a man through the swamp, which pretty much surrounded the prison for miles in every direction; they always got their man. He told them some other rules and instructions, then he told the guards to get on with the day's duties.

Billy could see and hear the other prisoners being told by their bosses what their work details would be for the day. Their barracks boss stood in front, looking over them. He said his name was Ed, but they were to call him Boss Ed. He had worked at this prison longer than anyone else, even the warden. He was here when it first opened and probably would die here, just like most of them. He split the prisoners into two groups. The group Billy was in had the job of cleaning the barracks, top to bottom, and making any repairs that needed to be addressed, such as holes in the screens on the windows, patch any holes on the roof, and sweep out the entire barrack, except his room. They were told not to go into his room. The other group

his

from ~~their~~ barracks, along with all the other prisoners in the camp, lined up and walked out the main gate.

By the end of the day, the repairs were done, and the barracks was cleaned. The prisoners were sitting on their bunks, talking to one another about where they had come from, how they ended up there, and how long their sentence was. Billy was the only one with a murder conviction and a lifetime sentence, while the others had ten to twenty years.

The other half of Billy's barrack's prisoners came into the barracks; they looked like they had been working in the dirt all day. They were tired, hot, and smelled like sour mud. Some of them headed straight for the showers and didn't even undress, while the others lay on the floor or their beds.

Boss Ed yelled from the porch, "Okay, girls, it is time to eat, line up outside."

They had not eaten all day and Billy wondered if there would ever be breakfast or lunch. Billy found out later that there was coffee in the morning and maybe some corn bread, if there was enough time before the work detail. Lunch was questionable; it depended on the work detail and if the cooks felt like making it. There was always an evening meal, but sometimes it was just soup made from the leftovers of the day before.

Everyone jumped up and ran outside and formed a line and waited for instructions, scared to say anything or move. Boss Ed waved his stick to follow him, and they followed as Boss Ed walked to the long building at the far end of the compound. Inside there were long tables with benches that seated about twenty people. Just inside the doorway were two small tables; the first one had round metal plates in stacks, wooden spoons in a small bucket and tin cups in stacks of about ten each. At the other table were four men in white shirts and pants standing in front of two large pots, one small pot, and a flat tray with what looked like corn bread on it.

After the guards moved through the food line, the prisoners were told to move along to get their food. No one spoke as they slowly moved through the line and found a seat. Billy had no idea what he was eating, except for the corn bread. He had not eaten all day, so he ate everything he had been given without question. Being a new prisoner to the camp, Billy watched the old meat, as they were called, finish their meals and sat without saying anything. When the guards finished their meals, they picked up their plates, cups, and spoons and headed to the double doors, dropping the plates in one bucket of water while dropping the wooden spoons and tin cups in another bucket of water. They turned and called out their barracks number, and the prisoners of that barracks stood up. They made a single file and walked to the door. They dropped their plates, cups, and spoons in the same buckets as the guards and followed their bosses out the door.

Boss Ed was the last to call out, "Barracks number 3!"

All fifteen prisoners jumped up, grabbed their plates, cups, and spoons, and did the same as the other groups, hoping they were doing it correctly. They walked across the camp yard to their barracks and were told to stand in front of their beds. Boss Ed walked to the middle of the barracks and told everyone to get to bed you are going to need all the rest you can get. Your work duties tomorrow would be spreading gravel on a county road. Billy's group had been assigned to cover five miles of road, and they would get it done even if they had to work after dark—no lunch, and cold supper, if any at all. Some stripped off and took quick showers, while others went straight to bed. Billy did not shower; he just got undressed and lay on top of his bedcovers. He started thinking of home and how much he missed his family, especially Sarah, who he would never see again, and his daughter. After a while, the men in the showers came back to their bunks and started mumbling to one another about the work that would be done tomorrow. It took about thirty minutes for everyone to settle down, and other than a cough or a moan from someone, Billy eventually drifted off to sleep.

Billy was startled awake the next morning by Boss Ed, as he walked down the middle of the hall, banging on a pan with a wooden spoon and telling everyone to get dressed and be in the yard in five minutes. Billy jumped up, got dressed as fast as he could, ran out to the yard, and took his place in line. He thought, *at least we're going to get breakfast this morning before starting the long and hard day of shoveling gravel.* He was used to hard work, but this work was going to be different. Everyone knew if they said or questioned anything, it might mean a slap across the back with Boss Ed's cane or even time in the hot box. No one had any idea which it would be, and everyone did as they were told and headed across the prison yard to the mess hall. They stood in line waiting as the other prisoners from barracks 1 and 2 went first, which seemed to take forever. Billy began wondering if he would even have time to eat. As the line moved slowly forward, he grabbed a tin plate, a wooden spoon, and a tin cup. He moved to the first man serving what looked like oatmeal; then the next man gave him a piece of toasted bread, and there was a large kettle filled with something that looked like black coffee.

Billy walked to the long table and sat down. Looking at his plate, he wondered if he should eat it, or would he get sick if he ate it? In the middle of the table was a wooden bowl with a wooden spoon and something that looked like sugar. One prisoner put some on his oatmeal but quickly found out it was salt. Billy ate his without salt or sugar and without hesitation. He ate half of the toast and drank the warm strong coffee, knowing that this was going to be all he would get until lunch, if he got lunch. Boss Ed came to the table, told them to finish up and be outside in five minutes, ready to work. There was no time for the restroom, and everyone hurried out to the prison yard and formed two lines, following the lead of the other prisoners.

All the prisoners moved forward to the barbed wire gate. Just outside the gate, there was a road that ran, in a somewhat-north to south direction, in front of the prison. About one hundred yards south down the road was a fork with another road leading off in another direction. Boss Ed, sitting on his horse, pointed and said, "That way."

Barracks number 3 followed one of the trustees sitting on a wagon pulled by two mules. It seemed as though they had walked a couple of miles when the wagon stopped, and Boss Ed told everyone to get a shovel or rake from the wagon. Two prisoners were told to get into the back of the wagon and start shoveling the gravel out of the wagon onto the middle of the road. The rest of the group used shovels and rakes to scatter the gravel covering the entire surface of the road. This was their job for the day, and five miles of road had to be covered no matter how long it took.

By noon, Billy and everyone else was exhausted and welcomed the short lunch break. Billy got a slice of bread, a piece of tough meat, and a cup of water but was glad to get what was offered. Some men ate fast, then lay back in the grass to get a little rest. Billy ate slower, trying to make the bread and meat last as long as possible.

He had just taken his last sip of water when Boss Ed yelled, "Time's up, girls, back to work."

All of them grabbed their shovels and rakes and headed to the back of the wagon. Billy and another prisoner were told to replace the two men in the wagon, and they looked forward to the change. After a couple of hours, Billy wished he was back on the ground raking. The continuous bending over and shoveling was taking its toll on his back. As the prisoners rounded a curve in the road, there was a white flag about one hundred yards ahead. Billy hoped that was the end of the five miles of graveling the road.

As they approached the flag, Boss Ed said, "That's it for today. This is the end of the five miles."

Billy didn't know if boss Ed felt sorry for them or if they had done a good day's worth of work, but he told all of the prisoners to get on the wagon for the ride back to the prison. Maybe Boss Ed wasn't such a bad person after all, or maybe he just wanted to get there in time for a hot supper. Whatever the reason, Billy was glad to be riding instead of walking.

After reaching the prison yard, Boss Ed said, "Thirty minutes before supper."

Everyone jumped from the wagon and ran inside, stripping off their clothes as they ran for the shower. Knowing it would be crowded, Billy waited, knowing that everyone could not be in the shower at the same time. He lay down on his bunk and fought sleep. He knew falling asleep would mean missing supper. Seeing some of the men coming out of the shower, he ran in for a quick rinse with cold water and got dressed just as Boss Ed told them to chow up. This time, no lines formed in the prison yard; everyone headed for the chow hall, but they still ate at the same assigned tables.

Someone asked one of the older prisoners, "Why didn't we form groups outside like before?"

The old-timer said, "On workdays, when prisoners are taken outside the camp to work, they don't have to form groups and wait their turn for supper. The guards want to eat as soon as they can while it is hot. Barracks groups are only formed when there is work to be done inside the camp."

Barracks number 3 finished eating, and Boss Ed said, "Head to the barracks and get some sleep. We start on the next five miles first thing in the morning."

Billy lay on top of his blanket; the nights were getting hotter, and he wanted to stay as cool as possible for as long as he could. This had been one of the hardest days of work he had ever done. This was what he had to look forward to for the rest of his life. Tears started to roll down his cheeks, but he wiped them away, hoping no one saw him. He made himself a promise that someday somehow, he would get out of this place and find out who killed Luke Hampton. For now, he needed to get to sleep and as much rest as he could; tomorrow would be another long day.

CHAPTER 3

❧

Ole Red and the Escape

After a few weeks of prison life, most of the new prisoners had the routine down. They worked most days spreading gravel, mending roadside fences, swinging a sling blade cutting the grass along the roadside, digging ditches, cleaning them out—anything the county needed done, they did it. Sometimes there was lunch, and sometimes there wasn't. Most of the time, there was a hot supper, but there were times when supper was only a cold sandwich. This was usually when someone on the crew messed up or spoke back to Boss Ed or one of the trustees, and everyone was punished with a cold supper.

On one particular day, Billy and a few other inmates were repairing barbed wire fencing along the road and had it pulled as tight as they could. A couple of prisoners were told to start nailing it to the posts. Either they didn't hear to start nailing, or they didn't start on purpose. Billy wasn't sure, but someone yelled okay, and the prisoners holding the wire tight let go. It flew back in a coil and hit one of the trustees in the face, which sliced his cheek open. All the prisoners on that work detail were punished—no supper, and two days in the hot boxes. That was the worst two days since he had arrived at the prison. The two days seemed like a week. He did not know if he would make it. A slice of bread and one cup of water in two days, but he survived.

During his first year at the prison, several prisoners attempted to escape. Every escapee was caught and put in the hot box. They would spend one to two weeks in the hot box; most survived, but three of them died. One of the survivors was never the same; he just went around talking to himself. On one occasion, the trustees and guards in charge of tracking an escapee came back in the evening without the prisoner. The prison warden, Calhoun, came out of his office, stood on the porch, and demanded a reason why they came back without the escapee. One of the guards who had been transferred from another prison blamed it on the hounds and started kicking the hound that was on the end of the leash that he was holding.

Billy had been working on the warden's porch and was standing at the end of it when the guard started kicking the dog. Billy never liked anyone mistreating animals, so he jumped down and grabbed the leash from the guard's hand and jerked the dog away. The guard raised his nightstick and hit him across the shoulder. Billy dropped to the ground but still held onto the leash, and the guard started kicking the dog again. Billy rolled in front of the dog and took the kicks. Finally, the warden yelled enough and told the young guard he was through; go inside. The warden told his assistant to pay the guard and told the young guard to get out he was done at this prison. Billy slowly got up and checked on the dog. It could not get up. He tried to pick the dog up, but it yelped. One of the legs appeared broken, and its ribs were probably cracked or broken as well, because it yelped when Billy felt the dog's side. The warden asked Billy what was wrong, and he told him what he thought. The warden said he's no good if the leg was broken and told one of the other guards to shoot it, and he did.

Billy gave the warden a hateful look and said, "I wasn't sure it was broken; it was just a guess. It might have been fixable."

The warden looked at Billy and said, "You should have made a better decision about its condition." Billy felt like he had sentenced the dog to death. He felt sick, got up, and started walking to the barracks without looking back. The warden yelled out, "Don't you walk away. I wanna see you in my office now!"

Billy turned, looked at the warden with a stern look on his face, and walked up the steps into his office. He stood in front of his desk, waiting to see how many days he was going to get to spend in the box. Billy heard him come in, and the door slammed shut. He walked to his desk and flopped down on his big swivel chair. Billy thought it was going to break the way he sat down hard on it.

He looked at Billy for a long time and said, "Boy, I could put you in the hot box for your actions out there in front of the other prisoners, and I should, to show the other inmates this prison does not tolerate that kind of disrespect."

After a little more than a year at the prison, this would be the second time he was going to spend time in the box. Billy had always tried to do what he was told without question and never step out of line, even though there were many times he knew what was going on wasn't right or fair, and kicking the dog was one of those times. But this was a prison, nothing was fair, and there were no rights, just time.

The warden asked his name, and he replied, "I am Billy Bersha."

The warden asked, "What are you in here for?"

Billy replied, "Murder." But did not say anything about not doing the killing; that would have fallen on deaf ears.

"Tell me about yourself, where you are from," the warden asked. Billy thought the warden would have known about all his prisoners but come to find out, he didn't really care about who they were or why they were in prison. For him, they were there to do time. Billy told him that he was from Hardwood, Georgia, and had worked in a lumber mill, and in his spare time, he trained hunting and tracking dogs and never thought it was right to mistreat animals, especially dogs. This caught the warden's attention.

"How long have you been training them?"

"Most of my life. I love dogs and hated to see any dog being abused, that is why I spoke up out there in the yard. I didn't think it was right to kick the dog for something it may not have done. Maybe it just wasn't that good of a tracker."

Billy could see the warden's face soften a little.

"I, too, have a soft spot for tracking hounds and love to hunt. I have done it all my life. I just had a hound shot because of a broken leg or a supposedly broken leg. I need to replace him, along with a couple of others that are getting too old to track. Would you take on the job of training young pups to track?"

Billy stood there thinking, *this might get me off the hard work details every day*. Then he thought, what would happen to him if the hounds didn't take to tracking? Would he end up on even worse work details? Before Billy could answer, the warden said, "I have a hunt'n friend, and his best female Majestic Tree hound was bred to one of Georgia's champion hunt'n and track'n hounds. She had a litter of six pups, and I get first pick of three of them as soon as they were weaned. It's now time to go pick them up. Do you want the job?"

Billy did not get a chance to respond, the warden yelled, and a guard came through the door. Warden Calhoun told the guard to find Boss Ed and bring him to his office. A few minutes later, Boss Ed and Billy were standing together in front of Warden Calhoun. He told them how he wanted them to go pick up the young dogs. Billy was to pick out three pups that looked the most promising to become trackers. They were to bring them back, and Billy would start training them. Calhoun looked straight at Billy and said, "Don't even think about trying to escape. Boss Ed is a good shot, and even if he misses, you will be caught. No one has ever escaped from my prison."

The following day, Boss Ed and Billy got in one of the prison work trucks and headed out on a three-hour drive to a farm where the young hounds were. They arrived around noon, and the warden's friend took them to the side of his barn where there were several pens with dogs in them. All the dogs were yelping for attention and ready to get out. The last couple of pens had the younger dogs in them. He stopped in front of one and pointed to the pups that were jumping around, yelping and barking for attention. He said pick out the three dogs they want. Billy noticed two of the pups were jumping up and down more than the others, and one just sitting on its butt, looking up. Billy thought, *this one doesn't look like it has what it takes to become a good tracker*. But there was something in his eyes when the dog looked up at Billy that said, *take me*, so he did, along with the two jumping pups.

The dogs were put in a cage that was strapped to the flatbed of the prison truck, and they headed back to the prison. Billy suggested stopping a couple of times on the way back to give the dogs some water and thought Boss Ed would not agree, but he did, which surprised him.

On their ride to and from the dog farm, Boss Ed and Billy had time to talk, and he did listen to Billy's story about Sarah and Luke and how he came to be in prison but didn't say whether he thought Billy was guilty or not. Billy found out that Boss Ed had been sentenced to ten years for robbery, but he didn't actually do the robbing; he was the lookout. After being sentenced, he was placed in their newly built prison and he eventually became a trustee. The first warden of the prison wasn't there very long when Warden Calhoun replaced him and had taken a liking to Boss Ed. When Boss Ed's time was completed, Warden Calhoun asked if he wanted to stay on as a full-time guard, and since he had no family, he stayed and has worked there ever since. It seemed as though Boss Ed was not as strict as the other guards, probably because he had served time too. But Billy still did not want to be on his bad side.

They got back to the prison around 5:00 p.m., just in time for supper. Billy wanted to take care of the young dogs and get them settled in before he ate, so he missed supper. Boss Ed noticed this and relayed it to the warden, how Billy thought of the dogs before himself. Billy guessed that was one of the reasons why he had a pretty easy time after being assigned to training the tracking dogs.

Each morning after breakfast, Billy would head for the dog pens, get out one of the pups and start the training. Besides training the new dogs, he had to fine-tune the other older dogs; they had acquired some bad habits that needed to be trained out of them to make them all work as a team. Sometimes the warden would come out, watch, and ask how the new pups were doing or if Billy needed anything. Billy told him it was going well, the one that he thought would not make a good tracker was really coming along, and he had named him Ole Red. Billy told the warden when he first saw the pup, he didn't think he had what it took to be a tracker. Now after six months, Red was leading the pack; he had one of the best tracking noses he had ever seen.

Billy would drag an old shirt or piece of cloth around the prison grounds, then tear it in half and leave the torn piece for the dogs to find. He would take the other torn piece to the dogs and let them smell it and say, "Track'm dogs," and off they would go, with Red in the lead. Red always led the pack right to the piece Billy had hidden the other torn half of cloth. *place*

After about a year of training the dogs inside the prison grounds, the warden gave him permission to go outside the prison compound and let them train in the fields around the prison. This gave Billy a chance to use one of the trustees in training. He would get a piece of clothing from the trustee, tell him to hide in the field or at the edge of the swamp. After giving the trustee time to hide, he would let all the dogs smell the piece of clothing from the trustee and say, "Track'm dogs," and off they would go. They started out with short tracking's, which eventually turned into two, sometimes three-mile hunts. There was always a guard or trustee with Billy, the warden had not quite turned him completely lose on his own. Red always led the pack and was the first to find the trustee, usually up a tree so he wouldn't get bitten by the hounds. Ole Red had tracking blood in him, and Billy had told the warden that he was the best tracking hound he had ever seen.

A group of new prisoners came in late one evening. The next morning, when they were called to the camp yard for their instructions and rules of the camp, one prisoner was missing. The warden told Billy to get the dogs; he came back with six of them on leashes, and one of the trustees gave him a sheet from the escaped prisoner's bed. He let all the dogs have a good smell.

The warden said to Billy, "This is your first real test." And off they went.

The prisoner was caught in less than five hours. He thought that by running across the field to the edge of the swamp and running in the water, the dogs would lose the sent. He then doubled back onto the road for easier going. Red never missed a scent; in and out of the water, back onto the road, and with the guards on horsebacks, they caught up with the prisoner and brought him back. He got a week in the hot box.

Over the next year, the prison population grew, probably due to the Depression that the country was experiencing. There were more attempts to escape, and with Ole Red leading the pack, they were all caught. With the escapes slackening off, the warden would get bored and call everyone into the yard and sing out in a rhythmic tone, "Come on, somebody, why don't you run, Ole Red's itchin' to have a little fun, get my lantern, get my gun, Ole Red will have you tree'd before the mornin' come."

Billy was sure the warden went to bed singing that little song to himself. At night lying in his bunk, Billy would catch himself singing that short song and wonder if someone was going to try a breakout during the night. There were a few more over the next few months, but as good as Red and the other dogs had proven themselves, prisoners were not as anxious to try, knowing they would be caught and would spend time in the box.

It was 1936, Billy had been in prison a little over three years. Sam would drive down to see him as often as he could and kept Billy up to date with the local news and tell him about Sally Ann and how big she was getting. Sometimes Bobby Jo would come, and would tell him how she was raising Sally Ann; it was like Sally Ann was her own daughter. She always left with tears in her eyes, which made Billy feel even that much worse. On one of the visits, Billy told Sam the warden was letting him take Red out by himself, and the two of them would run a couple of miles down the road to where it turned and headed south from the prison; when they reached the curve in the road that was just out of sight of the prison, they would turn around and head back. They had been doing this for the last couple of months.

Billy and Sam were sitting away from everyone and while Billy was explaining all of this; Sam's mind was working and he whispered to Billy, "I might have a plan to get you out of prison, and we can talk about it the next time I come to visit. I have to do some scouting around on my drive back home first."

Billy did not want Sam to risk being arrested for trying to help him escape, but he knew Sam, he was a planner; Billy was looking forward to hearing the plan.

On Sam's next visit, they found a place far enough away from everyone else so that they could talk freely, without being noticed.

They were talking softer than usual. Sam told Billy he had a female hound that should be coming into season in a couple of weeks and Sam explained the plan to Billy. The next time he came to visit it would be on a Monday. Sam would bring the female hound down and set up a little camp site back in the woods off the road a few miles south of the prison. For the next couple of days, Sam would drive to the curve in the road south of the prison and out of sight of the guards and wait there for Billy and ole Red. Billy would bring ole Red and let him play around with the female hound, then Billy and ole Red would head back to the prison yard. They would do this until Friday to let Ole Red get used to it. Then on Friday morning Sam would clear out his camp site and head to the place where he would pick up Billy on the north side of the swamp the following Monday. On Friday morning when Billy rounded the curve, he would turn Red loose, knowing ole Red would head for the place where he was used to being with the female hound. Billy would then run north across a small field into the swamp. Since they were usually gone for about an hour, that would give him some time to get as far into the swamp as he could before Ole Red figured out the female wasn't there and run back to the prison yard without Billy. It would take a little time for the guards to figure out Billy was gone. Sam's plan sounded too good to be true, but it was a good plan. Billy agreed to the plan and looked forward to the next time he came down.

It was starting to be the hottest time of the year. For the next couple of weeks before the planned escape, Billy had been putting a jar of water and some food in a small bag, slinging it over his shoulder, and when the guards checked it, he told them it was for Ole Red. After a while, they didn't question the small pack slung over his shoulder, and they would wave him on through.

On the Monday before the planned escape, Sam showed up for his visit. They tried to act as natural as possible while talking, even though Billy felt as though he was shaking all over. Sam told Billy he had set up the campsite in the woods, out of sight of the road and prison. For the next few days, he would have the female hound down the road, just out of sight of the prison, Billy would bring Ole Red so the two could spend time together. On Friday morning Sam and the female hound would not be there and Sam told Billy where he would meet him that following Monday after Billy got through the swamp.

Friday morning came, Billy had put in extra water and food, knowing he would be in the swamp for a couple of days as Sam and he had discussed. He hoped the guards would not notice the extra bulge in the bag. As he approached, one of the guards held up his hand. Billy stopped; the guard reached down and gave Ole Red a pat on top of the head, "Have a good run," and waved them on. Billy felt like his heart had stopped beating. He did not say anything and headed south, down the road as usual toward the curve that would put them out of sight.

As soon as the guards could not see them, Billy turned Red loose, and off he ran, heading south down the road as hard as he could go. Billy headed north toward the edge of the swamp. It was about fifty yards across a field of high grass and small bushes, which helped to keep him somewhat out of sight before he reached the edge of the swamp. He was out of breath when he reached the swamp but knew he had to get as deep into the swamp as he could before Ole Red found out his lady friend was not there and ran back to the prison without Billy. Billy could hear Ole Red barking and felt sure he had made it back to the prison. Sure enough, he heard the escape bell ringing. It would take the guards and trustees a little time to gather the dogs and come after him. He only hoped Red would head south down the road, still looking for his lady friend. From the sounds of the barks and howls, Ole Red did just that and headed south.

Billy heard dog howls and barks, which became fainter as they headed south; this gave him a little more time to get deeper into the swamp. He ran as fast as he could, trying to step in small pools or would run in small streams to wash away any scent as best as possible. Billy knew Red always found the scent. He tried to avoid placing his hand on trees or grabbing vines, anything that would hold a scent. He slowed to rest and listen and heard Ole Red; it sounded like Ole Red had come back up the road and had picked up Billy's scent where he had run across the open field; soon they would be heading into the swamp. This would slow them a little, but Billy too, had to slow down. The sun was setting, and its light was creating long shadows across the swamp floor, which made it hard to see where to take his next step.

It was around five or six in the evening, and he could still hear the faint howls and barks of the dogs. Billy knew the guards would not want to be in the swamp after dark, and they would head back to the prison without a prisoner, which would mean the warden would be handing out punishments. The guards would probably get their pay docked, and the trustees may get time in the box, but he knew the warden would have them back on the hunt at daylight.

With the light fading fast, he searched for the safest place to spend the night, preferably off the swamp floor. Looking around using the dimming orange glow of the sun that penetrated through the swamp's canopy, he spotted a cypress tree that had a deformed trunk with two branches that crisscrossed one another and looked wide enough to hold him through the night. He walked around the massive base of the tree, looking for a way up.

Small cypress knees, about two or three feet tall, were sticking up all around the base. If he could balance on one, he might be able to make a short jump, grab the end of the large vine that was hanging down about six or seven feet from the swamp floor. If the jump succeeded and the vine held, he could use the vine to climb up the tree base to reach his place of refuge. He took off his brogans, tied them together, and slung them over his shoulder, along with his small life pack. Balancing as best he could on a cypress knee, while also stretching out his arm to brace against the tree trunk, he took a deep breath, pushed off the stump, and grabbed the vine with his other hand. He began inching himself up the vine toward his bed for the night, using his toes to feel for any foothold on the tree trunk. It was not an easy climb. Exhausted and weak from running in the swamp, he slowly climbed the old cypress until he finally reached the fork in the tree. This was going to be Billy's bed for a few hours, where, hopefully, he could get a little rest that he desperately needed.

Sleep did not come quickly. With every bit of sound emitting from the swamp, his eyes snapped open to dark surroundings. Now with only the faint light of the full moon piercing through the treetops, it was hard for his eyes to focus on anything. He tried to relax as best he could while balanced in the deformed fork of the old cypress tree. He had wrapped himself in some small vines to help hold him in place, and the sounds of the swamp finally became more and more distant. As he drifted off to sleep, his thoughts jumped from one event in his young life to the next. He thought of the hunting trips with his best friend, Sam, their hunting hounds, his parents and grandparents, his baby daughter, but most of all, Sarah, his murdered wife. The one thought that kept popping into his mind was what the county judge had said on the last day in the courtroom, *"William J. Bersha, you are hereby sentenced to ninety-nine years to life."*

Billy woke himself up, yelling out, "I didn't do it." He knew he had to figure out a way to prove his innocence, or he would be on the run, looking over his shoulder, for the rest of his life. He finally drifted off to sleep.

CHAPTER 4

Sam to the Rescue

Billy was jolted awake by a loud snapping, probably a tree limb breaking off. If it had not been for securing himself with surrounding vines as best as he could, he would have rolled off his makeshift bed, and the escape plan, or possibly his life, would have been over. If the fall wouldn't kill him, he could have broken an arm or leg. His arm or leg could also have gotten punctured by a limb or stump on the ground. Fortunately, this did not happen. After a moment or two, his breathing slowed, he released the tight grip on the vines and remembered where he was.

In his younger years, he had gone to church with his grandparents, but as he got older, he had stopped going regularly. Unconsciously he thanked God for not letting him fall. He sat there remembering the patchwork of dreams and wondered how long he had slept. He felt rested but worried. Were the guards and hounds back on the hunt, or had they given up? He heard no barking or howling, only the eerie sounds that crept from the swamps floor: frogs crooking, a bird chirp, and, off in the distance, a low grunt, probably from a wild hog.

It was early dawn, and with little light, he started to untangle himself from the vines. He pulled on one of the larger vines hoping it was the one used to pull himself up the night before. Billy pulled hard on the vine, and it seemed to be secure; easing himself off the fork of the tree, he began his descent. He lowered himself as close to the swamp floor as possible. He pushed off the tree trunk with his foot, swung out, let go, hoping to miss the cluster of cypress knees at the foot of the tree, and landed on a small patch of dry ground. His first thought was not of the safe successful landing but of the scent that would be on this patch of dry land. Would they pick it up? He stood still, listening to the sounds. Other than usual swamp sounds, he heard no hounds. The golden-red glow from the early-morning sun had started to creep into the forest. Having no idea of the time and barely enough light to see by, he leaned against the tree, took the high-top prison boots hanging from his shoulder, put them on, and laced them up. They were still damp from running in the swamp water the day before. He continued his trek through the swamp toward the place where Sam had told him a train would pass by.

In Sam's reconnaissance of the area, he said there were some railroad tracts of a small railroad line that ran along the north side of the swamp carrying lumber out of the surrounding forest to a saw-mill outside of Waycross. He had driven a road that ran alongside the rail line and if Billy could get to the rail line, hop on a flatcar loaded with lumber, ride it to the dirt road that led to a small town, he could jump off, hide, and wait for Sam to pick him up.

Billy wasn't familiar with this swamp, but from listening to guards and other inmates, he guessed it was about ten to twelve miles in a northerly direction to get out of the swampland and reach the railroad line that ran along the north side of the swamp. Sam found out it was a small private rail line with no caboose and only an engi-neer and fireman in the engine cab at the front. It made various stops along the edge of the swamp where flatcars were loaded with logs and, when fully loaded, would head nonstop, northeast to the sawmill, just outside of Waycross. Every Monday, around noon, it ran past where Sam planned on picking him up. It never reached much speed due to the twists and curves, so it never got over five to ten miles per hour. It would be easy to hop on and off without being seen when it rounded a curve. Sam had planned the escape for Friday morning, which would give Billy two and a half days to get through the swamp to the railroad tracks and the pickup point. He would need to get to the railroad tracks by Sunday evening, before dark, to find a spot where the train had to slow down for a curve. He would have to stay hidden from the engineer and fireman before jumping on when the train passed by sometime Monday morning. After jumping on, he would ride it until he saw an old abandoned water tower. It could be recognized by the weathered sign with missing letters. It spelled out "H mpt n L mber." They both knew it was once spelled "Hampton Lumber." Hampton Lumber once had a sawmill there but had shut it down a few years earlier and moved north to its present location. Billy would need to jump off the flatcar just after the engine rounded the curve past the water tower and stay hidden until the train was out of sight. Sam would be waiting on far side of the dirt road on the other side of the tracks at the edge of the tree line.

Billy took out a piece of dried meat and the small jar of water from the bag to subdue his hunger and quench his thirst. He knew he had to conserve the food and water for the hike, hoping he had brought enough for three days if it took that long. With the sun up, shining enough light through the treetops, he aligned himself so the sun was on his right side. That way, he would be facing north. Since there were no sounds of hounds barking and howling, he decided to take the risk and would try to stay on dry ground as much as possible. Traveling in water slowed him down, but sometimes it would be necessary to stay in a northerly direction.

As he worked his way through the swamp, dodging what looked like deep pools and stepping into shallow pools ever so often to help wash away any scent, he remembered the events from the day before. He tried to estimate how far he had traveled after entering the swamp and stopping for the night. How far into the swamp had he gone yesterday? It was hard to tell. He had been more concerned about trying to cover his scent than how far he had traveled. If the prison was fifteen miles from the northeastern side of the swamp, and he was cutting through the swamp in a northerly direction, this should cut off a few miles. He guessed there were maybe eight to ten more miles in the swamp before he reached the rail line at the edge of the swamp. He had traveled in the swamps back home, but it was always in a small flat-bottom boat. On foot, he estimated he would probably be able to cover maybe five or six miles a day, putting him at the swamp's north edge in two days if everything went right. He had been walking, and sometimes jogging, for most of the day, and the light from the setting sun was getting dimmer as it filtered through the treetops. He thought this should be Saturday evening, and thought he had made good travel time. He needed to find a place to spend the night. Up ahead, through the trees, was a small clearing, and on the other side was a tall tree with what looked like a deer stand built in it. That was where he would spend Saturday night if the old deer stand would hold him.

He and Sam had decided to plan the escape on a Friday for two reasons. First, the train with the loaded railcars would be heading north to the sawmill on Monday morning. It would pass by where Billy could jump on and ride to where Sam would pick him up. The other reason was that the weekend guards were not as experienced as those during the week, and they would be working Saturday and Sunday. So, if there ever was a good time to try for an escape, it would be on the weekend. Billy would get as far as he could in the swamp on Friday, then get an early start Saturday morning. He would try getting as far as he could before dark. Then hunker down Saturday night and start out early Sunday morning. This would allow him to make it to the railroad tracks along the edge of the swamp by Sunday evening. He would need to get there before dark to find a suitable location where he would not be seen as the train passed by Monday morning. He also had to figure out where he could jump on one of the flatcars loaded with timber without being seen.

After spending a fairly restful night in the deer stand, he woke up with the early-morning sunrays hitting his face, he opened his eyes to the dimly lit forest. He was still somewhat exhausted from running in the swamp and tried to remember, had this been his second or third night in the swamp? If last night was Saturday night, he was on time. If it was Sunday night, he may be late and would miss Sam. Panic started to set in. He sat on the tree stand, leaning back against the large oak tree trunk, looking into the clearing. He took out some tough jerky from his pack and slowly started to chew on it, trying to relax and clear his head. Opening the small jar of water with only a few swallows left, he took a small sip. It was hard to get the days figured out—was this Saturday or Sunday morning?

After a few restful minutes, he put together the events since Friday morning. The first night, Friday, he slept in the deformed tree branches. The second day would have been Saturday and after trekking through the swamp, he felt he had made good time and had found this deer stand, where he had spent last night. This had to be Sunday morning; he had not missed the train or Sam. He breathed a sigh of total relief and swallowed the second bite of the jerky.

He climbed down from the tree stand, and after walking for a couple of hours, the swamp started to change. There was more dry land, and walking became much easier; he could now make good time. By the way the sun was sitting in the sky, it was probably getting close to midafternoon. Just up ahead, he saw a small clearing. Staying just inside the wood line along the edge of the clearing, he looked across to the other side and saw some railroad tracks. Had he found them? If they were the ones Sam had told him about, he had made it. He needed to find a secluded spot to hide and wait for the train. After walking for several hundred yards along the edge of the tree line that ran adjacent to the railroad tracks, he was fairly certain these were the tracks Sam told him about. He needed to find a good vantage point that was out of sight but still gave him the ability to watch for the train that would pass by in the morning and rounded a curve so he would be out of sight and could jump on.

Off to his left, and about twenty feet from a swamp channel, was a thicket on a small mound that would put him high enough to watch for the train yet conceal him. Closer to the tracks sat a little hut, about the size of a two-seater outhouse, that Sam had told him about, so he was certain these were the right railroad tracks. He was concerned that the little shack might be too close to the tracks, and someone may be using the shed for something. The mound was about fifty yards from the tracks, where the railroad tracks started to make a fairly sharp curve to the north. After the engine rounded the curve, the engineer nor the fireman would not be able to see the end of the train. He hoped the train would be long enough and traveling slow enough for him to make the run and jump on one of the last railcars loaded with lumber. Once on, he would conceal himself as best he could behind the long round tree trunks chained to the flat-car. He had no idea how far he would have to ride before coming to the old water tower. His concealment needed to have a good vantage point for him to watch for the old water tower and the curve in the tracks where it crossed the dirt road where he was to jump off, and Sam would pick him up.

As Billy approached the thicket on the small mound, he noticed a small trail leading up to the mound; it was a gator trail. The mound was a nest, the kind a female gator builds and uses year after year to lay her eggs. Over the years, the undergrowth had grown up around the nest, which helped to conceal it. It was the perfect place for her eggs to incubate. The path looked well used, but he saw no gator on or around the nest, but it was that time of year when gators laid their eggs. He approached the mound with caution; she could be lying only a few feet from the nest, and he would never see her until she lunged. Shoving his hand down into the center of the nest and feeling around, there were eggs. If he spent the night here, there would be no sleeping as he would have to watch for the mother gator. It was almost dark; he looked at the small hut a few yards from the tracks. It was missing a few sideboards, and the door was barely hanging on. It looked as if it had not been used in some time, but he was not sure.

As he approached and looked inside, it appeared to be a shed where tools to repair the railroad tracks had been stored at one time. There were a couple of rusty shovels, pickaxes, and a long pry bar used to move sections of the rail. It appeared they had not been used in some time; cobwebs were on all the tools. He would risk staying in the shed instead of spending the night on the lookout for the mother gator. Folded up in the corner was an old tarp. Using the pry bar, he slowly lifted it up, checking for any creature that might be using it for refuge; luckily there were none. There was a small loft above that would be a perfect place to spend the night wrapped in the old tarp and off the ground. He would also have a good view to watch for the train. This would definitely be better than trying to sleep on top of a gator nest. He stacked a couple of old wooden crates on top of each other, climbed up and threw the tarp and his pack on the loft floor, and eased his way onto the loft, praying it would hold.

Luck followed him again; it held. He spread the tarp out, took out his jar of water, and drank half of what little water was left. He would have to wake up before dawn and watch for anyone that might be coming while waiting for the lumber train to pass by. Lying there, he thought how good it would feel to get in Sam's old truck and get as far away from South Georgia as possible. He thought who had stabbed Luke. But most of all, he thought how hard it would be to start a new life without Sarah and his daughter, Sally Ann. Sleep finally overcame him.

Awakened by what he thought was scratching at the old wooden door, he thought it was a dream. From the loft, he heard it again and squinted, trying to look through the cracks of the shed. The sun was coming up, and he had no idea of how long it had been up; had he missed the train? Hearing the scratching again, he looked down at the door. It was probably a skunk or possum looking for a place to spend the day sleeping after searching all night for food, but the shadow was too large for either of those. He tried focusing through the cracks on what was just outside the door, and it appeared to be a large-sized animal. Was it a coyote or maybe a black bear? There were black bears in this part of the country.

Then he heard whining, he knew it was a dog. He thought he recognized the sound, it sounded like Ole Red. His first thought was, he had been found. Panic set in. He listened more intently, but he didn't hear any other hounds. Slowly slipping down from the loft, he slowly walked to the door and peered through the crack. Looking as best he could through the small gaps between the boards, he did not see anyone. Then looking down through the cracks in the boards, he saw Ole Red looking up at him and heard a low soft whine. He knew Red was a good tracking dog, but he didn't know how good he really was until now. He slowly opened the door, and Ole Red pounced and began licking his face. He was glad to see his old companion but started worrying. How far behind were the rest of the hounds and guards? Straining to listen for distant howls and barks, he heard none and concluded that Ole Red had taken off on his own to find his master and had succeeded. The guards must have just given up trying to catch Ole Red, and they, along with the other hounds, had given up the chase.

Billy was glad to have his companion back but knew this would make it more difficult to jump onto the lumber car. Somehow, he would manage. He was not going to leave this dog that had helped him escape and had found him after two days of tracking through the swamp.

With the sun up higher in the sky, he needed a place as close to the tracks as possible to hide until the engine was out of sight to jump on. Sam had sat in his truck on his last visit and watched the loaded lumber train pass by. He said it usually passed by the little shack in the early afternoon, around one or two o'clock on Mondays. The train would slow down to make the curve, and as soon as the engine was out of sight, he should jump on. By the way the sun was sitting in the sky, him thought it was probably around noon, and began to relax. While waiting for the train, he still had doubts that he was not safe. Had he missed the train, or would it even come by today? He and Ole Red sat side by side. Billy gave him the last bit of jerky and water. The dog ate the jerky, then drank the last of the water in a couple of tongue laps. Billy rested his arm over the dog's back and began to pet his head. "Will I ever be able to rest, knowing there may always be someone looking for me?" He said out loud.

Billy heard the sound of a train whistle; he hadn't missed it. With Ole Red by his side, they crawled to a little bush next to the railroad tracks and waited for the lumber train. Now the question that remained was how to get Ole Red on the railcar with him. As the engine passed by, Billy lay on top of Red to hide them as best he could and keep him still. The train was slowing down for the curve, and he noticed it was pulling a lot of flatcars loaded with logs. This would put the engine further around the curve and out of sight of Billy and Ole Red when trying to jump on. Billy had buried the little bag he had brought along to cover his scent in case he was still being tracked. All he had to worry about was getting himself and Ole Red onto one of the flatcars. After a couple of railcars had passed, Billy noticed the logs were stacked unevenly which created small openings where he could crawl back in and hide, but how to get Red on with him?

Red had a thick leather collar around his neck. Billy tightened it up so his head would not slip through. He had planned on jumping on and hoped that Ole Red would run alongside the flatcar, and he could reach down and pick him up by the collar and pull him up onto the flatcar. Watching the cars go by and looking back at the end, he could see the last ones approaching. In a flash, Billy thought that pulling Red up by the collar might break his neck. With the last couple of cars approaching and the engine now out of sight around the curve, Billy would be out of sight when he jumped on the flatcar. With the train going slow and only two cars left, he picked up Ole Red, ran along the side of the flatcar and pitched Ole Red onto the end of the flatcar, then ran to catch up, grabbing hold of a log chain used to hold the logs in place, he pulled himself on. He was thankful that Red stayed on the car while he ran along to catch it. He crawled as far back under the logs as he could get. Red followed, curled up beside him, and laid his head on Billy's leg. Being tucked under the logs and out of sight, Billy would not be able to see the water tower when the train approached it, so he had to crawl out and check every few minutes. Thankfully the log train was long, and he could peek out over the logs without being seen and could watch for the water tower.

After driving on the dirt road beside the railroad tracks, Sam told Billy the little shack was about an hour's ride to the abandoned water tower. Billy had some idea when to be on the lookout for the water tower and was continuously peeking over the logs as the train rounded each curve. It seemed he had been riding for hours when he looked through the gaps in the logs and saw the water tower. He got Red ready, peering through the logs, he watched for the engine to go out of sight around the curve. He jumped off the car and ran along, trying to get Red to jump off into his arms. He was hesitant to jump but finally did. Billy caught him, and they both hit the ground and rolled down into the ditch. He lay there, with Red in his arms, hoping neither of them had broken any bones. He let go of Red, who stood there while Billy got to his knees and looked around. They were on the downhill side of the tracks, with the dirt road on the other side of the tracks. Sam said he would be waiting in his truck about a half mile north of the water tower.

Staying in the ditch, Billy ran as fast as he could, hunched over, trying not to be seen, while Red ran along behind him. When he thought he had run about a half mile, he stopped, crawled from the bottom of the ditch, up to the top, where he could look over the railroad tracks. Sam's truck was sitting on the other side of the tracks off to the side of the dirt road just inside the tree line. Billy could see Sam standing at the back of the truck and waved to him. Sam gave Billy a circle-motion wave, letting him know that he would drive the truck over so Billy could get in. Billy patted his leg for Red, and he came running; and by the time he was by his side, Sam had the truck in place. The two of them jumped in the back, lay down, and Billy pulled a tarp over himself and Ole Red. Sam drove until sunset, and Billy felt the truck slow down. He knew Sam had pulled off the road and was heading into the forest, to the place he had picked out to spend the night. When the truck stopped, and he heard Sam get out, he threw the tarp back, sat up, and saw Sam standing there, as well as Bobby Jo, who was holding a small child. Billy knew at once it was his daughter, Sally Ann, and he started to cry. Ole Red and Sam's female dog were running back and forth to either side of the truck waiting to be told to jump out of the bed of the truck. Sam dropped the tail gate, Billy and the dogs all got out.

Billy had never felt such relief when he grabbed Sam and gave him a hug.

"I thought it was just gonna be you?" Billy asked.

And instead of answering, Sam said, "And I thought it was only going to be you." He looked down at Ole Red.

"Looks like your friend came along in hopes of finding his girl-friend, which he did."

CHAPTER 5

―――――― ❦ ――――――

Off to Idaho and Meeting the Smiths

After the hugs were over and the crying subsided, Sam said, "Bobbie Jo was not going to be left out or behind. I told her no, but she insisted and was bringing little Sally Ann. Her father needs to see how big she has grown."

On the one hand, Billy was thrilled to see his daughter and Bobbie Jo, but on the other, he did not know how he and Sam were going to travel with them along. Sam had contacted a childhood friend who lived in Tennessee and was now a foreman of a small lumber-cutting company and would be willing to put Billy to work. Sam had not told him Billy's last name nor his troubles with the authorities. He simply told him Billy needed to get away from Hardwood, Georgia, because of family problems. Billy needed to work and save as much as he could to move as far away from Georgia as he could. But now, with Bobbie Jo and the baby, there needed to be travel changes.

The seat in the pickup was going to be crowded with all four of them, so Bobbie Jo and Billy took turns holding Sally Ann, who slept most of the time. Sam suggested they head back to Hardwood; he would drop Billy off at the little hunting camp he and Billy had used for years, then take Bobbie Jo and Sally Ann to the Williamson's house. Sam would get some supplies, then he and Billy would head for Tennessee. This sounded good until Bobbie Jo broke in with some bad news. One of her close friends, Tammie Watkins, back in Tennessee had written her a letter asking that since her brother was coming to town, would she be coming up with him, and if so, Tammie would love to see her. Sam soon realized that his friend in Tennessee had mentioned to others that he was coming back to town, and word got around, so his and Bobbie Jo's childhood friends wanted to see them. This news changed everything, and they had to figure out something new.

They drove most of the day, and it was time to start looking for a place to spend the night. They had passed through a couple of some small towns that had cabins for rent, but they did not feel safe, so Sam kept driving. Driving slowly, not knowing the road, his dim headlights lit up a sign that said campsite ahead, and he turned onto the road in the direction the sign pointed. He drove a half-mile through the woods and into a clearing and saw a couple of picnic tables and a rock firepit. Sam had brought a small tent just in case they would need to camp out, but he hadn't planned on Bobbie Jo and Sally Ann coming with him. Sam had planned ahead, but at the last minute, Bobbie Jo said she was come along with Sally Ann.

Sam set up the tent. It was small but would do for Bobbie Jo and the baby, while Billy started a small fire in the rock firepit to help take off some of the chill of the night. They ate some beef jerky and drank some water. Bobbie Jo had brought a small bottle of milk that she heated up in a pan of water over the fire along with some mashed vegetables for Sally Ann, who didn't really seem to like her supper. Bobbie Jo gave her a piece of jerky to suck on, which she seemed to like. Sam, Billy, Ole Red and Sam's female hound slept in the truck bed and shared one of the two blankets Sam had brought. Bobbie Jo took the other one for her and the baby. They were all tired, so it did not take long for everyone to drift off to sleep.

The next morning, as they were taking down the tent, Bobbie Jo told both Sam and Billy she was not going back home. She was going wherever Billy went; Sally Ann needed her father, and he needed her. That was a hard argument to go against. They all sat on the tailgate and discussed where to go. They did not have much money and only one truck, and the options were few. Sam tried to talk Bobbie Jo out of coming along, but she refused and would not budge from her plans to stay with Billy no matter where he went. She was out of school and old enough to make up her own mind. Sam decided they should drive back to Hardwood, tell his father what he had done by helping Billy escape, and get his dad's advice. It seemed like the most sensible idea. They loaded up and headed for Hardwood.

Sam dropped Billy and Red off at the little campsite. He left the tarp and tent and drove to his house, with Bobbie Jo and Sally Ann. Sam told his father about helping Billy escape and that he needed to get as far away from this part of the county as possible; Sam's dad agreed. Mr. Will, as Billy always called him, like Sam, was a planner. Unlike Billy's father, who did things on the spur of the moment, Mr. Will had been putting money back for an emergency, and to him, this was as good an emergency as could be. He told Sam he thought of Billy as a son, especially after his dad had died.

Mr. Will told Sam, "You can give your truck to Billy, along with the money I have been saving. Billy should head to Washington or maybe Idaho. They both are on the Canadian border, if he needs to get out of the country and there is a lot of timber-cutting there. Several men from around Hardwood had gone to the northwest to cut timber or work in the sawmills. Billy would need to change his name and have no contact with anyone back in Hardwood if he wants to stay free." Sam's dad knew, with Billy's experience, he would be able to get a job in a sawmill with no problem.

After hearing the plan, Bobbie Jo told her parents she was taking Sally Ann and going with Billy. They had taken in Sally Ann when Billy went to prison; she had cared for her like she was her own child, and she wasn't going to be without the baby or Billy. She told Sam and her parents that she had fallen in love with Billy the first time she saw him. She was of age and could make up her own mind. She knew he had loved Sarah Lou more than life itself, and she could never take her place, but she would do with second place if he would have her. If not, she was determined to take care of Sally Ann and be close enough to Billy that he could see her any time he wanted to. Her family tried to talk her out of it with no success. Sam knew how much Billy loved Sarah Lou, but Bobbie Jo had made up her mind, and nothing was going to change it. He knew how stubborn his sister could be and he finally agreed with his sister.

Sam, Bobbie Jo, with Sally Ann climbed into his truck and drove back to the campsite where Billy was waiting. Sam's dad followed so Sam would have a way back to town. Sam told Billy the plan about taking his truck and the money, and head to the northwest, on the condition that Bobbie Jo and Sally Ann go with him. Now it was up to Billy to have the final say.

When Billy heard the plan, he said, "Mr. Will, taking your savings, Sam's truck, and traveling with a baby that far, I cannot do it. I would rather turn myself in and go back to prison." Billy looked at Bobbie Jo holding little Sally Ann, with tears running down her face as she told him that she had always loved him. Billy had always known that she had feelings for him but never thought, or knew, how much until now; he was torn apart inside. Bobbie Jo told Billy she did not care if he ever loved her as much as Sarah Lou, but she had raised Sally Ann for over three years and was not going to give her up, but she was his daughter; he couldn't just abandon her. Bobbie Jo was right; she was his daughter and the only living thing he had to keep the memory of Sarah Lou alive, so Billy agreed to the plan.

After saying goodbye to his little sister, Sam turned to Billy. Billy told Sam how much he thought of his parents to do this for him, taking their savings, the truck, and now their daughter, who they probably would never see again. Billy walked to Sam's dad, Mr. Williamson. With his eyes full of tears, he gave Mr. Will a hug that seemed to last forever, all the time thinking of his deceased father. Billy told him he did not know how he could ever repay him for his love and kindness. Saying the goodbyes, knowing he would probably never see Sam or Mr. Will again, felt like his heart was being torn out of his chest. Billy knew deep down it was the right thing to do.

Bobbie Jo, Sally Ann, Ole Red, and Billy climbed in the truck and headed to the northwest to start a new life.

After driving a couple of hundred miles in Sam's truck, they stopped for gas. There was a car at the other pump, and an elderly man was having a problem getting the handle up to start the pump going.

Billy asked, "Need help with that?"

"If you don't mind, I'm not as strong as I used to be. For some reason, I cannot get the pump turned on."

Billy got the pump turned on for him and noticed the man had an Idaho sticker on his back glass.

"Are you from Idaho?"

"Yes, I am. It's a beautiful state, lots of mountains with timber everywhere."

"How's the hunting and fishing?"

"It's the best."

They talked for a bit longer, the man's wife came out from inside the station and approached them.

When she stopped, the elderly man looked at Billy and said, "I'm Elmer Smith, and my wife is Lois. I didn't catch your name."

"It's Billy," he said without thinking.

Lois said she was hungry, and the station attendant told her the café next door served a great lunch, and it was reasonable. The Depression was still going on, so reasonable prices were hard to come by. His wife looked at their truck and saw Bobbie Jo holding Sally Ann, waved at them.

"Your wife and baby."

Billy didn't answer right off, as she looked at him.

"Oh, sorry, yes, they are."

The elderly man asked if they would like to join them for lunch, but Billy declined. Billy was guessing the older gentleman thought maybe they couldn't afford it.

"You got the pump going so I could fill up my gas tank. The least I can do is buy you lunch."

Billy agreed and walked back to his truck to finish filling it. Billy told Bobbie Jo that the elderly couple had invited them to have lunch, and he had agreed. Billy also told Bobbie Jo that he told them that they were husband and wife and that Sally Ann was their child. A huge smile appeared on Bobbie Jo's face, and she squeezed Billy's hand. He felt a warm feeling that he hadn't felt in a long time. Billy said he had slipped and told the elderly man his name was Billy but hadn't said the last name.

"We need to come up with a last name," Bobbie Jo said.

As Billy pulled out of the station's drive and headed next door to the little café, Bobbie Jo noticed the store across the street with a sign above the door; it read Perkins Hardware.

"Perkins, Bill and Bobbie Jo Perkins from Waycross, Georgia, and Sally Ann Perkins."

"So now we are the Perkins," Billy commented.

"Yep, got it from a hardware store," Bobbie Jo said with a chuckle.

Billy parked the truck, picked up Sally Ann, and Red jumped from the truck's bed into the cab, curled up for a nap on the seat. They walked into the small café. There were only a few people, most of them sitting on stools at the counter, and all the tables were empty except for the one where the elderly couple had sat down. Billy handed Sally Ann to Bobbie Jo after she sat down. Elmer handed Billy a menu. He looked it over and handed it to Bobbie Jo. The waitress came to the table and asked if they had decided.

Elmer and Lois said, "We have."

And the waitress took their order. Bobbie Jo and Billy ordered ham sandwiches, water, and oatmeal for Sally Ann, with a little brown sugar and cinnamon on it, if they had it, and a small glass of milk.

"No problem," the waitress walked to the window to turn in their orders.

Lois asked, "How old is she?" As she pointed to Sally Ann.

"She's Four."

"She is very well mannered for four."

"Thank you."

"Are you vacationing?" Elmer asked.

"No, we are heading to the northwest to look for work. It is slow and hard to find work nowadays in this part of the country, with sawmills closing all around."

"What type of work do you do?"

"I worked in the timber industry, I cut down trees, I've loaded them on railcars and have worked at various jobs in sawmills, sizing lumber, etc. I heard the northwest had better opportunities for my line of work, so we decided to head that way."

"The northwest is doing better than down south. That is why Lois and I are in this part of the country. We are looking to buy a small lumber company that is up for sale. I own a large lumber company in Idaho. We cut the timber, ship it to one of our three sawmills to cut into usable lumber, then sell the cut lumber to independent stores all over the country. With the Depression the way it is, many small companies are going out of business or downsizing. I hate taking advantage of hard times, but I want to expand my business and thought this would be a good area to expand in. Since you worked in the timber business around here, you may know the company that I am thinking of purchasing, Hampton Lumber and Saw mill in Hardwood?"

"Yes, I've heard of them," Billy said, trying not to act surprised.

"Hampton is selling off some of their smaller sawmills, and I made them an offer, so we are headed to Hardwood, Georgia, to look at it. Lois and I have never been in this part of the country, so we decided to drive to see the county, and I wanted to see the sawmill for myself."

Billy was becoming more nervous and hoping it didn't show. Finally, the waitress came with their food, and he was praying the subject would change, but it didn't.

"Billy, you said you are headed to the northwest to look for work?"

"Yes, I am."

Mr. Smith took out one of his business cards, turned it over, and on the back, he wrote something, then handed it to Billy.

"Here is one of my business cards. If you don't find anything, get in touch with me, or go to one of my sawmills and give them this card. They should be able to help you out."

Billy took the card; it read Smith Timber Companies. He turned the card over to read it, "Hire him, he has the experience and is a nice young man that helped me in Georgia, Elmer Smith."

"Thank you, and I will be sure to get in touch if I don't find anything. Right now, we are just concerned about getting there."

Billy was afraid his past might follow him to the northwest if Mr. Smith buys the Hampton Company and talks to people in Hardwood about their meeting.

Billy and Bobbie Jo tried to say as little as possible about where they were from or about their families, but the Smiths kept asking about things that Billy did not want being brought up. They asked Billy if he grew up in Waycross, how long he had worked in the timber business, what sawmill he had worked for, things that Billy had to lie about and hoped he could remember if it came up again in another conversation.

Billy was becoming more and more nervous and noticed that Sally Ann had fallen asleep in Bobbie Jo's lap, which was a good excuse for them to leave. They thanked the Smiths for lunch and would keep the card just in case he didn't find work. Surprisingly both Smiths gave Billy and Bobbie Jo long hugs, told them to be safe, and told them if they ever needed help, the Smiths would be there for them. The Smiths told them they didn't have any children, but if they had had any, they hoped they would be as nice and thoughtful as they were. Billy thought, *if they knew my past and why we were leaving, they might not have said that.* Billy, held Sally Ann while Bobbie Jo got into their truck to resume their journey.

Looking at Bobbie Jo, he said, "I'm not going to be as helpful next time."

"You cannot help it. It's your nature to help people."

As they drove, Billy kept thinking about Mr. Smith, would he say anything to anyone in Hardwood about meeting a young couple named Billy and Bobbie Jo with a four-year-old child. Would he tell them they were headed to the northwest? Billy would have to get used to looking over his shoulder the rest of his life, and he hated that for Bobbie Jo and Sally Ann.

As he drove, Red sat between him and Bobbie Jo, who held Sally Ann, who were sleeping. Driving along, Billy had time to think and started to become depressed. Not only would he be on the run for the rest of his life, but now Bobbie Jo and his daughter would also be on the run. He did not like the thought of that. He had to get control of his thoughts and figure out the quickest route to Idaho, the state he had decided on as their destination. The map Sam's dad had given him was some help and showed roads between the larger cities as being a hard surface. This meant they may be concrete; asphalt or gravel and the secondary roads would more than likely be dirt. Billy could not be sure they would always be gravel.

After driving all day, they finally reached the Tennessee, Georgia, state line. Billy pulled over at a roadside rest area. The area had a couple of picnic tables and an outhouse. Billy sat at the park table, looking at the map, figuring out the shortest and easiest route to Idaho. After studying the map, he told Bobbie Jo that it would take longer, but they should stay on roads that go through larger cities. They would have a better chance of not getting lost, and the roads would hopefully be better; she agreed. The route he chose would take them through Nashville, to St. Louis, over to Kansas City, then north to Omaha, up to Sioux Falls, then west to Rapid City. From there, they would head northwest to Billings, Montana. From Billings, they would head for Missoula. Billy told Bobbie Jo the roads in Idaho would probably be mostly dirt, with maybe a few miles with gravel. It would be a hard drive through the mountains. The mountains would be a lot different than the small mountains they had in Georgia. Once they reached Missoula, the only road shown on the map going to the northwest led to Spokane. Billy was hoping, as they crossed the northern tip of Idaho, there would be roads leading off the main road to Spokane that would lead to small timber towns. He wanted to be in the northern tip of Idaho, as close to the Canadian border as possible, in case they had to leave the country.

After telling Bobbie Jo the route he had planned, her only comment was, "Sounds good, I trust you, Sally Ann and I are in your hands." Billy thought, Sarah Lou had trusted him with her life, and look where it got her. Billy started having significant doubts about bringing Bobbie Jo and Sally Ann, but they had come too far to turn back.

It took them three weeks to get to Missoula. Along the way, Billy picked up odd jobs to help pay for food and gas so as not to use up all the money Sam's dad had given him. The country's Depression was slowly coming to an end back east, but it had not hit this part of the country as bad. Most of the people in the mid and northwest were pretty self-sufficient. They grew gardens, raised their own meat, or hunted. Billy was always on the lookout for help-wanted signs and would ask around when he stopped for gas. The road between Missoula and Spokane went across the northern tip of Idaho, and as they approached the western border of Idaho, there was a sign that read "Sandpoint," and below it, "Bonners Ferry," with an arrow pointing to a gravel road turn off. They stopped and looked at the sign with the names of the towns on it. They both sounded like Georgia towns, so they headed north to what they hoped would be their new home.

When they went through the small town of Sandpoint, it looked nice enough, but there was something about it that neither of them felt comfortable with, so they drove on north to Bonners Ferry. It, too, was a small town with the main road running north and south. For some reason, it did not feel right to them either. Billy stopped for gas and asked one of the locals standing on the porch of the station, "Does the road going north out of town go all the way to the Canadian border?"

"Yes, it does."

"I am looking for work as a timber cutter or in a sawmill," Billy said.

"A few miles up the road, there will be a sign pointing to turn off which will take you to Hillside. There is a lumber company there, and they are always looking for extra help, good luck."

Billy thanked him, got back in his truck, and told Bobbie Jo to watch for the road sign that said Hillside. After a few miles, they came upon a sign that was partially hidden by a brush. It read "Hillside 5 miles" in faded paint. Billy turned onto a gravel road in the direction the sign was pointing, hoping he had made the right choice. When they pulled into the little town, it felt like they had found their new home.

Bobbie Jo said, "It feels cozy."

As they drove down the main street looking for a place to eat, they saw a few stores, shops, and a small building with a sign at the top, "Smith's Lumber Company office."

Billy said, "How lucky or unlucky could this be? Should we stay or go?"

"God has protected us all this way and brought us to this town that has a Smith's Lumber Company office. I say we stay." The decision was made they would stay, and Billy needed to find a job.

CHAPTER 6

Getting Settled in Hillside

B illy stopped in front of the Hillside Diner. All three went inside while Ole Red lay down on the seat of the truck for his nap. Shortly after they sat down, a middle-aged woman brought them a couple of one-page menus and asked, "Would you like anything to drink?"

"I'll have water and a small glass of milk," Bobby Jo said.

"I'll have some tea, thank you."

They looked over the lunch items; since it was midday, both decided on sandwiches. Bobbie Jo said, "I'll order some soup for Sally Ann, since she is just getting used to some types of solid food and probably will not eat much." The waitress came back, placed their drinks on the table, and took their orders. As they looked around, there were not many people inside, and Billy said, "I think I will ask her if she knows of anyone who needs help of any kind."

"Since this looked like it is the only place to eat in town, she probably would know if anyone was hiring," Jo answered.

The waitress came with their food, and Billy said, "We are from out of town, and I'm looking for work. Do you know of anyone who needs part-time or preferably full-time help?"

"You're in luck if you can do carpenter work."

"Yes, I can."

"My husband wants to do some remodeling on our house, but he does not have the time with the work here at the diner. By the way, my name is Betty Campbell, and my husband is Tom."

"I'm Billy Perkins, and this is Bobbie Jo and Sally Ann."

"I will tell my husband, and I'm sure he will want to speak with you before you leave."

"That would be great."

Billy and Bobbie Jo had just finished their meal when Tom Campbell came to their table.

"Looking for work?"

"Yes, your wife said you wanted to do some remodeling and needed help."

"I spend most of the day here at our diner cooking and just don't seem to have the time to work on our house. I could use the help if you know about framing a room and hanging cabinets, etc."

Billy and his dad had helped their friends on several occasions to add on rooms to their houses, and he had learned a lot from his granddad and Sam's dad when they built his and Sarah Lou's little house, so he felt confident that he could do what Mr. Campbell needed to be done. The diner was empty, he and Tom talked about what needed to be done while Bobbie Jo and Betty talked and played with Sally Ann. Billy had watched his spending on the trip from Georgia, and with the money left over from what Sam's dad had given them, Billy told the Campbells they needed to find a small place to rent until they could save up enough money to buy a house. Betty told them there was a small house just outside of town that was for rent. She also told Billy that he could use her and Tom as references. Tom told Billy that as soon as he got settled in, he should come back to the diner, and he would show him what needed to be done at his house.

Billy and Bobbie Jo spoke to the owner of the little house and got moved got in. As the weeks went by, Billy got everything done that Mr. Campbell had requested. While Billy worked on the Campbell house, Bobbie Jo helped out part time at the diner at noontime and Betty let her bring Sally Ann. On Saturday, she worked all day full-time while a young girl that Betty knew babysat Sally Ann. Everything was going well, and with all the work done on the Campbells' house, Billy needed to find a full-time job. He found the business card Mr. Elmer Smith had given him back in Georgia and went to apply for a job at the Smith's Lumber Company after hearing they needed help. After speaking with the manager of this branch of the Smith Lumber Company, Billy handed him the business card Mr. Smith had given him back in Georgia. The manager read what Mr. Smith had written on the back, Billy got the job.

Billy and Bobbie Jo were hesitant for him to work for Smith Lumber, as they were afraid Mr. Smith or Mrs. Smith might have spoken to someone back in Hardwood and figured out who Billy and Bobbie Jo really were. If Billy went to work for Mr. Smith, and he found out that the young boy from Georgia had been hired, there was a good chance Mr. Smith would turn him over to the authorities. Billy needed a job so they had decided to take the chance.

One Sunday afternoon, Billy and Bobbie Jo got the baby sitter to watch Sally Ann, and with Ole Red sitting between them they decided to take a drive. They drove up a winding road to a spot where the Campbells had told them about some land that was for sale. It was a five-acre tract of land on the side of a small mountain overlooking the valley that the Kootenai River ran through, and they decided this was the place to build their cabin.

After a few months working at the Smith's Lumber Company, nothing had been mentioned about Billy being from Georgia or his past. Billy and Bobbie Jo assumed the Smiths never spoke to any-one in Hardwood about meeting a young couple with a child. Billy guessed that since the home office for the Smith's Lumber Company was in Spokane, and Mr. Smith rarely came to Hillside, he probably did not know that Billy had used the business card to help get the job. When Billy found out that the Smiths had died in a crash on a slick mud road back in Georgia, he knew that was probably the main reason nothing ever came up about Billy's past. Billy told Bobbie Jo about the Smiths and they both were deeply saddened to hear about the Smith's.

"They were the nicest couple, and we were so lucky to have met them," Bobbie Jo commented to Billy.

It took a while, but they saved up enough money to buy the land and a small travel trailer. It took almost three years for Billy and Bobbie Jo to build their small cabin. Billy's job at the Smith's sawmill kept him at work five, sometimes six, days a week, leaving only the evenings and Sundays to work on clearing the land and building the cabin. Most of his pay was spent on the purchasing of building materials and other things to make their little place a home. Bobbie Jo had started working full time at the Hillside Diner, and now she was even doing some of the cooking; and everyone loved her strawberry-banana-cream pie.

The small cabin was about the same size as most of the others in the area. Billy had designed the floor plan to almost match the one he had helped build back in Georgia. The only difference being a larger porch that ran the entire length of the cabin on the east side, with the main entrance door centered in the middle of the porch and opened directly into the large family and kitchen area. Billy had gathered large rocks from the riverbank and made a nice solid walkway leading to the stairway going up onto the porch, with handrails on both sides. The porch was Billy's favorite place. He would sit and watch the early morning sunrise over the valley. In the summer, he and Jo would sit on the cabin porch and be out of the late afternoon heat and watch Sally Ann play in the yard with Ole Red. Bill had never seen Jo so happy when they slept in their bed for the first time in their finished cabin.

The land was fairly cheap in this area because it was only good for timber, not farming or grazing. All of the land around his five acres was covered in timber and it would be hard to harvest because of the underbrush and no roads. He had chosen this place for exactly that reason, seclusion. The only cleared area was around the center of his five acres, where their cabin sat and along the road leading to their cabin from the county road.

Over the years, they purchased more land around their five acres, which now totaled a couple of hundred acres, with part of the land running down to the river's edge. A few years after building the cabin, he cleared a little more land to the side of the cabin and built a garage where he kept his pickup on one side and a small workshop on the other side for his tools. He also had added on a small covered area at one end of the garage where he kept a few items that didn't need to be put inside. He would sometimes park his truck under this covered area when he needed the garage area to work on something out of the weather.

Sally Ann and Ole Red had become close companions. Billy and Bobbie Jo very seldom worried about her playing in the yard because Ole Red always warned everyone with a loud bark or howl if something wasn't right. Billy could tell by Red's barking if there was any kind of danger. Most of the time, it would be a garter snake, racoon or a skunk, Bill seldom saw timber rattlers on his property. However, when a black bear or an elk would wander into the yard, Ole Red had a completely different sound, and Billy knew he needed to check on them. As Sally Ann got old enough to attend school, Ole Red would lay on the porch and wait for Sally Ann to come home so they could play or go for a walk along the trail in the woods.

As the years went by, Sally Ann grew into a fine young lady. After high school, she moved to LA and went to work for the same company that one of her close friends worked for. She married a sales representative named Keith Thompson who also worked for the company. After a couple years of marriage, they had a son named Trey. Sally and Trey visited as often as she could get free, but as Trey got older, his interest was more with his friends than spending weekends with grandparents. Keith very seldom came with them; he was usually on the road.

With Trey getting older and wanting to be with his friends, trips to his grandparents with his mother became less frequent, which troubled Bill and Jo. They missed seeing her and wanted to see more of their grandson, but it was hard for her to get away for long weekends because of her work. On one of her last visits, all three, Sally, Trey and Keith came up. Sally Ann told Bill and Jo that she had cancer, and the doctors said she had approximately a year to live. This hit Bill harder than when he watched Sarah Lou die in his arms so many years before. Sally Ann and Trey made a couple more visits but they were for the weekend. Sally was getting weaker, and it was hard to travel and get around, and she told them this would probably be her last visit. Most of her visit the last time was spent sitting on the porch talking with her father while Jo took Trey to Hillside or one of the other little towns for shopping or sightseeing. Bill wanted to tell his daughter about her birth mother and how she had died, and that he had spent time in prison, but his emotions wouldn't let him. This time was for his daughter only and not about him or the past.

For years after Sally's death, Bill sat rocking on the porch, agonizing over not telling his daughter about her mother, him going to prison, and how they came to live in Hillside. He felt as if he had betrayed his daughter. When he brought this up to Jo, her response was always, "For some reason, God did not want you telling her, and someday you will know and understand why."

This answer never satisfied Bill, but he knew Jo was right. With him getting older, he did not want to make the same mistake with his grandson. It had been over thirty years since their daughter's death and with Trey a grown man; Bill and Jo decided it was time to tell Trey about their past and what had happened years ago back in Georgia and that his granddad was an escaped convict. They did not know how well Trey would accept this since he had worked as a detective in the LA police department.

Bill and Jo sat at their small table in the kitchen, having their coffee after breakfast, and Bill commented, "I have been reluctant to tell you these past few months, but I have had a strange feeling that someone is still looking for me. I know it is probably nothing, the feeling just keeps popping up."

"Do you think after all these years they would still be looking for you?"

"I wouldn't think so, but not sure. In the eyes of the law, I'm still an escaped convict."

"After we tell Trey about our past, we can see how he takes it, maybe you can ask him about looking into seeing if they are still looking for you."

"I will do that, depending on how he reacts."

"When we go to town later today, we can call him from the diner and ask him if he has time to come up for a visit," Jo said.

"I would like to see if he can stay for a few days so we can spend some time with him, and I can take him to the river and do a little fishing."

"Sounds good. If he says yes, I will need to make a list of things to fix for meals."

As Bill and Jo finished their meal at the Hillside Diner, Jo asked Betty if she could use the phone to call Trey. "Not a problem, help yourself, take as long as you need."

Jo called. Trey answered and seemed excited she had called. After they finished asking each other how everyone was doing, Jo said, "Bill and I would like to know if you would have time to come up and spend a few days with us, since in one of your letters, you mentioned that you took early retirement from the detective department, and we are worried something might be wrong. We have not spent much time with you over these past few years and would like to get to know you better and hear what is going on in your life, and we would like to discuss things with you that we think you should know."

"There is nothing wrong. I took early retirement to lessen some of the stress that goes with the job. I also had the opportunity to go to work part-time for a small private investigating firm. I am still doing mostly what I did before, but the stress factor is a lot less. I work on divorce cases for attorneys tracking down people who are not paying child support or help with finding children who have run away from home. It's rewarding when I can find kids and get them back with their parents. You mentioned you wanted to discuss something with me. Is anything wrong?"

"No, nothing is wrong. Over the past few years, we have been thinking that you are probably our only close relative we have left, and we would like to spend some time with you."

"I will check with the office and find out if I can take some time off as soon as I finish with the case I am working on, but it will probably won't be for a couple of months. I don't think it will be a problem, and I will write to you to give you a date when I can drive up."

"Thanks, sounds wonderful. I will tell Bill, hope to see you soon."

Jo hung up the phone and told Bill that Trey would send them a letter to give them a date when he would be coming up.

There was not much conversation on their drive home, other than the excitement of Trey coming for a visit. Bill was looking forward to taking him to the river and spend the day fishing. He hadn't been fishing with his grandson since he was little. He thought, *I need to get my gear checked out and make sure it was all in working order.* Jo thought of the different things she could bake: *homemade bread, donuts, and, Trey's favorite, strawberry-banana-cream pie.*

The next week, they waited on Trey's letter. The two of them had more life in their step, but Bill was worried about how Trey would react to their past life. Finally, when his letter came, they found out the day he would be there. Jo told Bill she would need to go to town a couple of days before he got there to get things to do some baking. Bill said, he too, needed a few things. They were acting like a couple of young kids going to the city to buy toys.

CHAPTER 7

Dan and the Pups

Bill suddenly sat up and yelled out as he wildly slapped at his arm, trying to remove whatever creature had landed on it. His nightshirt was wet with sweat. He was breathing heavily. He rolled over onto his side, slowly swung his legs off the side of the bed, and sat up. In his eighties now, it was getting harder and harder to move in the morning. He sat there, trying to slow down his shaking, and realized it was just another bad dream. He was not in the swamp, but on his bed, in his own house. Glancing at the open window next to his bed, he noticed the curtain being slightly lifted by the early morning wind. He realized it was not a critter from the swamp that touched his arm, only a piece of shredded window curtain.

Jo heard his abrupt awakening and shouted from the kitchen, "Bill, you, okay? Did you have another one of your nightmares?" Over the years, she had replaced Billy with Bill.

"Yeah, this time, it seemed more real than any of the others." The nightmares had taken more control over his last few minutes of sleep these past few weeks. They came more frequently and had become more vivid with each dream. He wondered if it had anything to do with him feeling someone was getting close to finding him. Sitting there, he thought of his younger years and his short time with his first wife, Sarah, and their deceased daughter, Sally Ann. He knew it was time to tell Trey about the past, his time in prison, and how he had escaped. What Bill wanted Trey to know, most of all, was he had

69

been convicted of murdering a young man back in Georgia, but he did not commit the crime and did not know who did. Bill knew Trey had probably heard every convicted person say they weren't guilty; would his grandson believe him?

With stiff leathery skin and popping bones, Bill slowly shuffled into the kitchen. He breathed in the wonderful smells of his wife's cooking. She was making one of his favorites—sausage, eggs, biscuits, and gravy. He headed for the stove where the coffee was perking. He hated to admit it, but he was addicted to strong coffee. It was what he needed to kick-start his day. He had begun drinking the strong black coffee in prison back in Georgia, where it had been made in large cast-iron pots. The water and coffee grounds were brought to a boil, then turned down to simmer. After the coffee grounds settled to the bottom, one would dip his cup in, let the coffee slowly run into it, trying to keep out as many of the grounds as possible. These new coffee makers just didn't have the taste he liked. He still preferred coffee made by perking on the stove. To him, the old way just tasted better, even though it sometimes brought back memories of the times he wanted to forget.

Bill took his first sip and said to his wife of over sixty years, "Head'n' to the porch." He pushed open the screen door and headed out with cup in hand.

"Breakfast will be ready in about thirty minutes."

While rocking slowly, waiting for breakfast, he thought of Ole Red, the hound that helped him escape from prison and saved his life. Sally Ann, his deceased daughter, entered his thoughts as well, but he shook his head to try and erase those thoughts. Ole Red had lived a long life for a dog. Bill thought he was about twenty years old when he died, and Jo had told him he needed to get another dog or two. Bill had put it off. He did not want to get attached to another dog. The heartache was too hard when it was their time. But maybe it was time for him to look for another dog, but he wanted to get two. Dogs are pack animals, and they do better when they have a companion. As the old rocker made its noises with each gentle rock, he thought back to his early days growing up in Hardwood, Georgia. He thought of times when he and his best friend, Sam, had taken their hunting hounds out and would spend hours in the woods training them to track and hunt. He was lost in his thoughts when he heard Jo say, "Breakfast is on."

When they finished eating, he told Jo he was going to town to get a few supplies and asked her if she needed anything. She wrote down a few things, handed him the list, and watched as he walked to his truck and drove down their gravel road to the county blacktop that led to Hillside. She thought about how much she loved him and how it had only grown over the years.

With the shopping done, he stepped out of the general store and noticed an elderly man standing beside a mule hitched to a small wooden wagon. He was dressed in what looked like buckskin, had on tall leather boots, and a cap that looked like it had been made from a coon, but Bill wasn't quite sure. Bill noticed the man seemed out of place and appeared to be a little lost.

Bill asked, "Can I help you with something?" in a way he hoped wouldn't seem meddling.

The old man gave Bill a puzzled look and said, "You live on Lookout Mountain?"

"Yes, I do. I have a cabin in the clearing on the northeast side, about a half-mile from the river."

"Yep, thought it was you."

Bill was puzzled. He had lived on his property for many years and knew of no other cabins on his side of the mountain that were lived in full time. He hunted all over the mountain and fished along his side of the river that ran through the valley and had never seen this gentleman. There were a few cabins on the mountainside downstream from his land, but most of them were only used by hunting and fishing guides and only for a few days at a time. On his twelve-mile drive to work each day, Bill took the narrow winding two-lane blacktop that ran along the river and he would drive by several small homes; some wood, some brick, but most were log homes like his. He could not remember ever seeing an old man dressed like this or a mule at any of the houses.

Concerned, Bill asked, "Where have you seen me?"

The man was silent for a bit, then said, "At the river."

"Do you live on Lookout Mountain?" Bill asked.

"Nope."

Bill thought, *this is a man of few words*, and he seemed nervous. Bill remembered seeing men like this in prison, keeping to themselves, saying very little, not getting close to anyone. The old man reminded Bill of himself. Was this man hiding from his past like he was? Bill watched as the man turned, grabbed the lead rope hanging from the mule's head, and walked away.

A week after the encounter with the old man, Bill drove his pickup down to his favorite secluded fishing spot. He had found the spot one winter's day while hunting for rabbits and squirrels. Over hundreds of years, the river had cut into the mountainside, creating a gently sloping gravel bank down to the river's edge. The river became wide at this point with several small cuts into the bank. The mainstream current was about a hundred feet out. Where the slower water at the edge of the mainstream cut back to the edge of the riverbank, it created small eddies. This was a perfect place for fish to rest and wait for their prey. Over the years, Bill worked to clear a path wide enough to drive his truck to this fishing hole. The only way to get to this spot by vehicle meant you had to cross Bill's property and pass in front of his log cabin. You could walk from the blacktop road in the lower valley, but it would be at least an hour's hike through thick woods and undergrowth. This seclusion made it Bill's favorite spot, with no intruders and fishing usually good.

After unloading his fishing gear, he sat down on his three-legged stool and tied a lure to his line. The lure resembled a shiny smelt, one that kokanee salmon couldn't resist. Since the kokanee usually won't eat when they are moving upstream in the fresh water, he would settle for white fish, smallmouth, or rock bass. Maybe a kokanee would forget they are not supposed to eat when going upstream, and he would catch one. He cast the lightly weighted lure to the far edge of the eddy, just at the edge of the faster-flowing water, where it would slowly drift back into the calmer waters of the eddy. Maybe a white fish or bass would be waiting for lunch to drift by.

He had been sitting for several minutes, holding the line with his fingertips, waiting to feel any slight tug on the line, when he noticed movement in the tree line on the other side of the river. He had only caught a glimpse, but it looked like a man had stepped out from behind a large pine tree then stepped back behind it. Someone could have walked up from the blacktop road, but it would be hard to make it back to the road before dark. Again, he saw movement; this time, he knew it was a man.

The memory of him being chased by prison dogs and guards' years earlier flashed in his mind. This caused him to stiffen and put him on alert. The figure stepped out of the tree line, onto the gravel bank on the other side of the river. Bill recognized the hat the man wore and realized it was the old man he had met in town a week earlier. Bill wondered what he was doing here and eased his hand down inside his jacket and gripped the butt of his Colt .38 revolver.

The old man started across the river toward Bill, following the shallower water as best he could. He had a walking stick in one hand, the other was empty, hanging at his side. Bill watched closely while the old man approached, making sure he did not reach inside his unbuttoned jacket for a pistol. When the old man got within speaking distance, he stopped.

"Any luck?"

"No."

"What ya fishin' for?"

"Anything that will bite."

"Won't get a kokanee, they're on the move."

Bill was getting a little annoyed with the short answers.

"This is my land, and when you step out of the river, you're trespassing!" The old man continued to walk toward Bill.

"Mind if I sit a bit?"

Bill was hesitant but curious.

"Nah, have a seat." The man sat on a large boulder about six feet from Bill and laid down his walking stick. When he reached into his vest, which looked like deerskin, Bill pulled out his .38.

"Whoa, Billy boy, just want to offer you some deer jerky."

Bill felt a little embarrassed, laid down his fishing rod, and took the offering of jerky, still holding onto his revolver. This was the most

73

he had heard the old man say in one sentence. Bill was curious about this old man. Where did he live? What was he doing here? And he had called him Billy boy. Growing up back in Georgia, most people that knew him called him Billy boy, even though his given name was William J. Bersha.

Calling him Billy boy put him on edge even more. He gripped his pistol a little tighter, and they sat there, not speaking for a minute or so, just watching the water flow by.

Seeing the rod tip move and the fishing line tightening up, Bill grabbed the rod with his one free hand and set the hook.

"Looks like a nice one, fight'n' like a bass." Bill was having difficulty reeling in the fish while holding onto the pistol and didn't answer. Walking backwards to pull the fish onto the bank, he could see it was a rock bass but still a nice fish.

"What's your name?" Bill asked as he walked backward, pulling the fish onto the bank. Bill stood there, trying to figure out how to remove the hook while holding his pistol. Bill stepped back a few more steps, laid the pistol on the rock next to him, and started removing the hook. "Where do you live?"

"I'm Dan. I live in the cabin on the other side of the river a few miles upstream. My place is kind of hard to get to from the road. There's only a narrow cart trail off the road to my cabin."

"Got a last name?"

"Sorry," the old man said, "It's Dan Moran. Kinda rhymes, don't it, Dan Moran?" The old guy giggled a little. "Guess my parents thought it would be funny. It ain't."

"How did you know my name was Bill?"

"I keep my eyes and ears open and mouth shut when in town. I hear people talking about you and Mrs. Perkins and that you live along this part of the river."

Becoming very uneasy with Dan's presence and responses to his questions, Bill glanced down at his .38 lying next to him.

"No need for that, Billy. I'm no threat." Dan stood up, laid a piece of jerky on a rock next to him and picked up his walking stick.

"Well, Billy boy, guess I'll be head'n' back across the river. I have a couple of traps I need to check on the way home. I need to get started so that I can make it home before dark, I just wanted to leave you with some jerky, and introduce myself."

As Dan walked away, he asked, "Mind if I come here again? Looks like a good stop for bass. I could use bass in my diet."

"Don't mind, just don't let it out about this private fish'n' hole."

"I won't. Enjoyed our visit. See ya again up here."

There was something about Dan that Bill could not get a fix on. While gathering up his gear, it occurred to him—it seemed as if Dan had a slight Southern accent when he spoke. It wasn't much, but it was noticeable with certain words. Bill would have to be on guard about what the two of them discussed if they ever meet again. Bill told Jo about Dan Moran, and she was glad he had someone to visit with while he was at the river. She felt a little safer knowing that someone would be there if Bill needed help.

Over the next couple of weeks, Dan would show up, cross the river, share some jerky, and they would talk about the townspeople and how the world was changing. Not much about their past lives, or exactly where they came from were discussed in much detail. Bill told Dan he was from the southeast. Dan talked about northern California. He had bought the piece of land a few years back and would come up every few months and work on the cabin that was on the land. It was finished now, and he had been living in it full-time for close to a year.

Bill told Dan he had worked for different logging companies and sawmills in the southeast, and finally ended up in Hillside. During their talks, Bill would notice a slight Southern accent. In one of their talks, Bill mentioned that he had brought a hunting dog with him, and about fifteen years or so after arriving in Idaho, the dog had died. Being without a dog for all these years, he thought it was time to get another one. His wife, Jo, told him he needed to get another one shortly after Ole Red died, but he just didn't want the heartache of losing another companion. After hearing this, Dan said his American Fox hound had a litter of pups, and he had given them all away except for two little females. Their mother was a great tracker, and the pups were smaller than the others, but he thought they would turn out to be the smartest.

"Billy boy, you need the dogs. I will give you the pups if you take them both. I'm not going to separate them. They've grown attached to each other."

At first, Bill said no, but Dan persisted, and Bill gave in, "I'll take'm."

"I'll bring them with me next time, and let them get used to your smell, and see if they will accept you."

"What do you mean by that comment?" Bill asked.

"Well, you smell like a freshly washed shirt, and that may be the reason for your poor fishing and hunting. I can smell you a mile away."

"You could use a little spicing up yourself," Bill shot back. "I'll trade you a bar of soap and some aftershave for the dogs."

"You got a deal, Billy boy."

"I'll bring the soap and aftershave. See ya Friday, Dan the mountain man."

"Dan the mountain man sounds better than Dan Moran."

The next time Bill went to his fishing hole, Dan was there waiting with the two pups. Dan told Bill they were about a year old, and Bill could see they were small for their age. The first thing Bill noticed was how attentive they were when he spoke to them. They cocked their heads, and their ears perked up. That was a good sign. They tend to pay attention when spoken to, even at this young age. After running his hands over both the pups to feel for lumps or any possible bone disfigurement, Bill decided to take them. "Looks and feels like they're in good shape, and most important of all, they seem to have a good sense of attention, I'll take'm."

"Thought of any names?"

"I want to train them to track and hunt. I think I'll name them Tracker and Hunter."

"Sounds like good names for them."

Jo was in the kitchen when Bill pulled into the yard, and Jo heard him talking; she went to the door and saw the two pups standing on the truck's tailgate. They were not sure about jumping out.

"Looks like you have a couple of friends that need to learn how to jump."

"Yeah, I think they will jump as soon as they get a good smell of your cook'n.'"

"Guess those are the pups you traded the soap and aftershave for?"

"Yep, they're the ones."

"They look like miniature Ole Reds," Jo said.

"Yes, they do. I hope they will be as smart."

"They will have a good trainer. I have an old bowl under the cabinet for some water. I will fill it and bring it out."

"Have you thought about names?"

"Tracker and Hunter."

She thought the names were fitting as she watched the little American Fox hound's drink.

"Trey is coming next week, plan on telling Dan?"

"I told him I would be at the river day after tomorrow, will see what he thinks. I am sure he will be okay with it."

"I think you are right in checking with him first, and if he agrees, you can figure out some type of signal to let him know to come across the river to meet Trey."

"Good idea," Bill answered.

Since it was not suppertime yet, he and Jo sat on their rockers and watched the pups run around, sniffing everything. There were so many new smells they had to investigate. After running around, they came to the foot of the steps going up onto the porch. They sat there looking at Jo and Bill.

"Do you think they are afraid of the stairs?" Jo asked.

"I don't think so." Bill patted his leg and said, "Come on, Tracker, come on, Hunter." Both dogs sat there looking at him.

"Which one is which?"

"The one with the darker face is Tracker, and the one with the little white patch on top of her head is Hunter."

"Names sound good to me. Hope they don't change colors so we can tell them apart."

Bill patted his leg. "Come here, Tracker." The pup with the darker face slowly walked up the steps unto the porch deck and lay down beside Bill's rocker.

"Come here, Hunter." And again, Bill patted his leg, and the other little pup climbed up the steps and lay down beside the other dog.

"I think they already know their names," Jo commented.

"Looks like it. I knew they were smart the first time I saw them, made eye contact, and spoke. They both cocked their heads as if they were waiting for instructions."

"Guess you got your newfound friends now. I'm curious to see if they can bring home their own food."

"I'll teach them everything they need to know."

"That will be something I don't want to miss. You down on all fours showing them how to track a rabbit."

"I'll have'm tracking in a month, no more going to town for dog food or meat."

"Can't wait," Jo said.

CHAPTER 8

❦

Anxiety about Grandson Trey's Arrival

Bill and Dan had been meeting at the river for several weeks now and had become fairly good friends, they just knew not to talk too much about their early lives or exactly where they had grown up. This morning he was going to tell Dan about Trey coming to visit. Bill pulled his pickup up to the shed by his cabin, got out, and as soon as he dropped the tailgate to load his gear, Hunter and Tracker both jumped in. "Guess you two are ready to go, but I didn't invite you."

Bill realized he was talking to dogs that did not answer back. Both dogs were looking at him with excitement in their eyes and tails wagging waiting for the invitation. They were his constant companions. Bill had learned early that dogs are not at all like humans, and they are always glad to see you; they do not care what is happening in your life, good or bad. All they require is your companionship, food, water and love. He had seen people who mistreated their dogs, and for some reason, the dogs are always forgiving, unlike most people. Bill's memory flashed back to prison and the guard kicking the dog. If it had not been for that, Bill would have never gotten the chance to train Ole Red and escape from prison.

On his drive to the river to meet Dan, Bill thought of the sermons the preacher gave when he attended church with his grandparents in his youth. "Love your enemies and forgive those who have done wrong against you," he would preach.

This was hard for Bill to do after what had happened to Sarah so many years ago. He had prayed about forgiveness, but it didn't seem to ease the pain of losing Sarah or being put in prison for something he did not do, even after all these years. Vengeance and anger always seemed to take over his thoughts.

"I need to work on this forgiveness stuff," he said out loud as dropped the tailgate and started to unloading his fishing gear. Dan was already there. "How ya doin', ladies? Ready to sniff out some rabbits, 'cuz I know you can't catch no fish."

Bill let out a short laugh and said, "Don't bet on that. They've figured out how to chase carp in the shallows by teaming up and cornering them next to the bank then one of them grabs it and hauls it out of the water. They have gotten pretty good at, but I don't care to eat carp. I'll stick to salmon, bass, catfish or perch, and I haven't tried to smoke carp, so I'm not sure the pups would eat smoked carp, they love my smoked salmon."

"That's the way I like mine, too, and you smoke it just like I like it," Dan said.

"Guess I have got all three of you spoiled. How about you three catch the fish while I sit and relax, and if you catch anything other than carp, I'll smoke it."

"Naw, I want to see if you still know how to fish."

Both men sat down on their stools and began putting bait on their lines; they were baiting up for perch or bluegill, but any fish would do.

"Dan, my grandson is coming to spend some time with us, and I wanted to tell you about him before he gets here. He was a detective for the Los Angeles Police Department but took early retirement, and now he is working as a private investigator."

"Oh, what kind of private investigator?"

"From his letters, he is with a small firm that works with divorce cases and runaway kids. They look for people not paying child support or alimony, cases the police don't really have time for or are not interested in pursuing, but people still need answers. He also helps families find their lost or runaway kids."

"I guess he is good at what he does if he left the security of the LA Police Department," Dan said with a bit of sarcasm.

"If you don't want to meet him, I understand."

"Billy boy, I would be glad to meet him."

"He'll be here for about a week. Since our daughter died and he's grown with a life of his own, we have not spent much time with him but want to get to know him better. Show him how life is out here, hunt'n, fish'n you know, he has lived in the city all his life. When his mom would bring him up, it was only for a day or two, and they wouldn't stay long so we didn't get to fish or hunt that much. His dad seldom came I think because for some reason I always felt his dad didn't care for me that much," Bill said sadly.

"What do you mean he didn't like you? You're the most sociable guy I know. You've got how many friends, let's see, one human—me—and two dogs."

Both men sat on their stools for some time without talking.

"Bill!" Dan broke the silence. "I got another one, it's a bass, looks like a good one."

"You're right. It's a rock bass, that makes four bass and three bluegills. One of us will need to catch one more bluegill so we can split them evenly between us."

At that moment, Bill's line tightened, and the line started unspooling from the reel.

"I don't think this is a bluegill or bass. It is taking the line out too fast, and my line drag is not holding it."

Just as Bill got the fish to the bank, Dan jumped up to get the dip net, and at that moment, the line snapped. The fish headed back to deep water.

With disappointment in his voice, Dan said, "That was a big catfish, one of the biggest I've seen here, that would'a been good eat'n."

Bill let out a sigh. "Guess he just didn't want to be fried."

"Guess that's a sign it is time to head home. Bill, I'll take one bass and one bluegill. You can have the rest as you have more mouths to feed. I will let you and Trey have some time together before I meet him. I'll check our spot here every few days, and you can let me know with a wave when the time is right to cross over."

They said their goodbyes. Bill started putting his gear in the back of his truck as the dogs jumped in.

As Dan walked home, he thought, with Trey being a private investigator, he might ask questions about northern California and maybe more personal questions. He would have to watch what he said to Trey.

"Did you get Dan's approval?" Jo questioned as Bill walked into the kitchen.

"Approval for what?"

"To meet Trey."

"Oh yeah. I think he is okay with it, but when I told him that Trey was a retired detective and now a private investigator, he seemed a little nervous."

"I'm sure he will be okay with it." She turned back to the counter, where she was rolling out some dough.

"What are you making dough for, bread or my favorite, donuts?"

"It's for both. I'll use half for bread, for the other half, I will mix in some sugar and cinnamon for donuts. I will let it rise overnight and bake it tomorrow. It's been some time since I made it. I wanted to practice before Trey gets here."

Bill got a cup from the cupholder and poured coffee from the pot on the stove. "Just like I like it, hot and strong." And he sat down at the end of the table.

"It will be about an hour before supper if you want to take a nap."

"Naw. I'll sit here for a bit, then help you with supper."

"I know you like to help, but you tend to clean things and put back in their place as you go. By the way, did you clean the fish or just leave them in the bucket?"

Bill stood up. "I forgot, I'll clean them and come back in to help you with supper."

"That's okay. I'll manage in here. Take your time cleaning and doing whatever you need to do outside, explain to the pups why I would rather fix supper without your help and I'll have it ready when you come back in."

Bill finished his coffee, washed out his cup, hung it on the cup tree, then walked to door leading to the porch. Tracker and Hunter were both lying in front of the door. They were looking inside, keeping an eye on what was going on in the kitchen.

"Okay, girls, let's clean fish." They both lay there. "Well, guess I will do it myself." They still lay there. They knew it was about suppertime, and they weren't moving.

Shortly after Bill had finished cleaning the fish, Jo cracked the screen door open and saw Bill wiping off his fish-cleaning knife. "Supper is ready if you are."

"I'll be in as soon as I put my cleaning table in the shed." Bill wrapped up the fish in a towel, folded up the table, rinsed off his cleaning knife and fish bucket, and put them all in the shed. He had a place for everything, and he believed everything should be in its place. This made Jo a little crazy sometimes because when he helped her in the kitchen, he would put things away when she knew she would need it again. But she always knew where things were when she needed them. She wasn't as organized as Bill but had gotten better over the years, living with him.

She loved him more than anything, even with the few habits he had that sometimes annoyed her. He was her husband and also her closest friend. She had always known Sarah Lou was his first love, and he still loved her even though she died years ago. Jo had accepted this a long time ago.

Bill entered the kitchen with a handful of cleaned fish and asked, "Can you get me a pan and put some water and salt in it so the fish can soak before I freeze them?"

"I already have. It's on the little table by the freezer."

"I have taught you well over the years."

"You're right. Now if you could only teach those hounds of yours to fix their own meals, that would be a trick and would give you more time to help me."

Bill started to say something. Jo held up her hand and said, "Nah, on the other hand, I work better alone."

"Great." He headed out the door with bowls of dog food.

"I cater to you just like you cater to those pups. Maybe you could start spending the night in the shed with them."

"I don't think so. Who would warm up the bed before you get in at night?"

"You're right. I would miss that, but don't get any ideas about the pups sleeping in the bed and taking over your warming job."

Changing the subject, "Bill, I'm worried."

"About what?"

"I am worried about how Trey will react when you tell him about our past and you being an escaped convict."

"I'm a little worried as well, not only about our past but about the feeling that someone is still looking for me. I want to ask him if he can check around and see if I am still being hunted. I know he's a grown man and I know he has seen and heard a lot in his line of work, I'm sure he will be okay with everything after I explain to him what happen to Luke Hampton."

"Except when he hears you didn't do it, will be from family," Jo said.

Jo couldn't help but think how Trey would react. She thought quietly to herself as they both continued eating without talking. After telling their grandson what happened back in Georgia, would he tell Bill he needed to turn himself in? Or would he take a softer approach and maybe have some suggestions as to how to ease their worry about being found. Her thoughts were getting more and more confusing.

Bill looked over at Jo, "Looks like you still have worries about Trey?"

"I do, but I am going to pray about it and let *God* take over. I need to have faith that it will work out for the best."

"Sounds good to me. I will pray about it as well, cuz you know how much I pray. Maybe he will forgive me for not talking to him as often as I should and help us with this problem."

Jo picked up their plates and took them to the counter.

Bill wanted her to have some time alone. He told her he would finish cleaning up the kitchen; she could head on to bed, and he would be there shortly. Hoping he had put everything back where it belonged, he looked out the back door and saw the dog bowls were licked cleaned. Hunter and Tracker were just going through the little rubber door flap on the side of the garage. It was their bedtime as well. Bill flipped the light off and headed for the bedroom where Jo, for once, was already in bed but not asleep.

When he got settled in bed and told her, "Don't worry. I am sure everything will be okay." They gave each other a short kiss. Bill grabbed Jo's hand and squeezed it and told her again, "It will be okay."

"I know."

They both lay there in silence, holding hands. After a few minutes, he felt hers relax. Bill heard her heavy breathing and knew that she had drifted off to sleep, but he could not. He thought the last thing he wanted to do was alienate his only grandson. He had not told Jo that he was more than a little concerned about telling Trey he spent time in prison. Would his grandson rely on his experience with other criminals who said they didn't do it, or would he believe his grandfather?

As he lay there, he could see the full moon every time the breeze moved the curtain and thought of his past. His emotions got the better of him. Tears formed in his eyes and slowly rolled down his cheeks. He wiped them away and, for some reason, knew he needed to ask God for help. For the past few years, Jo had suggested they should find a small church and start attending. She also reminded him that they both needed to pray more and be thankful for all they had and for God protecting them all these years. Laying on the nightstand, next to his side of the bed, was his grandmother's little Bible that he had brought with him to Idaho. She had given it to him years before, when he was saying his goodbyes before getting on the bus that took him to prison. He had put it in his pocket on the day of his escape. He laid his hand on the Bible and whispered so that he wouldn't wake Jo. "Dear Lord, please give me the wisdom to say the right things when telling Trey about my past. Thank you, Lord, for protecting us all these years and for what you have blessed us with. I ask you to ease our worries about Trey's visit, amen." He drifted off to sleep.

The next morning Jo checked on the dough, which she had put on the counter by the stove to keep it warm so it would rise. As she started preparing breakfast, her thoughts turned to Trey. His visits in the past were only for a day or two every few months when he came with his mother Sally Ann. After their daughter passed away, his visits became less frequent. His dad couldn't or wouldn't take off work long enough to drive to Hillside for a visit, and Bill knew Trey's dad, Keith, did not want to bring him for a visit.

Bill came into the kitchen, got his coffee cup, filled it, and sat down at the table.

"I heard your prayer last night."

"Sorry, I didn't mean to wake you."

"That's okay. It was nice to hear you ask God for help and thank him for protecting us all these years and blessing us with everything we need. Thank you for your prayer, it eased my worries."

"I felt much better after saying it as well. Guess it is true. When you ask God for help, he is there, and I slept better for it. Like you have told me in the past, I need to do more of that, and I will try to remember to do so."

Jo put a plate of pancakes on the table in front of him, kissed him on the cheek, sat down, and asked, "What's on your schedule for today?"

"I am going to move some things around in the garage so Trey can park his car inside. I will put my pickup under the carport."

"Are the pups going to help?"

"I doubt it. I think it is their day of rest. They did a lot of chasing in the woods when we went to the river yesterday."

"Did they bring anything back to help restock what we feed them?"

"No, nothing to eat, probably just a few fleas and ticks."

"Guess you will have to check them over after you do your truck shuffling."

"Yeah, I may even give them a bath since they did not get in the river yesterday."

"I'm sure they will enjoy that. Just don't let them get near the bedsheets that I am going to hang out later this morning."

"I'll tell them to stay clear of the clean laundry."

They finished their breakfast without much more conversation.

Bill and Jo tried to stay busy throughout the day getting things ready for Trey's visit, and by the end of the day, both of them were tired. Jo had made some sandwiches and a pitcher of ice tea and suggested that they have a light supper on the porch. They could relax in the cool evening breeze and watch the trees in the valley as they created their long shadows as the sun was setting. It was always peaceful to watch the birds and other little critters scurry around before sunset, getting settled in for the night. Every once in a while, Tracker and Hunter would jump off the porch to chase a squirrel that would come down from a tree to search the yard for nuts. They never caught any. They always scampered back up the tree and would sit on a branch chattering, just out of reach of the dogs.

"I am getting a little chilly. I think I will get ready for bed. Busy day tomorrow going to town, getting stocked up before Trey arrives," Jo said.

"Yes, it will be busy but enjoyable to see Trey again. I'll be in shortly. Want to make sure the pups don't accidentally catch that squirrel."

Bill sat rocking slowly, sipping his tea and thinking about his deceased daughter, Sally Ann. He could barely make out where her grave exactly was in the moonlight. He knew it was up the hillside a little way next to the old tree stump, her favorite sitting spot. He missed her and wished she could have lived long enough to see how her son, Trey, had grown up. He wiped his eyes and headed inside.

CHAPTER 9

Trey's Arrival

As usual, Jo was already in the kitchen when Bill slowly walked in and got his cup of the strong black coffee that Jo had brewing on the stove.

"How's that for service early in the morning?" she said.

Bill took a sip and said, "As good as it has ever been." Then he sat down at the table. He looked out the screen door and saw the pups eagerly waiting for him to come out and sit on his rocker as he usually did, but he decided to eat first.

"I'll be out in a bit, ladies, and will give you your instructions for the day." The dogs cocked their heads as he talked to them.

"Do those dogs ever answer you?" Jo questioned.

"Sometimes."

"Well, they never answer me when I ask them a question."

"Maybe they don't understand you; you have to know hunt'n track'n dog talk?"

"Guess you'll have to teach me in your spare time."

"I'll put that on my bucket list. Are you still concerned about Trey?"

"Not as much. Been doing a lot of praying. It helps."

"Me too."

She flipped the eggs over.

"Wish we had one of those phones everyone carries around. That way, Trey could call us when he gets close to town."

"Sometimes I think we should have gotten one as well," Bill said.

"Someone would have to teach us how to use it." Jo set the plate of eggs and ham down on the table.

"Maybe we can talk to Trey about it. I'm sure he knows how they work. In his letter, he said he would be in Hillside midafternoon and would meet us in front of the hardware store and follow us home. Do you want to ride back with him, or do you want me to?" Bill asked.

"You can ride back with him, and you two can talk about those phones and how they work."

"Good idea." With no more conversation, the two of them finished their breakfast. Bill took his cup of coffee outside and sat on the porch with the pups and thought about the phone while Jo cleaned up the kitchen.

As he started rocking, he thought about when he, Jo, and Sally Ann first arrived in Hillside and how they wanted to be as self-sufficient as possible. They needed to live off the grid, as people called it, with as little contact with people as possible. They needed to be invisible.

Bill finished his coffee, walked back into the kitchen, washed his cup, and put it back on the cup tree. He said out loud to himself, "A place for everything and everything in its place."

Jo was standing in the hallway. "I'm ready." She looked at the clock on the wall. "We have a couple of hours before Trey gets to town. You better get ready so that we won't be late."

"Remember, Trey said it would be midafternoon. If we leave now, we will be sitting for longer than I want to," Bill replied, a little too sharply. "Sorry," he said, "guess I'm a little nervous."

"We can kill some time. I have a short list of things I need. You can look around for new and exciting tools at the hardware store and maybe one of those phones."

"That means we have to go to three stores—one for groceries, the hardware store, and the Dollar Up store?"

"Oh, I forgot how much you like to shop," she replied. "You get in, get what you need, and leave."

"Guess we can skip the hardware store," Bill said.

"With such a large selection of stores in Hillside, we could visit them all and be head'n' back home in less than an hour," Jo said.

"My kind of shopping." He finished getting ready and said, "Let's head out." They walked onto the porch where Tracker and Hunter were waiting. "Not this time, girls, we'll be back before dark."

As they were getting into the pickup, Jo said, "You sure talk to those dogs a lot."

"Well, they never talk back, and they know I am always right."

"I need to have a heart-to-heart talk with them and set them straight about you always being right."

"I thought you said they never answered you?"

"I can at least tell them. They can decide to answer me or not."

"They probably won't." Bill started the truck.

Over the years, Bill and Jo had learned to tease and joke with each other, never taking it too far and knowing when to stop. Bill knew this was one of those times.

Hillside was about a thirty-minute drive due to the road following the many curves of the river, so they would be there by lunchtime. Bill had suggested they eat lunch at the Hillside Diner and not at one of the fast-food drive-throughs; Jo agreed. She enjoyed not having to cook. She liked the little place and the people who owned it. It's where she had worked when they first got to Hillside and while they built the cabin. There was a stop and go convenience store where Bill bought gas with some ready-made sandwiches, slices of pizza, hot links, and a few other food items; but this was a special occasion, and he wanted it to be just that. It was Saturday, and this was when people came to town to stock up on supplies and visited with neighbors they had not seen in a couple of weeks. They parked in front of the Hillside Diner and went in. Bill pointed to a table in the corner by the window so he could see the hardware store across the street and watch for Trey. They sat down, and Betty, the wife of the owner of the little restaurant, came to their table.

"Jo, it is so good to see you. We've missed you. How have you been?"

"I am doing fine, been busy at home getting things ready to plant a garden, ya know, all the stuff you do in early spring."

"What brings you to town? You here for the town picnic?"

"No. Didn't know there was one. We're here to meet our grandson, Trey. He is going to spend some time with us."

"That's nice, and you might want to stay for the big get-together, looks like there will be a lot of people and food, and I am sure I could have sold all the strawberry-banana-cream pies you could make."

"We'll see, but Trey might be tired from his drive up from California."

"Good to see you too, Bill. Tom asked Dan about you when he stopped by a while back for some scraps for his traps, they had a long conversation about you and the pups you gave him. Dan wanted to know if Tom knew where you had learned how to train hunting and tracking hounds. Tom guessed your dad taught you when you were young. The long visit was unusual for ole Dan."

"Tell Tom hi."

"What'll ya have?" Bill and Jo both knew what they wanted and placed their order.

After Betty left, Bill whispered to Jo, "Wonder what else Tom and Dan talked about?"

"You're too paranoid, Jo said."

"Maybe some people just want to know how we are doing. Remember, we lived in town for a few years and did make a few friends, other than Betty and Tom, but not close ones. And maybe if we had had more people over for wine and cheese, played a round of bridge, we would have had more friends," Jo said a little sarcastically.

"I don't even know how to play bridge."

"Never mind, you can play solitaire. You're good at that."

Betty set their glasses of water on the table. "Food will be out in a few, and Tom said hello. He would like to talk to you before you leave." Betty turned and headed to another table; Bill looked at Jo.

"Don't worry, you have done carpentry work for him in the past, and he knows you're retired from the sawmill. Maybe he needs a few things done."

"You're right. I'm sure it's nothing to worry about."

Betty set their plates on the table. "If you need anything else, let me know. Enjoy your meal." Bill and Jo ate in silence.

Finishing their lunch, Bill paid the bill, and Tom came out of the kitchen and told Bill since he had some new pups, for him to stop by and he would give him some scrap to give to the pups.

Jo said, "see you had nothing to worry about, Tom was just being friendly, offering you the scraps."

"You're right," and they walked out onto the sidewalk. Hillside was a small town and was filling up with people. Across the street was the hardware store with a lumberyard in the back. There was an insurance business on one side and a real estate business on the other. Next to the restaurant where they ate was the Dollar Up store, which sold almost everything—a few grocery items, clothing, electronics, and some furniture.

Jo said, "Trey's not here. Let's look at those phones."

Bill didn't like the idea but agreed to look. It had been over sixty years when he and Jo had fled from Georgia, and he was worried that someone may be able to track them down if they started using those phones. How many questions would he need to answer to get one? They walked up to the glass case. There were several different colors and sizes; neither Bill nor Jo knew exactly how they worked. They had bought a radio shortly after they got electricity to their cabin, and a few years later, they purchased a small TV. It finally broke, and they bought a new one that worked off a satellite dish but did not really know how it worked. The young man instructed them on how to use it, but Bill nor Jo could figure out how to use all the buttons—record, pause, fast-forward, and so on. They had seen ads on TV about cell phones but did not know what they needed to do to get one. Finally, a young sales lady approached them.

"Can I help you?" Bill didn't answer. He didn't know what to ask and didn't want her to think he was ignorant about the phones. His pride kept his mouth shut.

Jo asked, "How do they work."

The young lady had dealt with elderly people before who had no idea how they worked, so she picked out one with bigger numbers and explained how it worked and what to do to get one.

She asked, "Will you be using it mainly for phone calls, or will you be sending texts, taking photos ect?"

Jo looked at Bill, then at the young lady.

"Just phone calls," Jo said. Bill wasn't enjoying this; he did not like not knowing how something worked, and Jo could tell he was getting anxious.

Jo said, "Thank you for your time. We are meeting our grandson in a little while; we will have him come in with us to have another look. Thank you again." They walked back outside where Jo saw a bench.

"Let's sit down. We can see the hardware store from here and watch for Trey. We need a phone," Jo said. "We are older and need to be able to contact someone if we need help."

"I know. I just hate getting old and maybe having to depend on you or someone else."

"We're not on our deathbeds yet, Bill."

"Well, it feels like it in the mornings when I try to get my stiff body out of bed."

"But you somehow managed to make it to the kitchen for my fine coffee and breakfast, then go out and have a long morning conversation with those dogs, discussing how you can mess up my plans for the day."

Bill replied, "I will work on that and make my conversations shorter."

"Thanks. That way, you will only mess up half of my day." Bill took her hand and squeezed it. "We'll talk to Trey about the cell phones and see what he thinks. After I tell him about our past, he will have a better idea of why we have wanted to stay hidden. He will know if using one of those phones can lead someone here to us."

They sat there watching the little town of Hillside fill with people. At the far end of the street, people were unloading long tables and folding chairs from trucks. They were setting them up, end to end, down the middle of the street.

Bill said, "The way they are setting things up, I hope we can get out of town."

"Maybe you should move our truck to the other end of town so we will have an exit."

"You're probably right. Wait here and hold our bench while I move the pickup. As busy as it's get'n, we could lose our sit'n' place." Bill patted Jo on the shoulder and said, "Keep an eye peeled for Trey, I'll be back quicker than chicken after a June bug."

"You sure have a way with words. I'll be right here."

She watched Bill walk away and thought of the first time she saw him back in Georgia. Over the years, she knew his love for her had grown, and now he would do anything for her. She looked up the street and saw a fairly new car that looked out of place for this pickup-and-four-wheel-drive town. Could that be Trey? As the car grew closer, she saw that the driver wore a ball cap, sunglasses, and looked to have a well-trimmed beard. When the car parked in front of the hardware store, and the driver got out, Jo was fairly confident it was Trey. It looked like him, but this man appeared taller; so, she wasn't sure. It had been a long time since they had last seen him and he was a grown man, so she wasn't sure. But the more she watched the man and the way he was looking around, the more she decided it was him but couldn't tell with the beard, glasses, and cap. Bill approached and sat down beside her.

Jo said, "See the man with the ball cap standing in front of the hardware store? I think that might be Trey." Bill squinted his eyes, trying to focus on the man.

"The way he is looking around, I think it is."

"Looks like that's an out-of-state license plate on the car." Bill grabbed her hand and stood up.

"Let's walk across the street and see if he recognizes us. As they approached, the young man turned and saw them.

"Papa Bill, Grandma Jo, so good to see you." He gave Jo a big hug and grabbed Bill's hand with both of his and gave a good squeeze, then hugged him.

"It's good to see you as well, Trey," Jo said.

"Lot more people here than I remember the last time I was here."

"Town's having their annual picnic later this afternoon," Bill said.

"That's nice. I guess small towns still act like family, unlike the big one where I am from, where everyone goes their own way, seldom speaking."

"We can stay if you like," Jo said.

"If you want to, that's fine," Trey answered.

"I think it would be better if we head back home. I don't want Jo driving the road home after dark, too many curves. I had planned on riding back with you, and Jo can drive the pickup home if that's okay?"

"That won't be necessary. I can follow you," Trey said.

"Well, let's head for home." Bill turned and headed up the street for his pickup, while Jo and Trey waited there.

After getting into their pickup and heading out of town, Bill made sure Trey was behind them.

"That seemed a little awkward and tense, don't you think?" Jo asked.

"It did, but remember, he hasn't seen us in a long time.

"I remember the last time he stayed longer than a couple of days. It was when Sally Ann and Keith brought him. That was when she told us she was sick, and they would be staying three or four days. I could tell Keith felt uneasy about staying that long," Jo replied.

Bill changed the subject. He didn't want to think about his deceased daughter. "I'm going to drive slower than usual because of the curves, and it is getting dark. I want Trey to be able to see us when we make the turn off the blacktop onto our gravel drive, it is easy to miss."

As they rounded the curve just before their turnoff, Bill checked the rearview mirror to make sure Trey saw them turn. He did and followed them up the winding drive to the cabin. Bill pulled between the cabin and his shop, under the covering, jumped out, and directed Trey to pull his car into the garage side.

"You can park here so your car will be out of the weather," Bill said.

Trey pulled in, got out, opened the trunk, got his suitcase out, and all three of them walked to the cabin without speaking.

Jo felt Trey's uneasiness and said, "I'll get supper ready while you and Bill have some tea out here on the porch and get reacquainted. I have the spare bedroom all ready for you. He may talk to the dogs more than you, but don't mind that. He does it most mornings to me." Trey looked a little puzzled.

"And they agree with almost everything I say, unlike you, Grandma Jo."

"Never mind him. Sometimes I think he is losing his mind." They both turned and saw the worried look on Trey's face.

Trey set his suitcase down next to the kitchen table and said, "Are you two all right? Are you having health problems, or maybe some small mental problems? Is that why you asked me to come and spend some time with you?" Trey asked.

"Oh, no!" Jo said. "I hope you don't think we asked you up here to talk about taking care of us."

"Well, your letter was vague about what you wanted to discuss, and I don't want to be rude, but sometimes people, ah, ah, older people—"

Bill interrupted Trey, "No, son, we are old, but we're in good health, and our minds are still sharp. We do move a little slower, though, especially in the morning, but we're fine. And no, we didn't ask you here to discuss taking care of us. Jo and I want to tell you about our past." Trey pulled out a chair and sat down, relief reflected on his face.

"That's great. I mean, about your health," Trey said.

Jo picked up Trey's suitcase and said, "I'll put this in your room and start supper while you and Papa Bill have your tea out on the porch." Bill filled two glasses with tea and headed for the porch. Trey followed.

In the hallway, Jo turned and said, "Don't feel left out when he talks to the dogs more than you."

Trey laughed and said, "I won't. I'll just sit, listen, and maybe put my two cents in when asked."

"Like grandpa like grandson," Bill said.

They both sat rocking for some time, looking out across the valley. The sun was setting and the long tree shadows started to appear across the valley.

"It is peaceful here. I can see why my mother talked about it so much, especially in her last few months," Trey commented.

"Yeah, when your Grandma Jo and I drove up here the first time, there was one little bare spot right here where the cabin is now.

We parked the pickup, dropped the tailgate, and sat looking out across the valley—just as we are now—and said the same thing, it is a peaceful view. We decided this would be our home. Your mom loved it here as well."

"When I got old enough to question, I would ask her to tell me about you and Grandma. Did you always live here in the mountains? It always seemed as though she was hiding something."

"She wasn't hiding anything. We just never told her our whole story. A few things and events were left out. I just wished we could have told both of you at the same time, but now she knows the truth."

Trey gave Bill a puzzled look and said, "What do you mean?"

"Your mother was the sweetest, kindest girl I have ever known, next to Grandma Jo. I know she is in heaven now, and everything has been shown to her, and someday I hope to see her again."

Trey knew that older people started thinking about death and what happens to them when they get older. They want to confess everything, good or bad. It began to make a little sense to him now why he was there.

"Supper is ready," Jo called from the kitchen. "Dogs are not invited." Bill and Trey got up.

"Tomorrow I would like to take you to my favorite fishing spot. It, too, is a peaceful place. I will tell you about our past if you want to hear it."

"Yes, it will answer some questions I have had for a long time."

They walked into the kitchen. Jo had their plates ready on the table. As they sat down, Bill and Jo both noticed that Trey was totally at ease now, and they began to eat.

CHAPTER 10

Bill's Early Years; Trey Meets Dan

The next morning Trey woke to a mixture of smells. The fresh air coming through an open window had the scent of pine trees and evergreen drifting in from the outside, while the smell of breakfast came through the bedroom door. He lay there, thinking about his mother, Sally Ann, knowing she probably had experienced the same smells? Lying there, he realized why she enjoyed growing up here. He also wondered what was so secretive about his grandparents' past. He was anxious to hear what they had to tell him. The bedroom window, where Trey slept, was at the far end of the porch and he could hear his Papa Bill talking. He didn't know if Bill was talking to Jo or to the dogs, but when he heard no reply, he knew Bill was talking to the dogs. From the kitchen, he heard, "Breakfast is on."

"Be there shortly," Trey yelled back as he was leaving the bathroom.

He remembered the stories his mother had told him about going outside to the outhouse when she was young and how happy everyone was when the bathroom was finally completed. It would have been so inconvenient to go outside every time nature called, especially in bad weather. Grandpa Bill was already at the table with his cup of coffee and a plate full of food.

"Breakfast smells great," Trey said as he filled his coffee cup and headed for the stove where Jo was ready to fill his plate.

"Hope you like scrambled eggs, sausage, gravy, and biscuits," Jo said.

"I do."

"The chickens out back made these eggs especially for you," Bill said with a chuckle.

"But the store in town made the sausage, flour, and milk for the gravy and biscuits," Jo said as she sat down.

Jo cleaned up the kitchen while Bill and Trey finished drinking the last of their coffee and Bill said, "I have the fishing rods all rigged up and ready to go if you are?"

"It's been some time since I have done any fishing. The last few times I was here with Mom, we sat around and visited but never went fishing. I think we all knew that she probably would not be able to make many more trips up here, and we never took the time to fish," Trey said as his eyes watered up, as did Jo's and Bill's.

They both got up and headed out the door. Jo handed them a basket. "Here's your lunch, see you at suppertime." She wiped her eyes.

Bill grabbed the rods propped against the side of the shed and pointed to the small tackle box on the workbench. "Do you mind grabbing that box and the ice chest to put the fish in?"

"Sure," Trey answered, "Think we'll have any luck?"

"I always catch at least two or three, maybe more, depends on how long we stay." Bill dropped the tailgate and put the gear in the pickup bed. The girls jumped in with excitement in their wiggles.

On the drive to the fishing hole, Bill told Trey that he had cleared out more brush to make it easier to turn the truck around. He had also built a firepit to keep warm if he stayed after the sun went down, or it became chilly during the day. Sometimes Jo came with him. She wasn't much on fishing but did like the open fire. She sometimes brought a book or magazine to read while Bill fished. When they reached the open area, Bill got out, dropped the tailgate, the dogs jumped out and headed for the edge of the river.

"Will they be, okay?" Trey asked.

"Yeah, they have to get a drink of water before they run into the woods to chase whatever they get a scent of."

"Do they ever catch anything?"

"Sometimes, but not often. I can tell by their howls and barking when they're onto something they want to catch, or when they find something, they shouldn't have been trying to catch, then I go and check on them."

"You can tell all that just by just listening to them?"

"Yeah, I grew up rais'n' hunt'n' and track'n' dogs back home. I can tell when they have something treed, chase'n' it or when they have lost the scent. Those two are American Fox hounds, they have a great since of smell and you can hear their barks and howls for a mile or more."

"Where is back home?"

"Let's bait the hooks, get lines in the water, get comfortable, and I'll tell all about back home."

Bill got comfortable in the wooden chair, propped his feet on the rock in front of him, and began. He told Trey about growing up and living in Hardwood, Georgia. He told Trey him about Grandma Jo being born in Ocoee, Tennessee, and how her family moved to Hardwood when she was in Jr high school. Bill told him about how Sam, Jo's older brother, had become his best friend and they did everything together, and Bobbie Jo always tagged along with them. Bill told Trey he always knew Jo liked him from the first time they met by the way she looked at him. She was starting the eighth grade; and was too young for him. Besides, girls weren't on his list at that time. With the town being so small, there were not many to choose from anyway, so he and Sam found other interests. One was training hunting and tracking hounds. He told Trey about his dad, who worked at the sawmill and how he died of a heart attack and his mother died about a year later.

"I wish you could have met my dad and Jo's dad. You don't find those kinds of men nowadays—hard workers, honest and true to their word. They both worked at the Hampton sawmill. Grandma Jo's dad had worked at a Hampton sawmill in Tennessee and was transferred to Hardwood when the mechanic at the mill in Hardwood quit. Jo's dad was well respected for his talent as a mechanic, and my dad oversaw the unloading of the logs before going into the sizing saws."

"What about your mother?" Trey questioned.

"She stayed home most of the time but did do various part-time jobs. One was doing the laundry and cleaning the homes for the Hampton family who owned the sawmill and the Bensons that owned the bank in Hardwood. My dad didn't like her doing it, but we could always use extra cash."

Trey asked, "Did you have any brothers or sisters?"

"Had a younger brother, but he died a few months after he was born. They called it a crib death. Mom got up one morning and found him in the crib, not breathing and cold. She never stopped blaming herself, everyone thought she just gave up living after my younger brother died." Bill said softly. "Now about your mother and biological grandmother," Bill said.

Trey looked at Bill with a puzzled expression on his face. "What do you mean my biological grandmother? Grandma Jo isn't my grandmother?"

"She's your step-grandmother. Your real grandmother was shot shortly after your mother, Sally Ann, was born."

"Did my mother know that Grandma Jo was her stepmother?"

"We never told her, but we think she knew," Bill said. "This too may shock you. I spent over three years in a Georgia prison for killing the man who attacked your real grandmother, Sarah Lou. I was convicted and given a life sentence. The problem is, I didn't kill him, and to this day, I don't know who did. With the help of your grandmother's brother Sam, and a prison hound named ole Red, I escaped." Bill said, looking at Trey and waiting for a reply. "Trey, I know you hear it all the time—'I didn't do it'—but truly, I did not kill the young man, Luke Hampton, and to this day I do not know who did. We never told your mother and now we truly regret not telling her."

Trey had been sitting at the edge of the wooden chair. He let out a sigh and leaned back and was silent for a few moments, trying to take in all that his grandfather had told him so far.

"How much more is there that I need to hear about?"

"As far as Grandma Jo and I know, you are the only family we have left. We cut off all contact with friends and what little family we had back in Georgia and Tennessee a long time ago and came here. For some reason, for the past several months, I have had an uneasy feeling someone is still looking for me, which is one reason we wanted you to come to visit. We wanted to tell you about our past, and I would like to know if you could find out if they are still looking for me?"

"I can make a few calls to friends that are still in the LA department and see what I can come up with," Trey said. "Right now, I would like to hear more about what happened to my real grandmother and the young man that was murdered." At that moment, Trey's fishing line started to unreel.

"Grab the rod and set the hook."

Trey grabbed the rod and gave it a jerk upward, and the end of the rod began to bend down as more line was being taken out.

"I think you've got a catfish."

Trey began to reel in the line with some effort. Bill grabbed the dip net as Trey got the fish closer to the bank.

"Keep the line tight, and I will walk into the water and try to get the net under it." Bill eased the net under the big fish and lifted it. "It's a big catfish, a real big one. I bet it will go twenty pounds."

Trey was like a little kid that had caught his first fish. He had caught small ones before—small perch and bluegill—but not a fish this size. It looked huge as it flopped in the net on the bank. Bill hit the fish in the head with a stick and pulled out his knife to gut it.

"This is the biggest catfish I've seen since I moved up here," Bill said excitedly.

Trey sat back down in the wooden chair and said, "Now I understand what people mean when they say they're hooked on fishing. That was exciting."

"This will be enough for a couple of meals." Bill had made a small wooden table a few years back and left it at the campsite to clean the fish. He laid the fish on a small wooden table and began to fillet the fish and put the slices in the ice chest. He handed Trey a small jar of cold tea as he sat back down on his chair.

"Do you want me to put the bait back on my line and try for another?" Trey asked.

"As big as that fish is, I think we have enough for today unless you want to fish more, or we can come back tomorrow and catch its brother or sister."

"With this excitement over, I would like for you to get back to our story, my detective curiosity is piquing. I want to know more."

They settled back down in their chairs, and with a smile on his face, Bill told Trey about the first time he saw Sarah Lou Benson and how the two fell in love and had to sneak around to see each other because her parents disapproved. Bill told Trey that he and Sarah got married after she graduated from high school, lived with his parents until they died, and had to move in with his grandparents.

Bill sat for a moment, holding back emotions about his parents and wife, Sarah, then finally said, "My granddad gave me twenty acres he had so we could build a small house of our own. We had been in our house for over a year and one evening coming home from work and walking pasted our front door headed to the back of our house, I heard your grandmother, Sarah scream. I ran in and saw Luke Hampton standing over her, she was naked. He pulled out a pistol and while we were fighting over it, the pistol went off, hitting Sarah. I chased Luke down a path and found him with a knife in his chest." Bill stopped his story when he looked up and saw Dan on the other side of the river. Bill waved for him to cross over.

"That's Dan the mountain man, as I call him."

"Looks like he is a real mountain man, the way he is dressed."

"Well, he would like to think of himself as a true mountain man, but he has electricity in his cabin, an old pickup truck, and a phone, so I think he may be half a mountain man."

"How y'all doin'," Dan shouted.

"We were trying to be as quiet as possible so as not to scare the fish."

"I can't see what difference being quiet would make since you ain't got no lines in the water. I'm Dan Moran." Dan held out his hand to shake.

"Pretty rhymey," Trey said as he grabbed Dan's hand with a firm grip.

"Since those introductions are done, what's in the bag?" Bill asked.

"Thought y'all might want fixings for tonight, see'n' you ain't got no lines in the water, so you probably ain't got no fish and it's getting late in the day," Dan said.

"Well, that's thoughtful of ya, but we already caught all the fish we need today." Bill flipped open the ice chest and showed the fillets to Dan.

"Trey caught this big catfish. I think it may be the one that got away from us a while back. I'll trade you some fillets for what you got in the bag," Bill said.

"Deal. I am out of fish back home, and I bet you haven't had deer meat in a while." They made the trade.

Dan sat down on the large rock next to the small fire that was about to go out. He tossed a piece of driftwood onto the fire and pushed it around with his foot to stir up the embers and get the fire going again.

"You're from LA, retired cop, right?"

"Yes, to all of that."

"Well, nice to meet ya."

"Same here."

"You two get caught up on all the family going's on, I guess? Don't want to intrude."

"Yeah, we pretty much got reacquainted."

"That's good. My family doesn't visit much, maybe been here three or four times since I moved up here. The last time they were here was about a year ago. They didn't think it was right for me to be here by myself at my age. If something were to happen, then what would I do? I just told them I'll die. Didn't get much of a response after that, so haven't seen them since.

Bill had never heard Dan speak of his family before, or even that he had family that had been here to see him. Trey's detective brain started to kick in. Bill had told Trey about Dan and mentioned that he thought he was from northern California, but Trey, too, had noticed a slight Southern accent on certain words but wasn't sure. Trey felt that he should be a little guarded with his conversations when talking to Dan, especially since Papa Bill had told him he felt people were still looking for him.

"Well, guys and gals"—he looked at the dogs—"guess I had better head back home so I can get this fish ready for the pan. Nice to meet you, Trey. Hope to see ya again before you head back to LA." He gave Bill the little bag with the deer meat in it.

"Same here," Trey said.

Dan picked up his walking stick, the bag of fillets, and headed back across the river.

After Dan was out of hearing range, Trey said to Bill, "He was kinda blunt and to the point about where I was from and that I was a retired cop."

"Yeah, Dan usually isn't that serious about anything, and yes, he did seem a little…what would you say, straightforward about you being a retired cop. It seemed as though he wanted you to talk more about it."

"Grandpa Bill, you mentioned that Dan did not talk much about his past or his family."

"That's right, and this was the first time he had ever mentioned the last time his family had been here to see him. It's strange that he brought it up. I have always felt like he, too, was hiding or running from someone or something."

"Maybe he is a little jealous that I'm here visiting, and his family doesn't have much to do with him."

"That could be. Let's put out the fire, gather up the fish'n gear, wake the pups from their evening nap, and head for home. Tomorrow I'll tell you about the trial, prison life, and my escape.

"I want you to know, no matter what you think of Grandma Jo and me, we will always love you and hope you do not stop coming to see us. Your Grandma Jo loves you as if you were her own flesh and blood. She loved your mother and raised her as if she were her own child. That's why we never told her that Jo was her stepmother. That may not have been right, but it is too late now, but not for you."

The silence was thick on the drive back to the cabin until they pulled into the yard. Hunter and Tracker had started running and jumping from one side of the truck bed to the other, howling and barking as if they were on the hunt.

Trey questioned, "Are they always that excited to get home?"

"No, they usually just sit in the back looking over the edge of the pickup bed until I drop the tailgate, then they jump out, go to the porch, lie down, and wait for supper. Don't know what's gotten into them." Trey got out first and started toward the carport to move a couple of things so Bill could drive in, when he heard Bill holler, "Trey, stop, stand still!"

Trey stopped immediately. "What is it?"

"It's a skunk by the dog door, behind the water bucket. Don't move, it might spray. That's what the dogs are excited about. I'll get out and make some noise and see if it will wander away on its way." Trey stood still and waited, praying the skunk would just waddle off and not be threatened.

"What about the dogs?" Trey said as softly as he could.

"They will stay in the bed of the truck until the tailgate is dropped. I just hope their barking doesn't startle it into spray mode."

The slow movement and noise that Bill was making seemed to be enough to get the skunk moving in a direction away from the building and toward the tree line. "I'll wait until it's in the woods and out of sight before I let the pups out, they sometimes have a mind of their own and head off after critters they see or get a good scent of."

Bill dropped the tailgate of the truck. Hunter and Tracker immediately jumped out and headed for the woods, hot on the skunk's trail. Bill gave two short whistles. They stopped, turned, headed back to the yard, went up the steps, and lay on the porch. Trey looked amazed; these dogs were better trained than any drug dogs used by the LAPD.

"Two whistles, they stop, come back, and lie down. That's amazing."

"Yeah, they know it's suppertime, and if they go into the woods and don't come back for a while, it will be a cold supper or none at all."

"And that's all it takes, food?" Trey asked.

"There's a little more to training than just food. I'll tell you more about hound training later and how it got me out of prison."

Trey let out a sigh and commented, "That would have ruined a good evening—skunk smell mixed in with the sweet smells coming from Grandma Jo's cooking. Grandpa, why didn't you just shoot it?" Trey asked.

"Well, I don't kill anything I can't use. I only do it for food, clothing, or protection."

"Seems like this would have been a time for protection."

"Na, it was just looking for leftover scraps or get'n a drink, no threat."

"I've heard skunks carry rabies, is that right?"

"Yeah, they do, but if it had had full-blown rabies, it would have been more aggressive. I think it just wandered in because of Grandma Jo's cook'n, looking for food, just like we are going to do as soon as we unload and clean up."

CHAPTER 11

Grandma Jo's Pie; Sam's Pocketknife

Both men headed to the mudroom at the far end of the porch to clean up. The closer they got to the kitchen, the more intense the smells got. Trey could smell fresh bread, what he thought was fried chicken, and a mixture of other smells all mixed together. He remembered in his youth, his mom asked, "Do you want to go see Grandma Jo?"

He would always say yes. "She's the best cook."

He didn't know it hurt his mother's feelings when he said it, but she was glad he always wanted to see his grandparents, and she knew there would be a time when she wouldn't be there to take him.

They both pulled out chairs and sat down. Jo had the food on the table and filled their glasses with fresh tea.

"This is the kind'a service I like—good food, fresh tea, and a beautiful waitress," Bill said.

"I'll expect a large tip when I bring the ticket," Jo said, as she gave Trey a wink.

"The times I came here, which I realize now, wasn't often enough. I always looked forward to your cooking. It was the best, and I would tell Mom that. Since she's gone, I have often wondered if it hurt her feelings when I said that, and I have tried to remember if I ever told her that her cooking was also good. With my new and less-stressful job, I have had time to reminisce about things I wish I had said or done while she was alive," Trey said with his voice breaking a little.

"Don't do that to yourself. We all think of things we should have said to loved ones after they have passed. It is part of life. It is God's way of teaching us to be better people," Jo said. "I think it is a good time to say a prayer before we eat. Thank you, Lord, for our health, for everything you have given us, and the love between us." This puzzled Bill; he and Jo believed in God, and they tried to do and act in the way a Christian would, but he wondered if there was something wrong with her health.

"Trey, your mom was a good cook, and I don't think she minded one bit when you commented about my cooking. She was delighted when you wanted to come for a visit and would tell me so. I know toward the end, she hated going back to LA. After finishing school here, she, like a lot of young people, could not wait to get away and out on her own. But I always knew a part of her missed being here, especially because of the peace it brought her. Now she is here for good, and I know she is looking down on us, seeing the love in this kitchen. Your grandpa Bill had her buried close to her favorite spot, where she would sit on that old stump and look out over the valley and be at peace." All three said nothing for some time. They slowly ate with watery eyes.

Now Bill was even more worried about Jo and her health. They had lost a daughter who had struggled for some time with cancer. She had not seen her son grow into the man he was. She died just before he started his law enforcement training. When Sally Ann found out she had terminal cancer, she brought Trey to the cabin as often as she could to let him enjoy the outdoors and be where she had grown up and get to know his grandparents better. It took her mind off of what she was fighting. Trey's dad, Keith, was not fond of Bill. There had always been some hidden tension between them, so he seldom came with them. Bill never knew the reason for Keith's dislike, but on one of their visits, Sally Ann and Keith were on the porch, and Bill heard his daughter ask Keith why he didn't like her dad. Keith told her that her dad was too secretive; it seemed as though he was hiding something. He seldom spoke of his childhood or where he was from and always changed the subject when it came up, and this worried him, He did not want any harm coming to her or Trey.

Bill was troubled after hearing this and wondered if he should tell his story to them. He decided not to. Again, he thought, that might have been the wrong decision, not to tell his story.

Before Sally Ann's small funeral in LA, which Bill and Jo did not attend, Bill called from the phone at the restaurant in Hillside and spoke to Keith. There had been a strong disagreement between him and Keith as to where to bury her—in LA or where she had grown up. Trey was in the room with his dad at the time of the conversation. The final decision was made when Trey went to his room and came back with an envelope that his mother had given him a few days before she died, he handed it to his dad. The envelope was addressed to him and his dad, and it said, "Do not open until after my death."

There were two letters inside: one for Trey and one for his dad, Keith. Trey had already read his. He handed the letter to his dad and talked to his granddad while Keith read his letter. The letters told each of them how much she loved them. The last comment written in both their letters solved the problem as to where she was to be buried. She had written:

> As my final request, I want to be buried next to Ole Red by the stump on the hill overlooking the valley. It was my favorite place to sit with Ole Red in the evenings and watch the sunset. I spent many evenings sitting on that stump, pondering the miracles of this earth, looking at the stars, and wondering what life had in store for me. The sky was so clear that looking into the sky at night, it was as if I could reach out and grab a star. I want that to be my last resting place, the place where I could look out over the valley below, feel at peace with myself and the world. I always cherished that place.

As this remembrance rushed through Bill's thoughts, he knew there must be something wrong with Jo, and he could barely listen to Jo and Trey as they continued talking.

"Do you need any more to eat?"

"No, it was all so good, but I have saved just enough room for a piece of your strawberry-banana-cream pie."

"And what makes you think there is a pie?"

"I don't remember a time when I came up here, and you had not made my favorite pie."

"Well, guess I had better get it so I won't break the chain of your favorite-pie tradition." They both grinned. "Bill, do you want a piece?"

Bill cleared the health thoughts about Jo from his head and said, "Sure, I never get tired of your pie."

She got the pie down from the top of the cupboard, where she had put it to keep it as warm as possible, and set it in the middle of the table. She pointed the knife at the pie and asked Trey, "How big?"

"That's just right," he said.

Bill said, "Same for me."

She cut herself a smaller piece, placed it on her plate, while Bill got three coffee cups. Jo had made Bill's coffee as he liked it, but she had made hers and Trey's in a coffee maker. She and Trey did not like theirs as strong as Bill.

"This tops off one of the best meals I've had in a long time."

"You need to come here more often. I will fatten you up," Jo said jokingly.

After taking his last bite, Trey asked, "Did your mother teach you how to make this pie?"

"No, it was my closest friend's mother, when I lived in Tennessee." Jo answered. "But before I tell you about the pie, I am guessing Papa Bill told you that I'm your step-grandma."

"Yes, he did, and that does not change how I feel about you. To me, you are and always will be my grandma."

Jo held back her feelings as best she could and started to tell Trey about the pie.

"I was born in Tennessee. When I was around twelve or thirteen, we moved to Hardwood, Georgia, where my dad took the job as the head mechanic for the Hampton saw and lumber mill. When we lived in Tennessee, my best friend was Tammy Lou Watkins.

It was her mother that taught me how to bake the strawberry-ba-nana-cream pie. Over the years, I added a few things, took out a few things, until I got it just how it is tonight."

Trey interrupted, "It is the best pie I have ever eaten. Did you ever think of baking and selling them?"

"Yes, at one time, I did." She continued her story, "When we first got here, I worked at the Hillside Diner as a waitress for a while. When the owners, Betty and Tom, knew there was going to be some-thing going on in town that would bring in a lot of people to their diner, they would hire me to help with the cooking and bake pies. The strawberry-banana-cream pie became a favorite dessert. For a while, I did bake pies for them to sell, but it got to be a lot of trouble taking them to town after I baked them, so I stopped."

Jo looked at Bill and said, "You know, Bill, come to think of it, I haven't heard from Tammy Lou in a long time."

Bill looked at her. "You have been talking to her?"

"No, the first few years we were up here, we wrote back and forth a couple of times a year to keep in touch."

"Jo! I thought we agreed when we arrived here and planned on making this our home, we would not have any contact with anyone back home."

Trey could sense some tension in Bill's voice.

"I know Bill, but she is the only one I had contact with, and it was the only way I could keep up with how my family was doing. Remember, she was the one that told me about Mom, Dad, and Sam dying in the house fire. I never put a return address on the letters I wrote to her, I didn't see what harm it would be, one or two letters a year."

"The fire was a long time ago, but you are still writing to her?" Bill said with a little disgust.

"Yes, I am, but not often. She is the only one I could trust not to tell anyone about us. The last letter I mailed was over a year ago, and I have not heard back from her. I'm afraid she may have passed away." The words were getting more heated between Trey's grandparents.

Trey spoke up, "Okay, let's all take a breath and calm down. Grandpa, I know you were in prison for a crime you say you did not commit. Grandma Jo, you are my step-grandmother, my real grandma was shot, that's a lot to take in." They all looked at one another, letting what Trey had just said sink in.

Jo got up and started cleaning up the supper meal. Bill picked up his coffee cup and asked Trey if he wanted more coffee. Bill filled Trey's cup, then his own, and sat back down at the table and looked at Trey.

"After being in prison a little over three years, I escaped with the help of Ole Red, Grandma Jo, and her brother, Sam. When Jo and I left Georgia, we agreed to change our last names." Jo spoke up "we got our last name from a hardware store, but that's another story for later." Bill continued. "We agreed not contact anyone back home so no one could find us. Jo and I had several talks about her contacting Tammy Lou in Tennessee. Thinking that no one in Hardwood knew about your Grandma Jo's friend Tammy, we agreed that it would be okay to write a letter to her letting her know we were okay, but not to mention where we were."

Jo broke in. "I learned in one of her letters that my entire family had perished in a house fire. I wanted to go back for the funeral but knew people would want to know where I was, what I was doing, was I married—you know, all the things' people want to know when you have been away and out of touch for so long. Grandpa Bill and I decided it was best for me not to go back. It was hard, but I knew it was to protect us."

"I can't believe the two of you have kept this secret life all these years," Trey said.

"It is just a secret about our lives before moving up here. We have not been a secret to people around here," Bill said. "We just avoid talking too much about our past."

"But you are concerned about your friend Tammy not writing back," Trey said.

"I am. I hadn't thought too much about her writing back, but it's been some time since I last wrote to her, and I haven't heard back. It is not like her. I am wondering if something has happened to her. Did she pass away?"

"I, too, am worried," Bill said. "Is she just late writing back, has she passed away, or has someone found out from her letters where we are, and she is scared to write back to you? I hope she has destroyed the letters you sent. I'm not sure, but maybe someone can use the envelopes in some way to track us down. What do they call the stamp the post office puts on the envelope?"

Trey spoke up, "The postmark."

"Yeah, that is what I was thinking of."

Trey explained, "In my line of work, I have tracked many letters by postmarks and have found that some small towns, such as Hillside, sometimes bag up all the letters and send them to a larger town where they are sorted through a machine that stamps the postmark of that town, and not the town where the letter was originally mailed. I can do some checking around and see if that is how it works in Hillside."

"I don't want you to get involved," Jo said to Trey.

"It's no problem. I have learned how to be very discreet when asking questions."

"It's getting late, and if you want to get to the river before the fish wake up, we had better head for bed," Bill said, as he looked out the back door and saw the tail of one of the dogs as it went through the dog door of the shed.

Trey hugged Jo and told her again how much he enjoyed her cooking and that his mom had a great teacher. Jo said thanks and told him she loved cooking for him and having him here and would see him in the morning.

"Grandpa Bill, I will see you in the morning, and even if we don't catch any fish, I want to hear more."

"You will, I promise. Just hope I'm not getting too old to remember everything."

Again, Trey woke to the delightful smells coming from the kitchen. Even after eating his fill the night before, for some reason, he was hungry again. He freshened up, got dressed, and headed for the kitchen.

"I don't know why I am so hungry after what I had last night."

"It's the country livin'," Jo said as she handed him a cup of coffee. "Grandpa Bill is on the porch, rockin' and talk'n'."

"He does like to talk to those hounds." He pushed the screen door open and walked onto the porch. He sat down in the rocker on the other side of the little table between the two rockers.

"I can see why mom loved it here. I know I have said this before, but it is beautiful looking out over the valley with the sun peeking over the mountaintop. It's peaceful here, it's like Mother Nature takes away all your pains, worries, and thoughts of how bad some people can be, and I've seen a lot of that over the years in law enforcement, this place is so much different than the big city."

"I'm sure you have. After we eat, if you want, we can go back to the river, build a small fire, fish, and talk, or we can stay here on the porch. Grandma Jo is going to town to do a little shopping, so we'll have all morning to talk."

Trey was silent for a minute or two, and finally answered, "Let's stay here. I want to enjoy as much of this peace and quiet as I can before going back to LA. I like just rocking here on the porch, it feels like my mother is right here with us."

Jo came out with two fresh cups of coffee. "I'm going to finish cleaning up the kitchen, then get ready to head for town. You two gonna be all right with me being gone all morning?" she asked.

"I think we will manage, as long as we don't stray too far from the porch," Bill said.

"You going to the river?"

"Na, we decided to stay around here today. I'm going to tell Trey a little more about Georgia, Sarah Lou, my time in prison and how you, Sam and especially Ole Red help in my escape."

Jo felt a slight bit of jealousy when Bill mentioned Sarah Lou's name. "Good," she said.

She headed back into the kitchen, and they could hear her cleaning up, and both men felt bad that she was doing it herself, but when Bill started to get up, Jo hollered, "You two want any more coffee? If not, I'll get dressed and head for town." Trey and Bill both said no thanks and went back to rocking.

Thirty minutes later, Jo came through the door, onto the porch.

"I'm headed to town with my list, do either of you need anything?"

"I am fine," Trey said.

"Me too." Jo headed to the truck; the dogs sat up.

"Not this time, ladies." They laid back down. Jo climbed into the truck and drove off. They watched her drive down the curvy drive to the blacktop that led to Hillside.

Bill slowed his rocking and said, "You know about your grandma Sarah getting shot, the fight between Luke Hampton and me, then how I found him along the path with a knife in his chest, now, as Paul Harvey would say, here is the rest of the story."

"Paul Harvey, I've heard that name," Trey said.

"Grandma Jo and I didn't have a TV for a long time, and we would listen to the radio. Paul Harvey hosted a radio program called *The Rest of the Story* in the late 1970s. We listened to it until we got a TV. He would tell the first part of a story or event, and then for the last part of his program he would say, 'Now here's the rest of the story,' and would tell what really happened or how the story truly turned out. It made you want to listen every day. So, with no TV, we listened. Now here is the rest of my story."

Trey said, "My curiosity has been piquing ever since I got your letter to come up for a visit, and you said you had something important to tell me before your time ran out. I thought something was wrong with one or both of you, I am so thankful nothing is wrong with either of you."

Bill continued with his story. "After finding Luke Hampton, I ran back to the house where I had left Sarah lying on the floor. When I ran into the house, she was still lying on the floor in a pool of blood. I knew she was gone. I sat there holding her head on my lap for some time, then I heard your mother Sally Ann, cry out. I ran to her, picked her up, and saw that she was okay. I put a sheet over Sarah and drove to my grandfather's home, with your mother in my arms. He drove us to the sheriff's office so I could tell him what had happened to Sarah and Luke. I told him I had no idea who killed Luke. I knew the sheriff would not believe me, and I would probably be convicted of his murder. I learned after the trial that two jurors could not vote for the death penalty. They understood why I would have been so angry at seeing my naked wife with Luke standing over her and were truly concerned why I had not used the pistole to shoot him. I never found out the names of the two jurors."

Bill and Trey sat for some time, not speaking, slowly rocking, looking out across the valley at the tall pine trees that were now creating long shadows from the early afternoon sun. Their thoughts and silence were broken by Hunter and Tracker suddenly barking and jumping off the porch; they looked toward the gravel road leading up to the cabin and saw the pickup approaching. Jo stuck her arm out the window and gave them a wave. Jo pulled to a stop in front of the porch as they walked down the a few steps to the rock pathway that led to the circle drive where she had parked. Bill looked in the back of the truck and saw a couple of bags that had been tied down so as not to fly out while driving home. Trey approached the passenger side and opened the door.

Jo said, "If you can get these bigger bags and take them to the kitchen, I will get the smaller ones out of the back of the truck." As Trey turned, he saw his Grandpa Bill with his arms wrapped around three bags and was trying to shut the pickup's tailgate.

"Grandpa, I'll get those. You can help Grandma Jo."

"Okay, I guess three may be a little much for me to carry, getting old, I guess, thanks." Trey did not like to hear either of his grandparents talk about getting old, but he knew that was life, but still didn't like it. At their age, Trey was amazed at how his two grandparents got around; they were in excellent shape for their age. As he carried the bags in, he assumed the reason for their health was due to living here in the mountains—growing their vegetables, eating fresh game and fish, and consuming as little store-bought food as possible.

After all the bags had been brought in and placed on the kitchen table, Bill sat down and commented to Jo, "Did you leave anything at the store?"

"I sure did—money. I needed to stock up on staples and also got some extra snacks that I thought Trey might like."

"You didn't need to do that. With what you have been fixing these past couple of days, I don't need any snacks. I will have to go on a strict diet when I get back home."

"No problem, the pups and I will help you devour them, we don't get treats like this very often. Maybe you should come up more often so I can have more store-bought food."

"Are you saying you don't like what I fix around here? It sure seems like there isn't much leftover after I fix a meal. You and the pups do a good job cleaning your plates. Sometimes I don't even think I need to wash the plates; they are so clean when you're done. Don't worry, Trey, I do wash them. You two go through the bag at the end of the table while I put the rest of this stuff away. I got a few things in there for each of you. Let me know if I need to take anything back."

"It isn't my birthday or a holiday," Bill said. "I didn't need anything."

"Can't I just buy you something because you're so sweet and good to me?" Jo said.

"I guess so, guess I'm not too good at being appreciative," Bill said, a little shamefully. While Jo and Bill had been talking about gifts, Trey had been emptying the bag. He laid out a couple of shirts and some socks on the table. Bill and Trey were picking out which shirt each wanted while Jo had gone to the back of the house and when she came back into the kitchen, she laid a small package wrapped in old brown paper tied up with a string on the table.

"This is for you, Trey," Jo said.

Trey started opening the package. As he was taking off the old paper, he could see an old box with a picture of a pocketknife on the top. Bill knew at once what it was and sat back in his chair and watched as Trey finished taking the old paper off. Trey opened up the box and saw it was a pocketknife with what looked like an ivory handle with a carving of a deer standing in tall grass on it. Trey sat there, looking at the knife and admiring the carving in the handle.

"You didn't buy this at the store. The box is too old."

"No, I didn't. It was my brother, Sam's, knife. I brought it with me when we left Georgia. He and your Grandpa Bill were best friends, and when we left, my brother gave it to me to give to Bill to remember him by. Somehow my brother knew he would never see us again."

Trey said to Bill, "This is yours; it was given to you. I can't take it."

Bill looked at Trey and said, "Your Grandma Jo showed me the knife when we got settled here. Sam wanted me to have something to remember our deep friendship by. I never carried or used it. I left it in the box and put it in the dresser by the bed. I would take it out once in a while and remember the good times Sam and I had growing up in Hardwood." Trey noticed a tear running down Bill's cheek. Trey knew that Sam and his Grandpa Bill had a profound friendship and felt even worse about being offered the knife.

Jo said, "Go ahead, Bill and I decided it should go to you, whether you take it now or later."

Trey took the small pocketknife out and looked at it more closely. He could not tell, but it looked like the handle was made of real ivory.

"Yes, it's ivory, and it's part of a set. The other was a fixed-blade hunting knife with a 6-inch blade, they cost my dad a day's pay back then. He gave them to Sam for his eighteenth birthday, and Sam gave me the pocketknife to give to Bill the last time we saw each other." Trey put the knife back in the box and wrapped the old paper around it and tied the string back.

Trey said, "I will accept the gift, on one condition—that it stays here, and someday, I hope in the distant future, I will take it with me."

"You mean put it in my will," Bill said.

"Yes," Trey answered hesitantly.

"That sounds good to me," Bill said as he got up, walked over to Trey, and hugged him with tears running down his face.

Jo watched as the two hugged; she too started to cry, remembering her brother and how close he and Bill were. She also thought of her mother, father, and her close friend Tammy Lou, all of whom she would never see again.

"We need to stop with the sentimental talk. It is getting depressing, and I need to start getting things ready for supper," Jo said. "You two head to the porch and get started on your rocking contest. Here's a couple of glasses for tea that's in the fridge. Bill, you'll need to take some water for the pups. I noticed their water bowl was empty when I came up the porch steps," Jo said.

"You mean they can't have a glass of nice cool tea?" Bill asked.

"If you want to give them yours, that will be fine, but you still need to fill their water bowl, and I bet they will share that with you, but you'll have to drink on all fours."

Trey was amazed at how the two of them could joke with each other, and neither got mad. But he guessed with them being together for this long, out here by themselves, this was their way of showing each other their love.

"Go on, get out of here. I'll bring out some water to fill the dog bowl. You two can settle in for the rock'n' contest, and I'll get things set out for supper. Before you two start your rock'n, can you go to the garden and pick some fresh vegetables I can use for supper? And while you're there, pull a few weeds, they are starting to take over," Jo asked.

"Come on, Trey, I'll teach you how to pull weeds and tell you about the trial and my prison time."

In the garden, doing a little weeding and picking some vegetables for Jo, Bill told Trey about how he sat in jail, waiting for his trial. He knew he would be found guilty and would probably get the death penalty, but as it turned out, a couple of jurors did not think he had murdered Luke Hampton. With this doubt, the jurors voted for a life sentence.

After filling up the basket with what vegetables they thought would be suitable for supper, they went back to the porch and the rockers. Jo came out, refilled their glasses with tea, took the basket, and said supper should be ready in about an hour.

"Just enough time to tell Trey about my prison time, training Ole Red, and my daring escape."

"Don't forget to tell him about my map-reading skills and how I helped us get here."

Bill did not go into much detail about his prison life, except he knew he had to escape; he would not spend the rest of his life in prison for something he did not do. He told Trey about training Ole Red and how Sam had it all planned out to use the dog to help him escape. The only flaw in his plan was Bobbie Jo demanded she came along with Sally Ann when they picked up Bill.

"Trey, your Grandma Jo made it clear she was not being left behind. She and Sally Ann were going with me no matter where I went. I tried to convince her I needed to travel alone, but she insisted. I have never had any regrets about her coming with me. I loved Sarah Lou, but over the years, my love for Jo grew, and looking back, I could not have asked for a better wife and mother to our daughter."

Bill told Trey how they met the Smiths on their trip here and how Mr. Smith's business card helped him get a job and then finding out about their death. He also told him how, over the years, he and Jo worked and saved money to purchase the land and build a cabin.

"Supper is on the table," Jo hollered.

"Grandpa Bill, this has been a very interesting couple of days with you telling me what has gone on in your life."

"I Always like to keep my audience riveted. Now let's eat."

CHAPTER 12

Trey's Research and Offer to Help

"If I stay here much longer, I'll be like those pups—eat, sleep, move to another spot, and sleep some more," Trey said.

"They are a pretty active pair," Bill answered as they went through the door into the kitchen.

"Go change out of those garden-dirt clothes, wash up, and by the time you've finished, I will be putting the finishing touches on supper."

"I think I'll take a shower if it doesn't cause you and Bill to wait on supper," Trey said.

"That will be fine," Jo said. "Take your time. We are in no hurry." Trey headed to the back to shower and get clean clothes while Bill washed his face and hands in the kitchen sink.

"He's making himself right at home here," Jo said, and Bill agreed.

"I sure like him being here. We have had nice long conversations. I have been able to get a lot off my chest about my, or I should say *our*, past?"

"I'm glad you have had time with him. I hope it will help you sleep better and maybe lessen your bad dreams."

"Me too," Bill answered.

"I know you are still concerned that someone is still looking for us," Jo said.

"I don't know why. It just pops in my head every so often that I'm being watched. I know it's silly, we don't have anyone that close that can watch us, but there is still that feeling."

"If someone were around, the pups would let us know right off," Jo said.

"You're right. They would be barking and running after who-ever was out there. They are a couple of the best hounds I have had, except for Ole Red. I sure miss my old pal."

"He was a great hound and so protective of Sally Ann. I never worried too much when she was little and would wonder out of the yard. Ole Red would grab her pant leg or sleeve and lead her back to the yard," Jo said with a lump in her throat.

Trey came into the kitchen, "Am I interrupting a deep conversation?"

"Naw," Bill said. "Just talk'n' about Ole Red and your mother when she was young."

"Sometimes sitting at home with nothing going on, I can pic-ture my mom running around here with that old dog chasing her. I can't count the times she told me how much she missed her dog; he was so special to her."

"And to me," Bill said. "Like I said earlier today, if it weren't for him, I wouldn't be here."

"Okay, enough sad talk. Grab your plates and fill'em up," Jo said. After they had sat down, Jo said, "Let's pray." And they all bowed their heads. "Dear Father God, we thank you for this food, for our family and friends, our health, and the love between us, amen."

Trey thought his grandma said almost that same prayer the other night. It is short, to the point, and covers nearly everything a person would ever need to say.

Trey broke the silence, "Grandpa Bill, you have mentioned sev-eral times you have had a feeling that someone is still looking for you and even feel you're being watched?"

"That's right."

"You also said you had no idea who killed—what was the young man's name?"

"Luke, Luke Hampton. Yes, I would like to find out before I go to my grave, but I am not going to take a chance on getting caught by going back to Hardwood, Georgia, and spending my last remaining years in prison."

They all were silent for a minute, then Trey said, "I have an idea or plan if you will hear me out?"

"It won't put you in danger, will it?" Jo asked.

"No, not at all." Trey started telling them his plan, "You know I retired from the LA Detective Department and now work part-time for a private investigation firm. I mostly track down people who do not pay child support or alimony. Sometimes I am asked to find someone, mostly by parents whose son or daughter has run away, so I have a lot of experience in finding people. I can write down as much information as you can give me—names, places, and dates if you can remember them. I can do some searching on the Internet on my computer and see what I can come up with."

"How does the Internet work?" Bill asked. Trey explained to Jo and Bill that it was somewhat like an electronic encyclopedia and phone book, which they seemed to understand.

"That sounds good, but I do not want you getting in the middle of this and jeopardizing your job or life," Bill said.

"Just doing a little research is not going to do any harm. Maybe I can come across some information as to why you feel you are being watched."

"I don't think it is a good idea, Trey," Jo remarked.

"No one will know why I am checking, and I will be careful. I can get started searching the internet as soon as I get back to LA. If you agree and don't mind, can you make a list of names, places, and dates? That way, I will have something to start with?"

Bill said, "We don't know exactly how the Internet works, but we can start on the list as soon as we get through with supper. Maybe Grandma Jo can help me remember some of the people and dates back in Hardwood."

"Great, I am looking forward to helping you start to relax and enjoy the next several years without this worry," Trey said.

Jo finished with the cleanup and sat down at the table with Bill and Trey.

She handed Trey a notepad and pen, and he said, "Let's start with the people back home." After half an hour of going through names, Trey said, "Now if you can remember the dates of some of the events that led up to the murder and your trial?"

Jo said, "Hold on." She left the room, came back with her Bible, opened the back cover, and pulled out a small notepad. She opened it and pushed it to Trey. He took the notepad and flipped the cover open to the first page. The page had a date at the top, and just below the date, Trey read to himself what Jo had written many years ago back in Georgia. It read, "Dear diary, my brother introduced me to the most wonderful boy today, and someday I'm going to marry him." There was nothing else on the page. After reading it, Trey looked at his Grandma Jo and saw that she was starting to cry. Bill had no idea what Trey had just read and asked Jo why she was crying.

Jo said, "I have not read from that diary in several years, and it is bringing back old memories of back home and how much I miss our family and old friends."

Trey flipped through more pages and laid the diary on the table. "This diary with the list of dates and what happened on each one of them will be a big help," Trey said.

"I didn't know you had all that in there," Bill said.

"I started writing it down the first day I met you and added to it every time I thought there was something important to remember. I brought it with me. This is one thing I was not going to leave behind."

Trey asked his Grandma Jo, "Do you want to go through the diary and discuss what you have written down under each date?"

Jo agreed, and Bill listened as Jo told Trey about each date and explained, as best as she could, why she had written what had happened on that day.

"Very impressive," Trey said. "You have even drawn lines under what appears to be the most significant dates. That's good. It will help me narrow down the chain of events and my search."

They spent another hour going over the list.

"This will be enough for me to get started, and if I need anything else, I'll call."

"That will be difficult," Jo said. "If you remember, we don't have a phone, and that's another thing we would like to talk to you about before you leave."

"Sure, we can talk about it in the morning, since I'm leaving tomorrow, I would like to get a good night's sleep." Trey answered and took the list. Then he headed to his bedroom.

"I sure hope he doesn't get into trouble," Jo said to Bill as they lay in bed.

"I don't think he would have offered if he thought he would get in trouble or get us found," Bill said as he squeezed her hand and kissed her on the cheek. They both drifted off to sleep.

The next morning at breakfast, Bill asked Trey if he would stop at the Dollar Up store on his way out of town. He and Jo would follow him to town and would like for him to take a look at the phones people carried around with them.

Trey said, "Sure, they are called cell phones and work off of cell towers and satellites."

Bill said, "I don't understand how that works. My concern is if we use them, can someone find us?"

"It can be done, but you don't go by your given name, so it would be hard to put it together," Trey said.

"That's a relief," Jo said. "We spoke with a young girl at the store but didn't understand what she was telling us, and we told her we would come back with our grandson, and she understood."

"At our age, we know we need to be able to get in touch with someone if we need help," Bill said.

Trey agreed, "Good plan, and I will be glad to help you with it and show you how to use it. They are pretty simple, especially if you are just going to use it to make calls. It can do a lot more than just make phone calls, but there is no need for you to know all the other stuff. The only thing is there is a monthly fee to have one. It's not much and I can add you to my plan so don't worry about the cost."

They finished their breakfast. Trey went to the bedroom, gathered his luggage, and took it to his car that Bill had pulled out of the shed.

"I'll meet you in town," Trey said as he pulled out of the drive. Jo and Bill were not far behind, and they parked next to Trey's car in front of the Dollar Up store. They walked in; he was talking to the young girl they had spoken with before.

He had a phone in his hand, and when they walked up, the girl said, "I remember you. Good to see you again."

Trey told them this phone was just what they needed and should consider getting one for each one of them. He pulled out his wallet, got out a credit card, and bought two phones.

Bill said, "You don't need to buy those. They're for us, and we should buy them."

"It's for all the good food Grandma Jo fed me, the great fishing lessons, the story of your past, but most of all, the special time I have had with my grandparents."

The clerk said, "That is so sweet. Kids nowadays don't want to spend much time with their grandparents. I don't have mine anymore, and wish I had spent more time with them."

Bill and Jo agreed to let Trey pay for the phones; Jo thought how lucky she and Bill were to have Trey for a grandson as they walked out of the store.

Bill said, "Let's go to the Hillside restaurant for a quick goodbye cup of coffee, and you can show us how to use the phones."

They walked across the street to the diner. At the table, Trey made a call on his cell phone and talked to someone about putting Bill and Jo on his family plan and got it worked out. He got a number for Bill and one for Jo. He programmed the phones, showed them how to make calls and how to get in touch with him or each other by simply pushing one of the buttons. He set up button number 1 for Bill, and number 2 was Jo, and he was number 3. All they had to do was flip the cover up and push the numbered button for the person they wanted to call. He also told them they could dial 911 for either the police or medical help.

He could see that Bill and Jo were a little confused and told them, just flip the phone open, hit the number 3 button, and it would call him directly, and he could help them with any problem they may be having with using the phone. Jo was so happy Trey had helped them with the phone. She now had a way to let someone know if they needed help. Trey told them he would take care of the monthly charges, which would not be that much since they were only using the phone to make calls and not texting or searching the web, which Bill and Jo knew nothing about. So, they agreed to let him pay for it.

With a little more discussion about the phones, Trey felt confident they knew how to use them.

"Well, I hate to say this, but I need to get going. I would like to get out of the mountains and on the interstate before dark."

Bill got up and paid for the coffee, and they all stood in front of the diner and said their goodbyes. It was hard for them to see Trey leave, but they knew he had his own life to live, as did they. They watched him drive out of town. They climbed into the pickup and drove home in silence.

It was a quiet evening supper. They barely spoke to each other, which was unusual. With supper over, Bill helped Jo clean up, then said he was going to his rocker on the porch to think. He sat there rocking and thinking of the past and back home, as most elderly people do. He wondered how it would have been if Sarah Lou had lived. Would he still be in Hardwood, Georgia? How would Sally Ann have turned out? Would she have gotten cancer? Would they have lived close to Trey so he could see him more often?

Jo came through the door and said, "Interrupting any good thoughts?"

Bill sleepily said, "No, not really. Just thinking about the past and the people back in Hardwood."

Jo instantly knew he had been thinking of his deceased wife, Sarah Lou, but she didn't mind, and it didn't bother her. She knew he had grown to love her just as much as he had loved his first wife. Jo too, had often wondered if things had been different, would Sarah Lou have followed Bill anywhere he wanted to go as she did?

They rocked in silence for some time. Jo got up. "Getting late, I'm go'na get ready for bed."

"I'll be in shortly." After he said this, the two dogs got up and headed for their flap on the side of the shed. They, too, were ready for sleep, even though Bill knew they probably had done nothing but sleep all day. He sat rocking for a bit longer and finally headed in. Jo was reading her Bible as he climbed into bed, and she closed it and laid it on her nightstand.

He grabbed her hand, squeezed it, and said, "We have had a good life here on our little plot of land."

"Yes, we have," Jo replied, and they drifted off to sleep holding hands.

By the time Trey got back home, it was Friday evening, and he would have all weekend to research his Granddad Bill's past. Trey was looking forward to it; he loved doing research and solving mysteries like this. What intrigued him the most was who killed the boy, Luke Hampton. Trey didn't know how good the record-keeping was back then, but there should be some files in storage that he could go through if he had to go to Georgia. He did not know how much would be available online, if any, and if so, could he even access them.

After unpacking and relaxing for a while, reading his mail, listening to his answering machine, he went to his desk and turned on his computer. After it went through its startup process, he typed in "Hardwood, Georgia." The only thing that came up was a map of Georgia, showing the location of the town of Hardwood and a couple of short write-ups of how the town got started. He typed in Bill's real last name, "Bersha." Nothing came up, although there was a comment, "see Hampton."

He typed in "Hampton, Hardwood, Georgia." The screen changed. There was a picture of a lumber mill with a short story about the lumber company's beginning. Reading further in the article, it told of the murder of the owner's son, Luke Hampton, in 1932. William J. Bersha was convicted of the murder and had gone to prison and had escaped about three years after being imprisoned and was never found. He tried other names—the Bensons, Sarah Lou's parents, the owners of the only bank in town. There was a short historic story about how Mr. Benson, from Chicago, along with his partner from New York, had bought the local bank, along with a few others in surrounding towns, because they wanted to expand their banking business to the southern part of the United States. It also mentioned that Mr. Benson and Mr. Hampton had been in business dealings together in cities along the East Coast. It did not go into much detail about what type of dealings or businesses these were.

The short article also mentioned that Sarah Lou, the daughter of Mr. Benson, was shot and died. At the time she was shot, she was married to William J. Bersha, the young man that went to prison for murdering Luke Hampton. This was the last statement of the article. Trey found no more helpful information. He tried to find if Hardwood had a local newspaper and if he could access it online. Hardwood had a paper, the *Hardwood Review*. It was printed out of Waycross, Georgia. Many small-town newspapers had downsized their business in their local town. The local newspaper would gather ads, write articles about what was going on in town and its people, then send this information to a larger newspaper who would do the actual printing. It was more cost-efficient. He tried to access the *Waycross Daily* website, but he would have to wait until Monday, he needed to sign up and get a username and password before accessing the paper's website. He was getting frustrated, so he decided to shut down the search and enjoy relaxing the rest of the weekend.

Monday morning came quickly. Georgia was three hours ahead of Pacific time. He called and subscribed to the *Waycross Daily*. With his username and password set up, he resumed his research. Trey found out that a reporter named Mike Simmons handled the *Hardwood Review* account; he sent Mike an e-mail, hoping he would get a quick answer. Trey told Mike in the e-mail that he was retired from the LA Investigation Department and now worked part-time for a small private investigating firm. Being a part-time job, he had some extra time and had always been interested in writing a book on unsolved or unusual crimes. Trey explained he had been keeping a list of various crimes over the years and now had time to review them in hopes of writing a book on one of them. He had narrowed his search down to the one that intrigued him the most—the murder of Luke Hampton back in 1932, in Hardwood, Georgia, and the escape from prison by the convicted murderer.

In the e-mail, he told Mike that over the years, the LA Police Department would get correspondence from other states to be on the lookout for criminals. Trey had been working on a case that involved a man and woman from Georgia. While going through the old Georgia file cabinet, he came across a folder dated 1935. It wasn't a large file and it contained a few newspaper articles about the murder of Luke Hampton, the prison escape, and the escapee had never been caught. What caught his interest and got his curiosity up was why a knife and not the pistol. Back in 1935, the LA Police received correspondence from George about the escape along with an old black-and-white picture of the escapee so they could be on the lookout for the escapee. Trey didn't go into any detail about any other of the crimes that he was interested in because there were none, but Mike did not need to know that. If Mike ever asked about other unsolved crimes, Trey would tell Mike that he had a couple other on the west coast, so as not to raise any suspicion.

It was midafternoon, and Trey was working on a case with his private investigating firm when a ding went off on his computer, letting him know he had an e-mail. It was from Mike Simmons in Georgia; he quickly opened it. Mike mentioned to Trey that he, too, had always been curious about this crime and had done a little research over the years, but since it was so old, he did not put a lot of time into it. Mike wrote that he thought there was a lot more to this crime than was being told or written in the files. Mike also noted the fact that it appeared the town of Hardwood had always had its share of corruption, and he thought some of it may still be going on. In the email Mike mentioned that if and when Trey had more time, he would like to tell him about a few things that had been going on over the years with some of the more prominent people of Hardwood, such as unexplained fires destroying businesses, unusual deaths or people just up and leaving town for no apparent reason.

Trey thought maybe Mike had found out somehow about his Grandpa Bill and sent someone to Idaho to look for him. Was that why his Grandpa Bill thought someone was watching him? Trey knew he would probably have to go to Georgia to be able to look through the court files concerning his Grandpa Bill's trial. He just wished he could take his Grandpa Bill and Grandma Jo, but there was no way. He would have to let them know he was going and would be extra careful not to raise anyone's suspicion. He would tell people in Georgia that he was doing the investigation for a book he was thinking about writing, and he would have a reporter from Waycross with him to make it more realistic. Trey was fairly good at convincing county clerks to let him look through a file that may not be accessible to the general public, and, he still had his LA detective badge.

If he went to Georgia, he would contact his old boss at the police department before he left and let him know that he was going to Georgia to find a deadbeat dad that wasn't paying his child support. So as not to tip off the deadbeat dad, Trey asked his old boss that if got a call from a clerk or official in Georgia to verify Trey's identity, to tell them he had taken some time off and was down there to do some research on a possible book he was thinking about writing.

Trey sent Mike an e-mail and asked if Mike could give him a call that evening after he got off work. Mike e-mailed back and said he would call around 5:00 p.m. California time.

Right on time, Trey's landline rang, and Mike's name popped up on the phone's caller ID screen.

"Mike, so kind of you to call."

They went through the usual greetings for people who have never met in person, and then after a few minutes of small talk about their jobs, family, and the weather in each other's part of the country, Mike asked, "So you want to write a book, what a challenge. I have always wanted to write a book but never could find the right subject nor the time."

Trey answered, "I have thought about it for some time, and now I have spare time. I am intrigued by the Hampton murder. I think people have a fixation on unsolved crimes, and this one in Hardwood, Georgia, has an additional twist. The convicted man escaped from prison and has not been found. I don't know how much I can write about his escape without finding him and getting the information firsthand, but it would be something if I could find him and get a story from him."

"That it would," Mike said.

"Now lets' talk, how much do you know about murder and the convicted murderer?" Trey asked Mike.

"Not a lot since it happened so long ago. I don't have much time to search the court files when I go to Hardwood. I usually take one day to drive down and back. I pick up ads and short articles from the owner or her son at the *Hardwood Review* office. In and out and head back to Waycross," Mike said. "I can tell you; it looks like the town of Hardwood has some shady dealings going on; drug business, money laundering, illegal aliens, etc. It appears there is a lot of money being funneled through that little town. Several people are living well above their means, and I don't see any industry around that would support that kind of lifestyle, there are only a couple of small independent lumber and saw mill companies around. When I ask Janice or Jack—the newspaper owners—they have very little to say and end up changing the subject. They don't want to comment on anything that goes on around their town, so I don't push it. I have mentioned to my boss about what I think is going on and should I do more investigating, he always says definitely not. We don't need to get involved. I think he knows more than he lets on about what is going on." Trey was getting more and more curious and knew he would have to go to Hardwood.

"If I come down to Waycross, could you take me to Hardwood, show me around, and introduce me to anyone that I might be able to talk to about the murder?"

"Sure, would be glad to. I think Janice or Jack might loosen up if we had time with them. We can only try."

Trey told Mike that he would get a plane ticket and let him know what day to expect him. Mike told Trey it would be best to fly into Jacksonville, Florida, rent a car, and drive to Waycross. It was about an hour's drive. Trey could call him when he got to Waycross and he would direct him where to go so they could meet up.

"That sounds good; I will get back to you in a day or two with information about my flight." They both hung up.

CHAPTER 13

———— ✑ ————

Off to Hardwood, Georgia

Trey sat back in his chair and thought if he had done the right thing by contacting Mike. He worked for the newspaper, and it seemed he had some knowledge of the killing of the young man and the prison escape years ago. He would have to be very vigilant and choose his words carefully, if and when the two met, so Mike would not become suspicious. The next thought that popped into Trey's mind, should he call his grandparents and let them know he was going to Georgia. Trey decided that he wanted to keep them informed as to as much of the investigation as he could. He was doing it on their behalf to ease his grandpa's uneasiness about being watched or followed. Trey turned on his computer and called up a blank word document, he started typing what he needed to tell his grandparents. He did this mainly to read over what he wanted to tell them so as not to make them uneasy. There were a few things that he did not want to tell them at this point, so he highlighted those thoughts to be sure and not mention them.

It was seven in the evening, and Trey was guessing Bill and Jo were sitting on the porch, watching the evening sun fade while rocking and talking about the events of the day. He made the call.

It took a couple of rings before Jo answered and said, "Hello, Trey, it's good to hear from you, sure glad we got these phones. Sorry, I was slow to answer. I had to go back to the kitchen and get the phone. I tend to forget to bring it outside with me. I haven't gotten used to carrying it around, and besides, we don't get calls."

"That's no problem. I'm just glad you have one so we can keep in touch." Trey explained to Jo how to put the phone on speaker so they both could hear what he had to tell them and his plans to go to Georgia. Jo followed Trey's instructions and laid the phone on the small table between her and Bill so both could listen and ask questions.

"Okay, Trey, we both can hear you now. What's on your mind?" Jo asked.

Trey started, "When I got back home, I started doing some research, and here is what I found, which isn't a whole lot." He told them by using the Internet, he had been able to find newspaper articles and got a few details about the murder and trial and that it listed a few more names and places than what they had given him. Trey told them he had read different articles about his Grandmother Sarah's death and how Grandpa Bill had been sentenced to life in prison. He told them he read why the life sentence was ordered by the judge and not a death sentence because a couple of jurors had their doubts as to why Billy had not used the pistol. Trey told them that he had contacted the Hardwood County Court's office and told the clerk in the office that he was researching for a book he planned on writing about the death of Sarah Lou Benson Bersha. The clerk told him that they did not have records on the Internet that went back that far, and he might try the *Waycross Daily* newspaper in Waycross, Georgia.

"I took the advice of the court clerk and contacted a reporter by the name of Mike Simmons at the *Waycross Daily*. I told him I was researching for a book I wanted to write about the murder of Luke Hampton but had run into a snag when trying to find information online. He agreed to help. I think Mike is in his early thirties, so he wasn't around when the murder of Luke Hampton happened, but the case had always intrigued him as well. In his spare time, he too had done a little research on his own about the murder and the escape of William "Billy" Bersha from prison, who was never caught, but had run into too many dead ends so he stopped." Trey waited for some reply from his grandparents. There was only silence, so he asked, "Are you still there?"

"Yes, we are still here, just taking in what you are telling us so far," Bill answered.

Jo asked, "What are you going to do now?"

"I am planning a trip to Waycross to meet with Mike. We will probably go to Hardwood, and I will look through old court records and possibly go to the newspaper office to see if I can dig up anything that might lead me down a path to who killed Luke Hampton," Trey answered.

"Do you think you really need to go to Georgia?" Jo asked Trey.

"Yes, I have gathered all the information I could using my computer, so the only thing left to do is to go to Hardwood. I will pull the court case of the trial and any newspaper articles, do some reading, and possibly talk with some locals that might still be around who lived there when all this occurred," Trey answered.

Bill spoke up, "I don't want you getting into any trouble by asking questions about what happened years ago. I don't know, but there might still be people around that want revenge."

"I understand, and I will be extra careful," Trey answered. "I plan on booking a plane flight sometime next week, depending on when I can meet up with Mike in Waycross. Mike told me he is pretty close to the people that own the *Hardwood Review*. He goes there once a week to pick up their ads and articles so his newspaper can print them. The *Hardwood Review* does not do its own printing anymore, it is too expensive. They have the paper in Waycross do it for them. The owners should be of some help. They should have articles on the jurors about their insight on the trial."

Bill asked in a somewhat worried voice, "How much does this Mike guy know? I am a little worried that he may get suspicious and start asking questions and figure out that you are doing more than just getting facts to write a book."

"Don't worry, Grandpa, I can act pretty good. I have had a lot of practice convincing people to go back home to their loved ones or telling a dad that isn't paying his child support that I am not a law enforcement officer, but here is what will happen if he doesn't start paying. Most of the time, I am successful, but there have been a few times things didn't work out, and I learn from my mistakes. I had better let you two go so you can enjoy the rest of the evening rocking and watching the sunset. I sure wish I was there with you, and I will keep in touch with you every few days. I will call and tell you when I get to Georgia. Love you both, good night, and don't worry."

They all hung up, and Trey went to his computer and e-mailed Mike to see what day would be suitable for him to fly down. Trey did not expect such a quick reply, but while he was reading a couple of his other e-mails, Mike replied any time will be fine. He just wanted to know so he can have that day set aside to meet Trey. Trey e-mailed back:

I will book my flight and let you know. Thanks for your help. I look forward to meeting with you.

Trey searched the web for a flight to Jacksonville, Florida. He was looking for one that would put him in Jacksonville as early in the morning as possible so he would have plenty of time to drive to Waycross. Trey found one that left LA at 6:45 a.m. on Monday, and with a short layover in Atlanta, he would land in Jacksonville around 1:00 p.m. This should give him plenty of time to rent a car and drive to Waycross. He would wait until morning to e-mail Mike back with the flight information. He was getting tired and always liked to lay in bed before going to sleep to think over things he had planned to do the next day. Trey did not think very long before he fell asleep.

Waking up feeling well rested, Trey made his coffee and sat down at his computer. He sent an e-mail to Mike informing him of the day he would fly down and the approximate time when he should be in Waycross. He sat staring at the computer screen, wondering what he found out in Georgia. He was also concerned about what Mike had told him about the little town and the possibility of organized crime. Trey, with his past law enforcement experience, could think of a couple of things. The one that was most obvious was drugs of some kind or maybe illegal aliens. Georgia had a lot of farming: peanuts, cotton, onions, chicken farms and lumber mills, all could use cheap illegal labor. Hardwood still had some lumbering going on around the town, some of the small lumber companies, saw mills or chicken farms, could be used to launder drug money. Maybe that was what Mike was talking about when he mentioned corruption. Trey's main concern was gathering as much information about the murder to help his grandfather solve the mystery, not the towns corruption.

Trey took a sip of coffee, and clicked on a file he had been working on to locate a missing girl from just outside Los Angeles. He wanted to get as much information in the file as possible before he gave it to one of the other investigators in the small firm since he may be gone for several days. He had just finished checking over the file for the last time before saving and closing it when he heard the ping that informed him that he received an e-mail. It was from Mike, but he had a different e-mail address and a different phone number to call when he reached Waycross. This seemed a little odd, but Mike said he was using his personal email and phone number, instead of the one at work, he did not want anyone at the newspaper accidently reading his email or talking to Trey on the papers phone. Trey appreciated Mike's concern. Mike's e-mail told Trey to go south from the airport to the 295 Beltway West, then watch for Highway 23 North; this would take him to Waycross. Mike told Trey that there were several good motels just before getting into Waycross, and once he got settled in, he should give him a call and he would come to the motel to discuss their trip to Hardwood. The instructions seemed simple enough, and Trey was getting more excited about the trip. He loved investigations, and this was going to be one that he wanted to solve more than any of the others.

Trey had a couple of days to try and relax before his flight, but what was he going to do? There were no repairs to do around his small duplex, his car was okay, he had no pets, what a boring life until now. He lived on the north side of LA, so he decided to drive to the Angeles National Forest. There are a couple of small springs with waterfalls, and he could hike around and take in some fresh air. The mountain and streams were not like the ones where his grandparents lived, but at least he would not be in the city. He packed a few things and headed out for a two-day-and-one-night trip. He would take along his notepad to jot down anything that might help him with his research in Georgia, but he mainly just wanted to get out of the city.

The open space at his grandparents continually tugged at his heart, and he thought about how his mother loved the country. After spending almost, a week there, he understood how she felt about where she grew up and how much he missed her. He tried to keep the thoughts of her and his grandparents as out his mind as he drove. Driving along he watched how the city started changing to the countryside, then into the small mountains with hiking trails at almost every turn.

When he got to where he would spend the night, he called his dad. After his mother died the two of them did not talk much. Trey wanted to tell him that he was taking a short working vacation back east for about a week and would call him when he got back home. His dad did not answer, so he left a message. Trey rented a small cabin, and while settling in, he thought how he and his dad were never very close. His dad seldom went with them when he and his mom went to see his grandparents or as far that that goes, he very seldom went anywhere with them. When he was young, he didn't know why his parents stayed together. They seldom did anything together; his dad worked continuously, family seemed to come second, so he and his mom spent a lot of time doing things without his dad. Maybe he was more like his dad than he thought. Work had always been Trey's first thought, and that may have been the reason why his relationships did not last very long. Being retired and work not being so fast-paced now, if he ever got in another relationship, he would work on being less work motivated and pay more attention to the person he was with. He realized he had received more than just fresh air and open spaces in the short time he spent in the mountains with his grandparents. He had seen how love and companionship between two people should really be. Trey sat down at the small table in the room. It felt like his mother's spirit had touched him; he remembered what she would tell him on one of their drives to see his grandparents, "*When you grow up, enjoy the wonders of the world, the people close to you and don't let work consume your life.*"

Trey had taken several short hikes on the nearby trails, sat beside the stream outside his cabin, and relaxed for two days. Now it was time to head back home. His flight was at six forty-five the next morning. He packed up and headed home. Getting home in the late afternoon, Trey unpacked and got out his list of things to take with him to Georgia. He always made a list of things to do or take when it came to work or almost anything he plan to do, he always wanted to be prepared. He always kept a notepad and pen on the lampstand next to his bed because when he started on a new case, he seemed to always wake up in the middle of the night with thoughts and would write them down so as not to forget them. This had become a habit. Several times it had helped him in a case, but he wondered, had work consumed his life that much? No, he thought, this was a good habit to have. It had helped him out more than once.

The next morning, he drove to the airport, boarded the plane, and settled in for the flight to Georgia. He arrived at Jacksonville a little after 1:00 p.m., rented a car, and headed to the 295 Beltway. It would take an hour to get to Waycross, and he would have plenty of time to find a motel and call Mike before dark. Waycross was not that big of a town, but Trey did not like going into a town, big or small, after dark.

As he approached Waycross, he started seeing motel signs and decided on the Comfort Inn. The ones he had stayed in before were reasonable and usually had everything he needed—good beds, continental breakfast, and, most of the time, good internet service. After getting everything situated in his room the way he wanted it, he sat down at the little desk and called Mike. He answered after a couple of rings. Trey told him what motel he was at, Mike asked him if he had no plans for the evening and was not too tired, he would stop by and pick him up, and the two of them could have supper. He knew of a small local restaurant where they would have privacy to discuss their trip to Hardwood. Trey said that sounded like just what they needed. Trey wanted to have as few people around while they talked about their trip to Hardwood. Mike had a couple of things to do before picking him up and would be there around 6:30 p.m.

Mike was right on time, and he drove a short distance to a small family-owned restaurant called Folks Home Cooking. "The country fried steak is my favorite, but all their food is good. They get most of their vegetables from locally grown farms," said Mike.

They ordered. Trey started telling Mike a little about what he wanted to do in Hardwood. He told Mike what he had downloaded from the Internet about the murder, and there was very little about the escape. He did not have much luck on the Internet looking at articles from the newspapers in the surrounding towns. Mike, too, had not found much over the few years that he had been with the *Waycross Daily*. The few times in the past that Mike had spoken to Janice at the *Hardwood Review* about the murder, she, too, had wondered why, if Billy Bersha had done it, why didn't he use the pistole he had. With a knife in his chest, Luke would have had to stop, turn around, he would have been an easy target for Billy. Mike told Trey he had spoken to Janice and told her that he and Trey would like to come down and do some research in the newspaper files, if that would be okay, and probably go to the court clerk's office as well. She had no problem with them coming to her office.

"When I spoke to Janice a couple of days ago, she mentioned to me, that in discussions she had with her grandfather in the past, he too had always wondered, why didn't Billy simply shoot Luke? Billy's reputation around town was that he was a good shooter with a rifle or a pistol. She nor her grandfather could not think of why Luke would have stopped and turned around, knowing Billy had a gun."

"I told her maybe Billy wanted revenge and thought a bullet would be to quick and easy."

Janice had told Mike that these questions were brought up in some of the newspaper articles pertaining to the murder, but she had not read the trial transcripts and would like to know what he and Trey find out.

During their supper, Trey told Mike about some of his detective work while he was on the LA police force and what he was now doing for the small investigation firm. With his work load not so hectic, he now had some time to start research on his book. This one especially piqued his interest, and then with the escape, that added even more mystery to the case. He doubted if he would ever get the chance to actually find the escapee and interview him, but wouldn't it be nice. Trey wasn't sure this case could be solved completely, but he would like to try and greatly appreciated Mike's help.

Trey hoped that he was convincing enough to have Mike believe his story about writing a book. He thought maybe by doing this research for the book, he may be able to prove his grandfather's innocence. They finished the evening meal; Mike drove Trey back to his room and told him he would pick him at eight the next morning. It would take an hour to get to Hardwood.

Again, Mike was right on time. Trey appreciated Mike's promptness. Trey thought of all the times in the past when he had to wait on people for a meeting that they had set up, and they were the ones always late. On the way to Hardwood, they decided to go to the newspaper first, and Mike would introduce Trey to Janice. Trey explain to her that he was now semi-retired and wanted to try his hand at writing. Trey hoped again that his story about a book would be convincing to Janice if she started asking too many questions. They reached Hardwood about 9:30 a.m., and Mike drove around the town and pointed out the courthouse, library and a couple of places to eat. They pulled in front of the *Hardwood Review* and parked. Walking in Mike introduced Trey to Janice and Jack, owners of the *Hardwood Review*. Janice looked to be in her late forties, and Jack was probably in his earlier twenties.

Trey asked Janice, "Mike said you are somewhat familiar with the Luke Hampton murder. Do you have any old newspaper articles I can read about the trial or any other information pertaining to the murder, as well as the escape by the convicted person?"

"Jack, can you take Mr. Thompson to the back room and show him the files with the old papers that have not been stored on the computer?"

Mike had a little more time than usual, and he asked Janice, "You have mentioned in the past that you think there may be some illegal dealings going on in Hardwood, but no one will or wants to discuss it?"

"Yes, and I try not to ask too many questions because of what has happened to some people in the past that have spoken to the sheriff. Some up and moved for no reason, while others simply shut their businesses down and move, and I don't want that for my newspaper."

"Do you think it's drugs or something else, possibly illegal aliens?"

"I think it is probably both, but I think it is mostly drugs. Once or twice a month, there are a couple of small white vans and a car with northeastern license plates that come to town and stay for a day or two. The people stay at the same motel and seldom purchase anything other than meals. They get in their vehicles, leave the motel, and are gone all day. They return late in the evening, then after of couple of days they leave town. I tend to think it is drugs that are being loaded into the small vans then taken up north. I don't know that for a fact, though. I think there are also illegal aliens being brought in as well, and they are kept them in the small white cabins just outside of town that housed slaves years ago. I don't know which would create the most revenue, but the county sheriff and his deputies tend to turn a blind eye when it comes to investigating any of it."

Mike asked, "Do you think they are being paid off?"

"I am sure they are. The county sheriff always has a new pickup for their personal vehicle, and his public salaries doesn't pay that much. There have been things in the past that have happened that should have been investigated in more detail but weren't. This has been going on for years and no one back then, or now, is going to take the first step. I don't want our conversation to get out."

"Thank you for what you have told me, it will not go any further. I do not want any trouble coming your way."

Trey and Jack came from the back room, and Trey said, "I think I have gotten all the information I can get from here, and I very much appreciate you letting me look through your old papers."

Trey thanked Janice and Jack again, and he and Mike headed for the courthouse to see if they could get permission to pull the old court files on the Luke Hampton murder case. On the way to the courthouse, which was within walking distance from the newspaper office, Mike told Trey some of what Janice had told him about drugs, illegal aliens, and other things that had happened in the past. She did not elaborate on those but seemed very concerned and troubled.

"She definitely does not want it getting out that she even spoke to me," Mike said. Trey said he understood and would not discuss any of what Mike told him.

CHAPTER 14

❧

Reading the Murder-Trial Transcript

On their walk to the courthouse, Mike told Trey where he had gone to school and how long he had worked for the *Waycross Daily*. He loved his job but got disheartened when he could not get information from a person about something he was reporting on; they would dodge questions or give him some generic answer. He was most frustrated when parties would not even acknowledge his calls or correspondence. He had hoped that someday he could work for a larger news agency, maybe a major network as an on-the-scene reporter, but maybe he did not have the personality for that. He, like Trey, loved investigative work, so he was thrilled when Trey asked him for help. He told Trey he had asked for a couple of days off so he could help with the research. Trey had to come up with some way to explain to Mike he did not need help but did not want to offend him. Although he might need his help in the future.

They enter the courthouse, and Mike led them down the long hall to the court clerk's office. Mike did not know the clerk personally but knew her name; Trey noticed it was also painted on the glass door. As they approached the counter, a young girl got up and asked if she could help them.

Trey responded, "Yes, my name is Trey Thompson and would it be possible for you to pull an old court case I would like to read through it? I have the case number, it is CV-0231-1932. It is a murder trial back in 1932, on the murder of Luke Hampton." When he said the murder of Luke Hampton, the elderly lady sitting at a large desk in the back of the room stood up and walked to the counter.

She asked, "Why do you need to review a case that old?"

Trey answered, "I don't want to cause any trouble. I am a retired LA detective, and I am doing research on a book that I plan to write on this case."

"Do you have identification?" she asked. Trey handed her his LA department badge along with his ID card that stated was with the LA Crime Investigation Department. She took it and looked at it with some skepticism. Trey noticed that she was a little concerned, so he told her she could call the number on the card and ask for Captain Palmer; he would vouch for him and for his purpose being in Hardwood. She handed the card and badge back to Trey and asked why this particular case. Trey told her that over the years, the investigation department that he had worked in got numerous cases, and when he was not working on a new case, his job was to go through old cold case files. When he came across a case that intrigued him, he would write down some information about it in hopes of doing more research and possibly write a book on it when he retired.

The elderly lady said, "The LA police department is investigating a case this old, and the murder happened in Georgia, not California."

Trey replied, "No, they are not reopening the case or investigating it. When I came across this case several years ago, it intrigued me, so after retiring, here I am, in hopes of doing a little more research for a book. As for the murder happening in Georgia in 1932, the LA department had been sent a photo back then of the escaped convict that was convicted of the crime so they could be on the lookout for him since he had escaped. Our cases are filed by last names, and while I was searching through the file cabinet under the *H*s for a different case I was working on, I came across this old case with the name of Hampton, pulled it, and I read through it in my spare time and thought this would be a great case to write a book on when I retire. So; if possible, I would like to see if I could get a little more information for my book, so here I am."

The elderly court clerk said, "I don't think there's a problem with letting you look through the old files, Anna, would you take Mr. Thompson to the file room in the back and show him where the old files are."

Trey responded, "I really appreciate your cooperation. I could not find much information online about this case. I guess it is too old. Being retired, I thought this would be a good chance to see part of the country I had never seen and maybe get a little more information on the case." Trey knew they could not keep him from seeing the case files, they were open to the public except in the cases involving juveniles.

Mike broke in and said he needed to meet with a couple of small shop owners about their ads, and he would meet Trey in about an hour at the little diner across the street from the courthouse.

Anna took Trey to the back room and pointed to the file cabinets and the shelves that held boxes with faded case numbers marked on the ends. Trey found the cabinet that held the case number he was looking for, pulled out the file, carried it to a long table in the middle of the room, and sat down. He took out his notepad and pen, then opened the file. On the first page was a picture paper clipped in the upper-right corner, who was probably his grandfather when he was young. He had a full head of dark hair and an unwrinkled face. He stared at it for some time when he realized Anna was watching him.

"You, okay?" she asked.

"Yes, it just doesn't look like the picture in the file back in LA."

"If you need anything, I will be in the next room," she said.

Trey started flipping through the pages until he came to the testimonies taken during the trial. He read there were no eyewitnesses to the crime, so the attorneys would only be able to call character witnesses for Luke Hampton and Billy Bersha, the accused.

Trey began reading the trial transcript, which was not as long as some he had read in the past. The district attorney, then the defendant's attorney, presented their opening statements. Trey read them both and thought that this was going to be a hard case for his granddad's attorney with no eyewitnesses. The attorney for his granddad called only two witnesses to testify. One was Sam Williamson, his granddad's best friend, and Mr. Williamson, Sam's father. The DA called three Hardwood townspeople as character witnesses, who all testified that they knew Billy, and he had grown up in Hardwood and seemed like a nice young man, as far as they knew he had never been in trouble. The deceased, Luke Hampton, and his family had moved to town from up north and had only lived in Hardwood for a couple of years. Luke's father owned the local sawmill and lumber company, along with others in the surrounding towns, and employed several people in the county. The witnesses stated that the Hampton sawmill and lumber companies were very good for the local economy, and they did not want what had happened to Luke Hampton to have a bad reflection on the hardworking people of Hardwood. Trey read where Billy's attorney asked each one of the witnesses if they knew of any reason Billy would have wanted to kill Luke Hampton other than seeing his naked wife, Sarah, lying on the floor, with Luke standing over her. They all replied no, but each one of them stated that the entire town knew there were bad feelings between Billy Bersha and Luke Hampton. As the last character witness stepped off the stand, she spoke out loud so the entire courtroom could hear her. "She should have married Luke Hampton instead of a common mill worker. She would have been better off, but she didn't and now look what it got her."

Billy's attorney objected, and the judge granted the objection. The witness had spoken out loud about what most of the town had been thinking. Trey knew that her comment was not permissible in a court of law, but the damage had been done. Trey imagined, in a small town like Hardwood, most people felt the same way. It would be hard to get a not-guilty charge and even harder to get his client a lesser charge than the death penalty. Trey read through some of the handwritten notes his granddad's attorney had put in the file. One stood out more than the rest. The note mentioned that the attorney thought Bill had a 50 percent chance of getting off with a life sentence and not the death penalty. He had to put as much doubt in the juror's minds as possible as to why Billy stabbed Luke instead of shooting him.

Trey read the testimony given by Billy's best friend, Sam. He had picked him up that morning so Billy could leave his truck for

Sarah to use if she needed to come to town. With Sam's dad's help, they finished loading the flatcars with lumber to be shipped out first thing Monday morning, and Sam dropped Billy off in front of his cabin around 5:00 p.m. He had stopped by a small store before going home. Sam was asked if he heard anything while driving off from Billy's cabin, he replied he had not, and he got to his house around 5:30 p.m. Sam's father's testimony told much the same story. Trey started to read from where the first day of the trial had ended, and no more witnesses were to be called. The judge told Billy's attorney that he could call Billy to the stand first thing the next morning. Then the attorneys would give their closing arguments.

Trey sat back in his chair and stared at the file and thought how it did not look good for his grandfather back then. There were no witnesses, and the attorney was inexperienced for a murder trial. Trey got up, walked to a water jug, got a small paper cup, filled it, and drank it down. He threw the cup in the trash and sat back down at the table staring at the papers in front of him. He picked up the trial transcript and began reading the second day of the trial transcripts. He read from where Mr. William Billy Bersha was called to the stand.

Billy's attorney asked, "Mr. Bersha, can you tell the court in detail all the events that occurred on April 17, of this year."

"Yes, I can."

It took Trey almost thirty minutes to read through the transcript in which Billy described the events of the day in question. As he read, he remembered a few weeks earlier, when he was on the porch with his grandfather, who told him about the day Sally was shot and how he found Luke Hampton with a knife in his chest. Trey was amazed at how good his granddad's memory was; what his grandfather told him then was almost word for word in the transcript he was reading.

It had almost been an hour, and Trey needed to get to the diner where Mike told him they would meet. Trey closed the file, put it back in the file cabinet, and walked into the front office. He thanked the two women and said he might be back tomorrow if that would be okay, and the court clerk told him that would be no problem. Trey thanked them again and walked out of the courthouse. He looked across the street and saw Mike going through the door of the little diner and thought, *He is prompt, right on time.* Trey and Mike sat down at a table for two in the corner that gave them a view of the main street.

Mike asked Trey, "Did you find out or learn anything new?"

Trey answered, "I read through most of the trial transcript, which wasn't as long as some I have read, but I haven't gotten to the closing argument. So far, it looks like the defense attorney, Jack Taylor, has a steep hill to climb to get his client off death row. I imagine Billy's attorney will put a lot of emphasis on the fact that Billy Bersha, used a knife instead of shooting Luke Hampton. That appears to be the attorney's only chance to avoid the death penalty."

Mike responded, "I guess he did put some doubt in the juror's mind because, by the articles in the papers, he got a life sentence instead of the death penalty. Are you going back to read more this afternoon?"

"No," Trey answered, "I don't want you to hang around here while I read. I know the way down here. I can drive back down tomorrow by myself so that you can have your last day off."

"It's no problem driving you back down here," Mike said.

Trey responded, "That's okay. With my own car, I can drive around, see the town, maybe talk to some people that might still be around when the murder happened. Hopefully get a little more personal insight as to what happened. It is always good to have more information than less, and I want my book to cover the community's thoughts about the murder and trial. I will probably drive to Jacksonville and spend the night there before my flight leaves."

They finished their lunch with small talk about their lives, with Trey being very guarded about how much he told Mike. Most of the talking was done by Mike, which was okay. Trey had learned over the years to be a good listener. There had been many times he let the person he was interviewing do all the talking, and it would divulge a clue or give him a lead in helping to solve the crime or find someone. Mike was not guilty of anything, Trey just wanted him to talk about himself so as not to think about wanting to help Trey with his research.

The drive back to Waycross to his motel room was fairly quiet, with only small talk about the scenery. Mike dropped Trey off and told him that if he needed anything, he should not hesitate to call. Trey thanked Mike for all he had done, went into his motel room, and sat down at the small desk. He pulled out his notepad and read over what he had written down earlier and thought about his Granddad Bill. How awful it must have been to hold his wife's head on his lap while she died, then be convicted of a murder he did not do.

Trey wondered, was his granddad telling him the truth, or did he really stab Luke instead of shooting him? Maybe Luke had stopped, turned around, and Billy had used the knife instead of the gun for an alibi. Trey thought not. With all that was going on, he did not think his granddad would have been thinking about creating an alibi at that time. Trey let that thought pass. He scanned through his notes a little more and jotted down a couple of reminders for the next day.

He took a shower and went to bed to get a good night's sleep so he would be rested for the next day. He thought about calling his grandparents but then thought otherwise. He would call them tomorrow evening after reading the closing arguments and possibly finding some old residents that may still be around that he could interview. He would have more to tell them after tomorrow.

CHAPTER 15

⁐

Closing Argument; Trouble in Hardwood

Trey was up early and went to the small breakfast area of the motel and had some coffee and a doughnut. Taking the first bite of the doughnut, he thought, *I am doing the exact thing people think we do—go sit in a coffee shop, have our doughnut and coffee before heading out. Glad I am not in a uniform, or I would be pictured as one of the doughnut-eaters.* He pulled out his notepad and read the first thing he needed to do when he got to Hardwood. It read, *"Read the closing arguments, write down the names of the people called in the trial and the jurors."*

Sam and his father were the defense's only witnesses, and they, along with Grandma Jo's mother, all died in the house fire. He thought it was a little odd that none of them made it out. But it was in the 1930s, with no smoke alarms and probably not much of a fire department in Hardwood. He made a note to check for any newspaper articles concerning the Williamsons' house fire. Trey sat there, watching people come and go from the little breakfast room; some would speak, but most would not. He thought the world had become more and more unfriendly, even in the small towns. He was accustomed to unfriendliness in California, but this was a bit of a shock to see it in this part of the country, so much for Southern hospitality, he thought. He finished his coffee and headed for his room.

Grabbing his briefcase, camera, and laptop, he walked to his rented car. He put his things in the back seat and slid behind the wheel. He then reached over to the glove box and pulled out a city map to make sure he would be taking the right road out of town heading south to Hardwood. During the one-hour drive, he thought about his grandparents back in Idaho and how they must have felt when they first arrived, not knowing anyone and not being able to correspond with family back home. They had agreed not talk too much about their past or exactly where they were from. They always had to be on guard when visiting with any new friends, they made.

Trey thought about his mother and how much he actually missed her. She had not gotten to see what he had done with his life, and he felt he had been cheated. He didn't blame God but wondered why he had taken her. She was the kindest person he had ever known, always helping anyone in any way she could when they needed it.

He drove on, trying not to think about the past and trying to focus on the scenery. He saw rolling green hills with pine trees and little valleys of tilled land where crops were growing. He did not know what kind of crops they were but suspected it was either cotton or peanuts. A few times, he would top a hill and, off in the distance, could see where a whole side of a hill had been clear cut and how barren it looked and thought what a shame. As he would get closer, he could see where small trees had been replanted. He was glad to see that some type of reclamation of the land was being done. He rounded a curve and saw a road sign, *"Hardwood 2 miles ahead."* He started slowing down. He did not want to miss the street that the courthouse was on.

Entering town, he remembered the turn from the day before and saw the courthouse flag a couple of blocks away. He found a parking spot in front and pulled in. After grabbing his briefcase from the back seat, he started to step up onto the sidewalk when he heard someone call his name. He turned and saw Janice across the street, standing in the doorway of her newspaper office and waving for him to come over.

They said their good mornings to each other, and she invited him in, saying she had something she wanted to talk to him about.

Trey was puzzled but answered, "Certainly, how can I help you?"

"I know you are a detective."

Trey interrupted, "A retired detective."

Janice said, "That is even better for what I would like to discuss with you, and I would like your cooperation in keeping our conversation confidential." Trey was thinking what could be so secretive that she did not want it getting out, did it have to do with what Mike had told him yesterday?

"I can promise you what we discuss here will go no further."

"I know you are here doing research on the murder of Luke Hampton, but if you have a few minutes, I would like to discuss some questionable things that have gone on in the past and are still going on to this day here in Hardwood." Janice invited him to sit down on a chair in front of her desk.

"I was told several years ago by my grandfather not to get involved or ask questions as to what is going on. He did not want his newspaper shut down or, worse, burnt down. So, I never commented or asked anyone about his or my concern. Since you are a detective, I thought you might be able to give me some advice as to how to bring this to light without harm to my business, myself, or family?"

Trey sat looking at her for a few seconds before he answered, "Let me think about what you have asked. I need to go back to the court's clerk's office and do a little more research, and I will get back to you after lunch if that will work for you?"

"After lunch would be a good time. That will give me time to get my articles ready for print. Thank you for your offer to help."

Trey left the newspaper office and walked to the courthouse. On his way, he walked by a building with a glass front which had, *Hardwood National Bank, a bank for the people,* painted on it and in the lower corner was painted, *est. 1928, owner Mark Benson.*

Trey remembered that his grandfather had told him that Sarah's maiden name was Benson, and he guessed that Mark Benson was probably related to his biological grandmother Sarah. Entering the courthouse, he walked to the court's clerk's office, and Anna approached him and asked if she could help him.

"Yes, I would like to look at the Luke Hampton case file again. I did not get to finish it yesterday, and it will not take long."

"Certainly," Anna said. Trey followed her to the back room, where he pulled the file and laid it on the table where he sat before.

"Thank you," Trey said and opened the file.

He turned to the last couple of pages of the trial transcript. He found the attorney's closing arguments and began reading. The county's district attorney reminded the jurors that the entire town knew there had been bad blood and feelings between Billy Bersha and Luke Hampton because Sarah had married Billy instead of Luke. With no witnesses to the murder, they only had Billy's word of what happened. They had fought, Luke had run down a path in the woods, and Billy found Luke with a knife in his chest. Trey began reading Billy's attorney's closing argument. He did not deny the bad feelings between the two young boys, but none of the character witnesses mentioned that Sarah was unhappy with her marriage to Billy. On the contrary, they all stated that she seemed happy, especially when the baby came. Jack Taylor, Billy's attorney, reminded the jurors that there were two bullets left in the pistol, so why would Billy use a knife instead of shooting Luke as he ran down the trail? Billy's friend, Sam, and Sam's father had testified that Billy was an excellent shot, so why use a knife? After jotting down a few notes, Trey closed the file, took it to the front office, and thanked the ladies as he left.

Trey walked to the small diner, sat down, ordered a tuna salad sandwich, and read over his notes. He was troubled as to what to do next. He wasn't sure if he should talk to Janice or should he stay out of whatever she wanted to discuss with him and focus on trying to help his grandpa Bill. Trey thought, who did kill Luke Hampton? Would he find out more if he went back to the courthouse to see if he would be permitted to pull an evidence box if they had one? After finishing his lunch, he decided to talk to Janice; she might have leads that he could use to help in his search. Janice was sitting at her desk when he walked in. He sat down in front of her desk.

"I have some time if you would like to discuss whatever you are concerned about. I am not sure I can help, but I will listen."

Janice began telling Trey about her grandfather. "My grandfather bought this newspaper in the early 1900s, and after my grandmother died, he lived with my mother and me. My mother worked at the newspaper as well, and when I got old enough, I started working here as well, and after my mother died, it was just me, Jack and my grandfather. When my grandfather died, I took it over and have managed it ever since. When I was old enough to truly understand right from wrong, I saw numerous things that should have been investigated by law enforcement but weren't. I would mention this to my mother and grandfather but was told not to question or express my thoughts or concerns to anyone. It involved men that did and would eliminate anyone that tried to interfere. Over the years, I figured out that some of the people and businesses in town had possible connections with organized crime from back east, and I think some still do. There have been sheriffs in the past that have tried to do some investigating only to find themselves being voted out of the office or quitting in midterm. One county sheriff just disappeared. His family never heard from him. His family had no idea what happened to him, but I have my ideas."

Trey asked, "Did the state or federal government look into his disappearance?"

"Yes, they did but gave up after a couple of months, I think because they got no cooperation from any of the townspeople." Janice answered. "This is not a rich town, and there are families here that are doing quite well, and I think it is because of organized crime, and since the owners of the bank, the lumber company, and a couple of other businesses keep a lot of people employed, no one was willing to help with what little investigation there was."

Trey said, "That seems all too reasonable for a small town when there are not that many employers." They both sat contemplating over what each of them had said.

Trey asked, "If it is organized crime, what kind of crimes do you think they are involved in?"

"I think drugs mostly, and there are what appear to be a lot of illegal aliens being shuttled through as well, but I cannot prove either of these."

Trey sat back in his chair and told her, "Through my many years in law enforcement and especially as a detective, you need eyewitnesses that are not afraid to come forward or photos to convince a district attorney to take on the case. Most of the time, this is hard to do. With this being such a small close-knit town, it is not surprising that no one will step up."

"I have tried to talk to a few people I thought I could trust, and they did not want to discuss it. Their response was leave it alone, our town is doing fine, don't get involved. I think they remember the sheriff that vanished and a couple of other townspeople that simply up and moved after reporting what they saw or heard to the authorities."

"So, you have had concerns about what has been going on for many years. Do you think organized crime had anything to do with the murder of Luke Hampton?" Trey asked.

"I'm not sure about that, but when I was younger, I knew there was a lot of moonshine being trucked out of the counties of Dawson, Lumpkin, Pickens, and out of here. I had heard it was going up north to Atlanta and further north to New York. My grandfather had mentioned this to my mother and he thought the Hardwood National Bank, owned by the Bensons, might have been doing money laundering for the gangsters from up north, but back then, I did not know what that meant. I know people did suspect Luke Hampton and Matt Benson of driving trucks north loaded with moonshine for extra money."

Trey thought out loud, "It might have been possible that Luke Hampton was keeping some of the whiskey for himself and the mob found out and he needed to be taken care of. They might have found out Luke was going to the Bersha cabin while Billy was at work, and they killed Luke knowing Billy would get the blame."

"That seems a little too coincidental," Janice said.

"Yeah, I guess you're right," Trey answered. He wrote this thought down on his notepad.

Janice then said, "One reason I think that organized crime of some type is still going on is that a couple of times a month, two or three small white cargo vans come to town, the drivers check in at the same motel and are here for only a couple of days. Each day the vans are driven out of town in the morning, are gone all day, then come back in late afternoon. At least once a month, a luxury car also comes to town with them. The driver pulls in front of the Hardwood

National Bank, and usually, two men get out carrying briefcases and go into the bank. They usually stay for about an hour. The same thing happens at the Hampton Lumber company's office."

Trey commented, "That does sound like some type of money exchange, but without actually viewing what goes on inside, we can only speculate. Do the vans come to town about the same time each month?"

"Yes, they come about every other week, and if my memory is correct, they should be here sometime this week." Trey leaned back in his chair; he had been leaning forward, listening intently to Janice, but his back had begun to hurt.

"I think I have done as much research in the courthouse as I can, and with the articles that you copied for me about the trial, I need to go back to my motel room and piece together what I have. With what I have so far, I don't think there will be anything that will link what you told me about the possibility of organized crime and Luke's death so many years earlier, but you never know. Stranger things have happened," Trey said. Trey gave Janice a list naming the jurors and the few witnesses that were called and asked her if any of these people were still alive, and if so, does she think any of them would be willing to talk to him.

Janice looked over the list and said, "Most of the people are deceased, and of the ones still alive, there might be a couple that would be willing to talk to you. Most people around here don't like talking to strangers, but maybe I can talk to them first and let them know what you are doing here."

"That would be very helpful, thanks," Trey said.

Janice scanned over the list again and said, "There are two women that I think would be willing to meet with you. One was a witness and the other, Mrs. Martha Boudreaux, was on the jury. I think she was one of the jurors that had doubts about Billy killing Luke."

Trey said, "I think she would be the first one I would like to speak with if she is willing."

"She is in her nineties and still pretty sharp for her age. She will be coming to our church tonight for our group meeting. I will pull her to the side and see what she thinks about speaking with you."

Trey answered, "I can be back in town tomorrow. Here is my phone number. Call me if she agrees and give me a time. I will be here."

As Trey stood up and thanked Janice for all her help, he turned and headed to the door. Janice stopped him by saying, "The vans are here as well as the car." Trey looked out the big front glass window and saw two vans and a black Lincoln pass by. They both watched as the vehicles drove to the corner and turned onto a street that led to the motel.

Janice said, "Right on time."

Trey told her thanks again, and he walked as fast as he could to his rented car without bringing attention to himself. He threw his briefcase on the passenger's side of the front seat, slid behind the steering wheel, slowly pulled away from the curb, and started to follow the vans and the car around the corner. He followed them for a couple of blocks until they reached the motel, where they pulled into the parking lot. He slowly drove by, trying to get a look at the license plates. He could not see the plates, so he drove on past, went to the corner, turned around, and drove back to the motel. He parked behind one of the vans waiting for the drivers to check into the motel. He wrote down the van's tag number and was hoping he could get the tag number of the Lincoln without drawing too much attention. After the men finished checking into the motel, they came back outside, stopped at the Lincoln's back window, and started talking to the man sitting in the back seat.

Trey got out and began to walk into the motel office so it would appear as if he was checking in. As he walked by the Lincoln, he looked at the license plate and hoped he could remember the number. As Trey walked past the car, the man in the back seat gave him a long hard look. Trey tried not to let the man notice that he saw him looking at him as he walked to the door of the motel lobby. Trey talked to the desk clerk long enough for the vans and the Lincoln to drive away. After he was sure the vans and car were out of sight, Trey got in his car and headed out of town toward Waycross.

As he was leaving town, he noticed that one of the vans was a few blocks behind him and wondered if it was following him. As houses gave way to timberland, Trey saw the van was about a mile behind him. He had an uneasy feeling, and when he reached the posted speed limit, he put the cruise control on to see if the van would stay the same distance behind him. After a few miles, the van turned onto a side road, and Trey saw dust being kicked up by the tires. He relaxed somewhat. He knew if he came back tomorrow or the next day, he would have to be extra cautious so that he would not draw too much attention to himself. He did not like the way the man in the back seat looked at him. Trey was not wearing anything that would lead anyone to think he was in law enforcement or had been in law enforcement. If these men were involved in crime, it's possible the man was just suspicious of everyone. Since Trey had sat in his car for a few minutes before going into the motel, it gave the man more reason to get a good look at him as he walked by.

As Trey drove, he continually glanced in his rearview mirror to watch the vehicles behind him to see if one of them was a van or possibly the black Lincoln. After several miles, he felt it was safe to relax, and he thought about his grandparents back in Idaho. He knew he should call them that evening and give them a short report. He didn't have much to tell them. He mainly wanted to let them know that he was okay and was making a little progress. He also wanted to tell them that he would keep them posted as soon as he found anything of interest. He drove on mostly without thinking, just admiring the landscape. Just as he pulled into the motel parking lot, his cell phone rang. It showed the caller as unknown. He answered and said hello.

"This is Janice. Can you talk?"

"Yes, I just pulled into the motel parking lot," Trey said.

"Good, I spoke with Martha just before our church group met, and she has no problem talking to you about what she can remember about the murder trial. I have her phone number, but I thought it would be better if you just met her here at my office. She said she would feel more comfortable if I could be there with her while you two talked if that's okay?"

"That would be fine. I want her to feel at ease. When do I need to be at your office?"

"I set the meeting for tomorrow at 10:00 a.m., if that will work for you."

Trey answered, "I'll be there at ten in the morning, and I appreciate all that you have done. I look forward to seeing you again."

After saying their goodbyes, Trey grabbed his briefcase, locked the car, and went to his room. He got out of his slacks and into his favorite lounge pants and shirt, sat down at the little desk, pulled out his notepad, and jotted down what he was going to tell his grandparents. Almost a half hour went by before he was ready to call them. He had decided to tell them about his upcoming meeting with Martha Boudreaux and wondered if they would remember her. It was 6:00 p.m. in Idaho, and they would probably be getting ready for supper, so he decided to call and have a pizza delivered to his room before he made the call to his grandparents.

While waiting on the pizza, Trey thought about Janice and her concerns about what was going on in Hardwood. He also thought about how she was an attractive, strong, and independent woman. She was running a newspaper and had raised Jack, a son on her own. Trey had no idea of how old she was, but she did not look old enough to have a son who looked like he was in his late twenties. Trey had dated a few women in the past, but with his job, he had never gotten too close with any of them. Most of them were in law enforcement as well, and conversations would always end up discussing cases. Trey did not want to spend the evening talking about work, so his dating became less frequent; and in the past few years, he had only gone out a couple of times. Maybe if he spends a few more days in Hardwood, he may learn a little more about Janice and possibly build up the courage to ask her out for a quiet thank you for your help, dinner.

Finally, the pizza arrived. He ate a couple of slices and glanced at the digital clock on the nightstand. It was 8:30 p.m. His grandparents should be finished with their evening meal, so he sat down in the chair next to the small table in the room and flipped open his cell phone.

After a couple of rings, Jo answered the phone, "Hello, Trey. Glad you called. Hope you're, okay?"

"Yes, I am doing fine. I just want to get you up to speed on how it is going down here. Do you remember how to put the phone on speaker so both of you can hear?"

Jo answered, "Yes, it is the button that has a picture of a speaker, right?"

"That's correct." He began telling them what he had been doing the past few days. After bringing them up to date, he told them he was going back to Hardwood in the morning for a couple more interviews. He asked them if they remembered Martha Boudreaux; Bill said yes. She had been one of his schoolteachers. He did not know her that well growing up but remembered her from the trial and how she would look at him with what he thought were sympathetic eyes. Trey told them he was meeting with her in the morning and would call if he found out anything important. They said their goodbyes. He hung up and got ready for bed.

CHAPTER 16

The Folders

Trey was up early. He showered and went to the breakfast bar for a coffee and roll. He tried to read the small Waycross paper but could only think of questions he wanted to ask Martha and to hear her story as a juror at the trial. He finished his second cup of coffee, went to his room, grabbed his small briefcase and laptop, got in his car, and headed south out of town to Hardwood. He had great expectations of what he was going to find out by listening to Martha's story. On the drive, he went over in his head what he wanted to ask Martha, with the main question being: did she think Billy killed Luke Hampton? He did not want to push her; he knew he had to be patient and listen to her story and not seem to be too inquisitive, and to remember she was an elderly lady.

Arriving in Hardwood, he parked in front of the *Hardwood Review* office. Stepping out of the rental car, he looked up and saw the black Lincoln drive by slowly, then stopping in front of the Hardwood Bank. Trey turned around and headed into the newspaper office. He did not know if the man that was in the back seat the day before noticed him or not, but he did not want to take a chance. Entering the office, he saw Janice at her desk with a nicely dressed elderly lady sitting in one of the two chairs in front of her desk.

Janice got up, stuck out her hand, and said, "Nice to see you again." In a tone that Trey thought was a little more than just being polite.

"This is Martha Boudreaux." Trey took her hand and told her how nice she looked and was glad to meet her.

"You are the gentleman that would like to talk to me about the murder trial of Luke Hampton?" Martha asked.

"Yes, I am. I am gathering information to possibly write a book on the murder, trial, and the prison escape."

"It is somewhat exciting to be telling you things that might someday be in a book," Martha said.

"If I do write the book, I will not be using anyone's real name of the people I interview."

Trey noticed Martha looked a little disappointed.

Trey said, "That is, unless I have their written approval. I am sure you have plenty of good information for me, so if you're ready, I would like to ask you a couple of questions before we get started."

She agreed, and Trey started. He asked her how long she had lived in Hardwood, was she married, did she work, and a few other personal questions mainly to get her to relax and feel more comfortable talking to him. Trey learned over the years of investigation that you need to show a personal interest in the person you are interviewing. He learned that you should make them feel as if you want to know about them personally before starting the questioning. After about ten minutes or so of getting acquainted, Trey asked Martha to tell him as much as she could remember about Luke Hampton and Billy Bersha.

Martha said she had known Billy Bersha most of his young life, and he had been in some of the classes she taught. She also knew his parents and grandparents they attended the same church she did; they were hardworking, honest, churchgoing people, like most of the people in Hardwood. As far as she knew, Billy had never gotten into any trouble other than maybe fishing or hunting on someone's property without permission. He also had never been in trouble with the police; he was a good kid. As for Luke Hampton, he had moved to Hardwood with his parents the summer before he was to start his last year of high school. His father owned the Hampton Lumber and Sawmill Company that employed most of the men and young boys in and around the town. She thought Luke had always seemed to think he was better than everyone else since his father owned the lumber company.

Luke, and Matt Benson, the son of the local bank owner, were best friends. Most of the young boys did not have much to do with either Luke or Matt. The few friends they did have, were the sons and daughters of the office personnel at the sawmill or the bank. Billy never had much to do with Luke or Matt, and as far as Martha knew, there had never been a problem between them until Sarah Lou Benson, Matt's younger sister, started showing an interest in Billy. Most of the townspeople thought that because Luke was the son of the largest business owner in the area, and Sarah Lou was the daughter of the owner of the only bank in town, they should be together.

Martha looked at Trey and said, "When Sarah started seeing Billy that was when trouble started between Luke and Billy."

"What trouble?"

"Sarah and Billy were spending a lot of time together. Luke, his family, and Sarah Lou's family did not approve of her seeing Billy. He was the son of a common worker, and she could do better. This was the town's thoughts and gossip."

Martha sat back in her chair, shook her head, and sighed.

"The whole town talked about Billy and Sarah Lou and how she should be with Luke Hampton. Billy, his family, along with his best friend, Sam Williamson, and his family, were, in a way, shunned by most of the townspeople. I myself was ashamed of my community in the way they treated Billy and Sarah Lou. The two were good kids. It wasn't a shock to anyone when Billy and Sarah Lou ran off to get married. Sarah Lou's family disowned her and did not acknowledge their own granddaughter when Sarah Lou had little Sally Ann. I could never have denied being with my grandchildren if I had had any. After almost two years, the gossip of the marriage between Billy and Sarah Lou and their new baby settled down, but I heard from some church members that Luke still held a lot of hatred for Billy and Sarah Lou."

"With what you have told me, do you think Billy killed Luke?"

"I don't know. As best I can remember, I had my doubts. I could never understand, if Billy had a pistol, why didn't he just shoot Luke?

This was one of the reasons why I voted no on the death penalty. This was the question that no one seemed to be able to answer. When Billy told his story, I felt like he did not do it."

As Martha sat there silently, Trey saw her face take on a sad impression, and he decided to try another line of questioning.

"At the time, did you know anyone else in town that disliked Luke enough to commit the murder?"

"I can't think of anyone, but it was a long time ago, and my memory, well, you know with age, is not as good as it used to be. There were a lot of young boys that did not like Luke or his friend Matt. But whether they disliked Luke enough to kill him, I don't think so."

"I have one last question, you and one other juror voted no on the death penalty?"

"That's right. The other jurors were not happy with us. It troubled both of us as to how our fellow citizens and friends treated us after the trial. There were a lot of friends that stopped having much to do with us after the trial. It took me some time to feel comfortable at church again. As for Betty, I think because she had no close family, and the friends she did have stopped communicating with her, she just wanted to stop living. She died a couple of years after the trial."

Trey closed his notebook and told Martha how much he appreciated her taking the time to talk to him. What she had told him will be of great help when he starts writing. If he completes his book and is fortunate enough to get it published, she will surely get one of the first copies. He hated lying to her about the book, but he had to keep the book-writing story going so that no one would suspect his true intentions, trying to help his grandparents. He helped Martha out the door, then turned and walked back to the desk where Janice was sitting.

"Will all of this information help with your book?" Janice asked.

"Yes, it will. It is almost noon. How about I buy you lunch?"

Janice replied, "I thought you would never ask."

Trey was surprised at her answer but also pleased. Janice looked around the office to make sure everything was turned off. They saw only a few people in town as they walked to the small family café.

They stopped in front of the café and as he held the door open, he saw the two vans pass by with the black Lincoln following slowly behind. The back window of the Lincoln was rolled down, and he saw the man in the back take a long stare at him, then the window slowly rolled back up. As Janice walked in, he watched as the Lincoln stopped in front of the Hardwood bank.

Trey and Janice were seated, and Janice asked him, "The man in the black car looked at you for a long time. Do you know him?"

"No!" Trey answered and handed her a menu. Janice wondered why Trey was so quick with such an abrupt no. Trey apologized for his quick answer and told her that he had followed them to the motel the day before, thinking maybe he could learn something about their presence in town; he did not. He told Janice the man in the Lincoln gave him the once-over when he walked past the car yesterday at the motel and was concerned when he looked at him again today. Trey felt as if the gentleman was making sure Trey noticed him watching.

"Guess my old detective habits are hard to drop. I just don't want any trouble coming your way or, for that matter, my way."

"It is nice to know that you are concerned, very thoughtful for someone you have only known for a couple of days," Janice said. She told the waiter what she would like to have for lunch. Trey gave his order, and they both sat silently for several minutes.

Trey wanted to tell her the real reason for being in Hardwood but now was not the time; he had more investigating to do. Waiting for their lunch to arrive, Trey's and Janice's conversation was about their past lives, the places they had been to, and a little about work. Trey told Janice how much he liked the view of the countryside, the rolling hills, the winding streams, the pine trees, but most of all, the friendly people that he had met so far. Janice commented that the country was nice to look at, but the people can be deceiving. She told him that not all are as friendly as they seem. She told Trey if he asked too many questions, the word will get around and suspicions will rise as to what he truly wants or who is he. This was the last thing he wanted. Janice told him that Martha Boudreaux was once a valued citizen, and many people in Hardwood respected her until the trial and the death of two out-of-towners a few years after the trial. Trey's curiosity was aroused, and he asked her to continue unless she had to get back to the news-paper. She suggested they finish their meal and go back to the office where she would pull some old files her grandfather Henry Weston kept in one of the file cabinets in the back room. Trey paid for the meal, and they walked back to the newspaper office, where Janice told him to wait while she got the files from the back room.

"As I mentioned yesterday, my grandfather and my mother ran the newspaper. When I got old enough, I started helping out and doing what I could. My mother died when I was a teenager, so I took her place at the office and home, doing the cooking, cleaning—you know, all the house and work stuff. My grandfather told me his life had been threatened several times, not in person, but by letters sent to him or notes slipped under the office door. He was told to stop prying into things that did not concern him. My mother tried to explain to him not to get involved, but my grandfather was a newspa-perman, so it was his job to investigate and report. I tried to remind him what my mother had told him, I also did not want him getting hurt, so he did stop asking questions but kept files on things that he thought were corrupt around town."

Janice had laid two large files on her desk. In bold black let-ters across one folder, it read, "Jurors of the Luke Hampton Murder Trial." The other folder read, "Question as to the death of Mr. and Mrs. Elmer Smith." Janice had forgotten their names but remem-bered it when she saw the file.

"As I told you when I was younger, my grandfather told me that Hardwood had always had some shady people around town, he also told me that a couple, Mr. and Mrs. Smith, died in a car accident before I was born, and he believed it was no accident, it was staged."

Trey picked up the folders and asked if he could take them back to the motel to read because it might shed some light on what went on in Hardwood in the past, as well as what appears to be going on even now. Janice agreed, and Trey picked up the folders.

"I will bring them back tomorrow. If you do not have plans for the evening meal, I would enjoy your company again." Trey asked.

"I have no plans. A new restaurant on the outskirts of town opened up a few months back. The few meals I have had were very good. One of their specialties was fried alligator tail, but I like their alligator gumbo best."

This did not sound that tasty to Trey, but he had enjoyed her company at lunch.

"Sounds great. I will be back in town tomorrow afternoon to do a little more research at the courthouse. I will meet you here at your office around four or five to pick you up."

"That would be fine."

Trey turned and walked out of the office to his car. Trey was anxious to get back to the motel and dive into the folders to see what secrets her grandfather had written down about the town of Hardwood.

As soon as Trey at the motel, he unloaded his things from the car and went to the ice machine for ice. Back in the room, he poured himself a soft drink, sat down at the small table, and opened the file marked "Jurors of the Luke Hampton Murder Trial." There were newspaper clippings with notes attached to them that were probably written by Janice's grandfather Henry. They were well organized by date, so Trey started at the earliest date—April 1932. Trey read several clippings but soon found out that reading the handwritten notes by Janice's grandfather proved to be more productive. Trey figured out that Henry Weston did not print in his newspaper what he really believed or thought. Trey read through the various notes on the trial and conviction of his own grandfather Bill and found that, for the most part, the town had convicted young Billy Bersha before the trial ever started. Getting a fair trial would have been almost impossible. Trey read the notes about Martha Boudreaux and realized that when the townspeople found out that Martha Boudreaux and the other juror had voted no on the death sentence, most of the town began to shun them, and Martha was asked to leave her church and stop teaching.

One of Henry's notes read, after speaking with Martha about her voting no, she had voted no on the death penalty because she knew Billy Bersha and his family and thought he could not have committed the crime. But her no vote had to do mainly with the knife issue. She had serious doubts about why Billy had used a knife;

there was just too much doubt. She thought there was more to Luke's murder than what was brought out in the trial, and she had mentioned this to the other jurors when they were deliberating the sentencing of Billy Bersha. There were a lot of things Luke and his friend Matt Benson were thought to be involved in around the town and she had mentioned this to the other jurors. They simply did not want to talk about it since they were the sons of two prominent businessmen. Trey leaned back in the chair and read more of what Henry wrote. Trey thought Martha probably said something during the juror's deliberation on the sentencing of Billy Bersha that she should not have said, which is why the jurors turned on her, and being a small town, word got out by some of the jurors about how Martha felt about Luke Hampton and Matt Benson.

Trey made a few notes but had second thoughts about speaking to Martha about it since it seemed as though the town had forgiven her, and she had been accepted back into her church. He will talk to Janice about it tomorrow. It was almost 8:00 p.m.; he closed the folder, slipped on his shoes, and thought he would walk to the little restaurant down the street and get a light supper. Getting some fresh air may help him gather his thoughts. While waiting on his order, he wondered why Janice had given him the Smith file. It did not seem to tie in with anything about the murder trial or Martha Boudreaux. He had not seen the Smith name in any of the court clerk's files pertaining to the murder trial. While eating, he became more curious about the Smith file. What could be in the file that caused Janice to give it to him?

He thought, *well, I am a detective. I should be able to sort through possible evidence.* He finished his meal and hurried back to his motel room.

When he got back to his room, he got into his comfortable lounging clothes, sat down at the small table, opened the Smith file, and began reading what Janice's grandfather, Henry, had put in the file. Trey saw again, that Henry had put every clipping in order by date. Just as he did in the juror's file, he also had handwritten notes to go along with the newspaper articles. He thumbed through the file, and there were several newspaper clippings from his own newspaper, as well as others from surrounding counties, reporting on the accident and death of Mr. and Mrs. Elmer Smith. Most of the articles did not go into much detail other than it appeared that the Smiths auto had slid off the road, rolled down the side of the embankment, and ended upside down in a ravine in about four feet of water. It was estimated that the Smiths had been there approximately four to five hours before anyone saw the auto in the ravine.

Trey knew that forensics in the 1930s was not what it is nowadays, so the accident could have happened several hours earlier. He read through all the articles, which mostly reported the same information. Trey then picked up the small notebook, which was also in the file. There had not been a notebook in the juror's folder. On the cover, Henry Weston had written, "Was Smiths' death truly an accident?" Trey wondered, did Janice's grandfather know something that he did not put in his articles about the accident, and the other newspapers failed to report or were not willing to report? Trey turned to the first page of the little book, and at the top, it read, "Reasons I believe it was not an accident."

Trey read through the half dozen or so explanations why Janice's grandfather did not believe it was not an accident. The notebook contained twenty handwritten pages, and Trey read through it all. What Henry Weston had written about the town of Hardwood was troubling, and Trey needed to get back to Hardwood early enough to talk to Janice about her grandfather's notebook. It was too late to make a call to his grandparents back in Idaho, so he decided to get a good night's sleep. He would talk to Janice tomorrow about the Smiths to see if she could share any more information as to her granddad's concerns.

CHAPTER 17

Secrets of Hardwood

Trey slept in later than he had planned. The motel phone rang and woke him up. It was Mike wanting to know how the investigation was going and if he had found out anything new. Trey told him about the interview with Martha Boudreaux but did not learn much more than he had already found out by reading the trial transcripts. Mike wanted to know if he was going back to Hardwood. Trey told him he was going back today, but it would probably be his last day. He would spend the night there and head to Jacksonville tomorrow to catch his flight back home. He could hear the disappointment in Mike's voice when he said goodbye, but Trey did not want people seeing him with a reporter from another town. Mike had been a lot of help, but for now he did not need any more help.

Trey got dressed, went to the motel office, and checked out. He got a cup of coffee to go, already-made sausage biscuits, and headed for Hardwood. He would get there earlier than planned, but he wanted to drive around the town. Being the detective he was, he wanted to do a little surveying of the surroundings, which might uncover more about what was going on that Janice was concerned about. Hardwood wasn't a large town, and he had not driven on the outskirts of the town except for coming in on the highway from Waycross.

As he approached Hardwood, he saw a sign that said truck route and it appeared as though it might go around Hardwood, so he took it in hopes it would circle the town. It did. After a mile or two, he saw a group of small white houses a couple of hundred yards off the road, all lined up in a row. There was one long narrow building at the edge of the forest. He saw a few people walking around but could not tell if all the buildings were occupied. He thought about driving in and asking for directions as if he were lost but changed his mind as soon as he saw one of the vans parked beside one of the little houses. A man was leaning against the front of the van, and the side door was open. Trey wondered if the man was waiting to put someone or something in the van, so he slowed down in hopes he could see what was going on. When the man leaning against the front of the van straightened up, Trey saw that he had a pair of binoculars and was watching Trey drive by. Trey increased his speed, hoping the man did not recognize his rental car from the day before. As the road curved, it put the little white houses out of sight, so Trey was not able to see if anything was being loaded into the van as he drove away.

Just as Trey thought, the blacktop road did circle the town of Hardwood, and he was approaching the Hampton Sawmill. It didn't appear to be a very large sawmill. There were a couple of railroad tracks leading in and out of the middle of what appeared to be loading ramps. There were piles of sawdust at one end of the property, a small office building, and two large buildings that were open on each end with railroad tracks going through the middle of them. Trey did not know much about sawmills, but he was guessing the reason for the warehouses being open was to keep the air circulating around the lumber. He did not see many workers but imagined most of them were out in the forest cutting down trees.

As he passed by, he saw the black Lincoln parked to the side what looked like an office, but wasn't sure if it was the same car he had seen earlier. He thought about turning around and driving by again but had second thoughts. The man in the back seat had stared at him pretty intensely the day before, so Trey drove on, hoping no one noticed him.

Another mile or two of driving, and he was back at the highway leading into Hardwood. He turned and headed into the town, wondering how many times his grandfather Bill had been down this road. He wanted to drive around to see if he could find where his grandfather and grandmother had lived when they first got married, but he had no idea where to start looking. He pulled to a stop in front of the *Hardwood Review*, sat there knowing he was a couple of hours early. He did not want Janice to think he was too eager to see her, but in a way, he was. He stared at the front door, wondering whether he should go in or not.

He was startled by a knock on the window of the car. He looked up, and it was Janice. As she walked to the front door, she motioned for him to come in. She was carrying some boxes, so he helped her with them and set them on a table she pointed to.

"Thanks," she said, "you're early."

"Yeah," Trey replied.

"That's okay. Jack helped me this morning. We got all the ads and what few articles there are set up and ready to give to Mike to print when he comes to pick them up."

Janice sat down behind her desk. Trey looked at the wooden block on her desk that read "Janice Weston" and instantly remembered her grandfather's last name was Weston and wanted to ask how that was. However, he did not have to ask.

Janice saw him looking at her wooden nameplate.

"Wondering about my name being the same as my grandfather's?"

"Well, somewhat, but it's none of my business."

"That's okay. The shame of what happened many years ago has long passed. I will tell you so you won't have to wonder and lose any sleep over it." Trey thought about how straightforward she was.

He sat back and said, "Okay, let's hear it." They both chuckled.

"My mother got pregnant with me after she was out of high school. Back then, situations like that were greatly frowned upon, and I guess my dad couldn't take the embarrassment, so he left before I was born, and my mother never married. We never heard from him, and to this day, I do not know where he is."

"What about your son Jack? Were you married?"

"Oh no, he is my adopted brother."

"Mike told me he was your son."

"No, my mother adopted him. About twenty-five years ago, a young girl got pregnant, had Jack and like my dad, Jacks' father up and left. The young girl did not want him either, so my mother, thinking of her past, took him in, and after a few years, the court awarded Jack to her. She always had a soft heart for unwanted things—dogs, cats, old newspaper clippings, and kids. After my mother passed, I have tried to treat him like a son, but I think he resents not having his real mother and father. He has a wild streak that sometimes gets him into trouble. My mother had more control over him than I do. I hope he grows out of the bitterness before it gets him into something he can't get out of."

Trey sighed and said, "I have seen too many young people go down the wrong path when their home life is not the way one would like to see it. In the end, everyone pays for the outcome in one way or another."

"My mother took him to church with her, and he seemed to enjoy being around the kids there. They weren't as cruel as others. When he started school, the real teasing began. It got worse as he got older and especially when he entered high school. Kids can be so mean. They teased him about his mother and father abandoning him and no one wanting him. Even though my mother and I did, it still had an effect on him."

"I'm sorry to hear that. Whatever he is into, I hope he and you can work it out," Trey said.

"Thanks, I'm sure we can."

Trey asked, "We have a couple of hours before our evening meal of alligator tail, and I would like to talk to you about your grandfather's folders. I read through the clippings but got more out of his handwritten notes than the articles.

"Yeah, that was granddad, a stickler for notes."

"I would like to know your thoughts as to what he wrote."

"Sure. And alligator is not the only thing on the menu at the restaurant. They also have boiled crawfish."

"Oh, those sound even more delightful," he said with a slight laugh.

"What do you want to know? Ask away."

"Do you know why the town turned on Martha? Was it just because she voted no on the death penalty? And did your grandfather talk to you in detail about the Smiths' accident?"

"One at a time. I remember some of what my grandfather and mother told me, but it was several years ago. Most of the town turned on Martha, partly because of her voting no to the death penalty but mostly because she spoke out about the criminal activity going on and around the town. She was a churchgoing schoolteacher and was very outspoken and concerned about how the children of the town were being exposed to the criminal elements and being drawn into a life of crime, especially Luke Hampton and Matt Benson. She tried to get my grandfather to report on what she knew was going on, but after he received death threats, he decided against it. He tactfully reported on some of the problems but in a way so as not to bring any more attention to the problem than possible. I guess it appeased many of the townspeople, especially the ones profiting from the questionable activities and the threats stopped.

My mother told me that Martha was very upset, and since the newspaper would not report on it, she attended city council meetings and school board meetings, trying to convince authorities to do something. Nothing was ever done, so most of the town thought she was a troublemaker and disrupter. She did not want the town to prosper. This was upsetting to my grandfather, and he told Martha he wished he could help, but he had to look out for his own business and our lives. Even at my age, I knew what was going on. The making of moonshine, then shipping it north was against the law. Also bringing in people from Mexico or other countries to work in the fields where corn and other crops were grown to make the moonshine, paying them very little—if anything at all—for their labor was wrong. I knew, as well as most of the town, these people were brought in, and they lived in the little white house's outside of town. What little money the workers did spend helped the small stores in town."

Janice took a sip of her coffee and continued. "The Hampton Sawmill and Lumber company prospered as well as the Hardwood National Bank. I knew back then, as well as today, that both these businesses are involved in some type of activity that needs to be looked into. It took years for Martha to gain respect back from the townspeople, but she finally did, and she was thrilled to be able to attend her church again without being snubbed."

Janice stopped talking, leaned back in her chair, took a deep breath, after which she said, "As for the Smiths' accident, I remember Granddad telling me he drove out to investigate and report on the accident. When he came back, he told my mother that he did not think it was an accident and was not going to report what he thought had happened. He told me the curve in the road where the automobile went off was a gentle curve and was wider there so people could make the turn without fear of running off the road. It had been raining that morning, but the road was well maintained by the local county prisoners, and a layer of small rocks was always kept on the surface for better traction. Mr. Smith lived in the far northwest and was familiar with driving on wet mountainous roads. He had driven from Spokane, Washington, to Hardwood, Georgia, so it was not like he had just started driving. Mr. Smith had come to Hardwood to speak to Mr. Hampton about purchasing the sawmill outside of town, along with some leased timberland and the small camp that housed workers.

In an interview my grandfather had with Mr. Smith, he told my grandfather that the purchase was to expand his lumber business into the southern part of the country. This way, he did not have to ship timber from his sawmills in the far northwest all the way across the country to the eastern part of the United States. Through their correspondence, Mr. Smith was under the impression that Mr. Hampton wanted to sell all of his holdings. After arriving here and meeting with Tom Hampton in person, Mr. Smith was told the small houses outside of town and the leased timberlands were no longer included in the sale. Mr. Smith told my grandfather he was frustrated that he had driven all that way to find out that these had been pulled from the sale, only the sawmill was for sale. When Mr. Smith questioned why, he was only told things had changed, and Mr. Hampton was sorry that the Smiths had driven all that way. Mr. Smith told my grandfather that when he pressed Mr. Hampton as to why it was now only the saw mill for sale, Tom Hampton became angry and said he had simply changed his mind. Mr. Smith did not think Mr. Hampton was being honest with him." Janice sat back in her chair as her face took on a saddened look.

"I take it your grandfather told you more and it is hard for you to talk about."

"Yes, my grandfather told Mr. Smith about the criminal activity going on and that he thought the leased timberland was used to hide moonshine stills, and the small houses were used to house Mexicans for cheap labor. Mr. Smith said he would have nothing to do with any type of criminal behavior and that he would be leaving in a day or two. The next day, my grandfather found out that Mr. Smith had told Mr. Hampton he had decided not to buy the saw mill or anything from him, he was not going to get mixed up in anything illegal. I don't know if Mr. Smith mentioned anything to Mr. Hampton about my grandfather telling him about what he thought was going, but on the way out of town two days later, the Smiths' accident happened."

"Was your grandfather worried that something might happen to his business or his family?"

"Yes, he was, but fortunately nothing ever did. Years later he told me that he had always thought something happened to the car or possibly that they were murdered somehow and the car was pushed off the road. I definitely remember my grandfather telling me that William Benson, owner of the Hardwood National Bank at that time, was very angry with Tom Hampton for the sale not going through and blamed the failure of the sale on Tom Hampton."

Trey said to Janice, "In one of your grandfather's notes, he wrote he had spoken in private with a bank employee that overheard Tom Hampton and William Benson in a heated discussion at the bank about what they were going to do for money. How were they going to get the funds to pay back the people up north since the Smith deal fell through. Your grandfather's notes did not reveal the bank employee's name, but I read where your grandfather wrote that the employee feared for his life if it got out, he had said anything to your grandfather about the quarrel."

Janice answered, "My grandfather heard rumors that money was being funneled through the Hardwood bank to fund mob dealings up north. The bank had used some of it so that Tom Hampton could purchase more timber leases and equipment for his sawmills.

177

Granddad thought that since the sale did not go through there was no way to repay the money to the mob. To keep the Smiths' from talking, he was sure the Smiths' accident was staged. Hampton and Benson did not want Mr. Smith telling anyone about the possibility of any criminal activity going on, so they silenced Mr. and Mrs. Smith. My grandfather just didn't have the proof that it was not an accident."

Trey asked, "Do you know if their bodies were examined for any type of wounds other than what may have been caused by the accident?"

"Are you referring to perhaps gunshots or some other way they may have died other than the accident?"

"Yes," Trey answered.

"I am not sure if there was ever any in-depth investigation into the accident. If a doctor looked for any other type of wound, I doubt it. I think it was an open-and-closed unfortunate accident," Janice answered.

"This may be something I can check into at the sheriff's office, that is, if they kept the accident records," Trey said.

"Good luck trying getting those from the sheriff's office. The sheriff is in deep with what is going on around here." Just as Janice made her comment about the sheriff, her brother, Jack, stepped into the front office from the little side room where he had been finishing up ads for the next newspaper edition.

Janice looked at Jack.

"I thought you had left for the day."

"Na, I was making sure everything was good to go for Mike to pick up."

Trey thought to himself, had Jack been listening to their conversation? He had heard no noise coming from the little side room. Maybe he was being a little too paranoid and thought he probably should not be digging too deep right now into the accident. He needed to focus on what he came to Hardwood to do in the first place, help his granddad clear his name.

The talk between Janice and Trey had taken up most of the rest of the afternoon, and Trey suggested, "Do you want to head to the alligator crawdad restaurant?"

Janice replied, "It has other things to eat as well, like roadkill opossum, squirrel and skunk, and another of my favorites—catfish."

"Sounds like a great roadkill menu. Except for the catfish, I don't think they are capable of crossing the road," Trey said with a smile on his face.

"You're pretty country sharp for a big-city person."

Trey opened the door, and they walked to his rental car. They both noticed the black Lincoln drive by with all the windows up this time, so there was no way to tell if anyone was watching them. Trey felt an uneasy feeling coming over him. They got in his car and headed to the Wildwood Palace restaurant on the outskirts of the town. Trey thought to himself, *what a name*, but was looking forward to an enjoyable evening with Janice and hopefully a good meal.

On the way there, he told Janice that he had checked out of the motel in Waycross and was going to spend a few nights at a motel in Hardwood before catching his flight out of Jacksonville. He had some last-minute record checking to do, and he had rescheduled his flight to leave out of Jacksonville in a couple of days. He may even have time to do a little digging into what Janice thought was going on and maybe look into the Smith accident without drawing too much attention.

There wasn't much of a crowd at the Wildwood Palace, but it was early for an evening meal. Trey was glad it wasn't too busy, this way, he and Janice could talk without being concerned about being heard. He wanted to learn a little more about what she thought was going on and about her. He did not want to admit it, but he was getting attracted to her. She was not like the women he had dated back in LA. She was down-home and seemed truly honest, nothing fake, the you-get-what-you-see type of person, and he liked that. The waiter took their order. While waiting, they talked about their lives and a little about their families. Trey told her about his mother, Sally, and how she died, about his grandparents that lived in Idaho on the side of a mountain, and how much he enjoyed visiting them, but he did not mention their last names.

The waiter arrived with their dinner. Janice did order the alligator tail, but Trey opted for a chicken fried steak. About halfway through their meal, Janice offered him a bite of the alligator tail, which Trey admitted was quite tasty.

Janice said, "You stay here any longer, and you will be surprised at how good the cuisine is around here."

"This chicken fried steak is nothing like back in LA, this is great. Food is one of the many reasons I like visiting my grandparents in Idaho. Grandma Jo is a great cook."

After mentioning his grandma's name, he was hoping Janice would not ask any more about her. Thankfully she didn't. They finished their meal, and the waiter had just brought them some coffee when Trey saw the man that had been in the black Lincoln, along with two other men, walk in. The man gave Trey another long look. This time, Trey thought it was a more threatening look and waited for the man to point a finger at him in the shape of a pistol. He thought to himself, *I am going to need to be more alert as to my surroundings.*

Trey and Janice talked quietly about events in their lives. She asked about LA and things to do there. She had not been out of the state of Georgia except for going to Jacksonville with Jack for shopping a few of times.

She softly asked him if he had any ideas about investigating what was going on without bringing too much attention to himself. Trey suggested a private eye, but with a town as small as Hardwood, he would probably stick out like a sore thumb. Trey told her he had a couple of friends he had worked with at the LA Detective Department and they had since taken jobs with the FBI, and he still kept in touch with one of them. He would contact him from time to time, asking for help in locating someone since he had access to a larger database when it came to locating last-known addresses. If she wanted, he would contact him, explain what she thought was going on, and let her know what he said. Janice thought that would be the best avenue to proceed, and hopefully, something could be done if there was any organized crime in the area.

With their coffee finished, Trey paid for the meal. They stood up to leave, and Trey noticed the man from the Lincoln giving him a smile with a look as if to say, *you need to be careful.*

Trey looked at him, again waiting for the man to form his fist into the shape of a pistol and point his finger at him, but the man didn't; he and Janice walked out the door.

Trey drove to the newspaper office and dropped Janice off at her car. Before getting out of the car, she leaned over and gave him a kiss, which he was not expecting but it was a pleasant surprise. She said good night and headed for her car. Trey watched to make sure she got off okay, then headed for one of the three motels in town. They were not high-dollar motels, but one was a Days Inn, which usually were not bad.

CHAPTER 18

A Surprise Encounter

It was dusk when Trey pulled into the motel parking lot. The motel had only a few cars in the parking lot, so he should have no problem getting a room. He parked his car under the motel's canopy, got out, and went to the front desk and requested a room for one. After checking in, he drove to the side of the motel where his room was and stopped in front of his door. The motel was one level; there was no second story to the motel, which was nice. He did not like rooms above him because people tend to stomp around in the room, which he found irritating. He always wondered if people stomped around their own home that way as he sat in his car thinking about the evening.

After a minute or two, he got out of his car, walked to the door, unlocked it, turned on the light, and took a quick survey of the room. Before he could turn around to go to his car to gather his bags, someone pushed him into the room and slammed the door shut. The push was hard enough to throw him facedown onto the bed. The next thing he knew, a knee was in the middle of his back, and both his arms had been grabbed and pulled behind his back. He could not turn his head far enough to see the face of the person pinning him down.

After a few seconds, he realized there were two people holding him down, and one of them said, "We know you are a retired detective from LA, and you say you are here gathering research for a book you want to write on a murder trial that took place several years ago, but the problem we have is you have been asking too many questions about things other than the trial, and we are advising you not to get involved in things that don't concern you."

Trey heard a different voice, "We want you to take this advice: You have done all the research you need to do here in Hardwood. Now it's time for you to head back to LA before you can't travel at all." The bedspread was then thrown over his head, and he was told not to move. Trey did as he was told, which was very much against his training, but in this situation, it was probably best that he obeyed.

He did not hear his motel room door shut, nor did he hear any vehicle pull away. He assumed they had watched and followed him on foot to his room. For all Trey knew, they may not even have had a car nearby, and they may have walked to the motel from down the street so as not to raise any suspicion. After a minute or two, Trey decided it was safe enough to sit up and collect his thoughts and settle his nerves. In the past, he had been accosted by people, but these guys seemed to be more professional than the street thugs back in LA. Maybe Janice was right in thinking organized crime was in Hardwood, and he had gotten a little too close, he thought of the man in the black Lincoln.

As he sat there on the edge of his bed, he wondered, how did they know he was from LA, had been a detective, was researching an old murder trial? Who told them? He cautiously walked to his car, got his bags and briefcase, and returned to his room, where he began to unpack a few things. After freshening up a little, he undressed and got into his comfortable jogging pants and sat down at the little desk. He pulled out his notepad and began making a list of all the people he could remember that knew he was there and what he was doing. He started from the beginning.

Mike Simmons, the reporter from the *Waycross Daily*.

The county court clerk and her assistant, Anna.

Martha Boudreaux, a juror from the murder trial.

Janice Weston, owner of the *Hardwood Review*.

Jack Weston, the adopted brother of Janice.

He could not think of anyone else; there were waitresses and motel clerks, but he did not mention to any of them his reason for being in Hardwood.

Trey sat there looking at the list, trying to eliminate one name after another while trying to think of a reason why one of them would want him to stop asking questions. Mike Simmons lived in another town and had a suspicion that something was going on in Hardwood and seemed eager to find out more, so why would he want him to stop asking questions?

Trey marked through the county court clerk and the assistant, Anna's, names; how would they benefit by him not asking questions. Martha Boudreaux was reluctant to talk about some things, but he felt sure she had given up on trying to bring things to light because the people of Hardwood had accepted her back into their community. And at her age, she just wanted to live out the rest of her life as quietly as possible. Next on his list was Janice, who he had gotten attracted to. Had she tricked him? If so, then why? What did she have to gain? She was the one that appeared to be the most concerned about organized crime in Hardwood, and wanted it cleaned up. The last person on his list was Jack, Janice's adopted brother. Trey thought back to when Jack surprisingly came out of the small side room while he and Janice were talking. Trey had wondered at the time; had he been listening to what the two of them had been discussing over the past few days and about what was going on around Hardwood? Janice had mentioned that Jack had made some bad decisions in the past, and she was afraid he was going to be in more trouble than he could get out of. Could Jack be involved with the bad elements that came to town? How could he approach Janice with this concern? Or should he even tell her about the attack? Should he just say his goodbyes to Janice in the morning and head out? His flight was not scheduled to leave for another two days, so he would sleep on what had happened. In the morning, he hoped to have a clear mind and would make his decision on whether to talk to Janice about the evening's encounter.

Waking up the next morning, Trey's shoulders were a little sore because of his arms being pulled behind his back; but other than this slight soreness, he was fine. What hurt more were his torn feelings for Janice. After dressing, he went to the little breakfast room off to the side of the motel lobby, got some coffee, milk, and a bowl of cereal. He ate and drank without any interruptions; a few people came and went, but none of them spoke, which he was thankful for. Taking the last swallow of coffee, he had decided to tell Janice about the attack. Maybe she would reveal something by which he could question her about her adopted brother and his possible involvement. He knew he would have to tread cautiously with any questions and also make sure Jack was not around.

It was almost 10:00 a.m. when he pulled up to the front of the newspaper office. He saw Janice and Jack going in the front door. He parked the car and waited for a few minutes while acting like he was getting things out of his briefcase. He looked up and saw Jack come out of the front door. Jack looked at him and nodded, then headed down the sidewalk with a bundle of papers under his arm. Trey walked into the office; Janice was seated at her desk; she was on the phone but hung up quickly when she saw Trey. He did not hear her say goodbye and thought that was a little strange as he sat down in the chair in front of his desk.

"What a nice surprise first thing in the morning. Yesterday evening was one of the most enjoyable evenings I have had in a long time. Thanks for inviting me out," Janice said.

"Same here. The meal was great, as well as the company." Janice gave him a sweet smile. Trey thought, if she had anything to do with what happened at the motel, she sure can put on an act.

"Are you here for more information about your book?" Janice asked.

"No," Trey replied, "but I do have something to tell you and a couple of questions." Janice looked pleased, then puzzled, as she looked at Trey more intently.

"After checking in at the motel and while starting to get things out of my car, two men pushed me into the room and pinned me on the bed. They suggested I stop asking questions and should probably leave town. I don't think the questions they were referring to were the ones about the murder trial."

"What questions do you mean?" Janice asked.

"I think it had to do with what you and I have been discussing about organized crime around town," Trey said.

Janice asked, "Have you spoken with anyone else about this?"

"If you're referring to the encounter with the two men, then no. If I have talked to anyone else about what is going on in Hardwood, the answer is no to that as well." Trey said as he watched for any kind of expression on her face. Other than a somewhat-surprised look, he could tell of none.

They sat there for a moment, neither saying anything, then Janice asked. "Do you think I had anything to do with what happened to you?"

"I am not accusing you of anything, but you and I are the only ones that have talked about what you think is going on," Trey said. "They knew I was from LA and had been a detective and were very adamant about me leaving, and to stop asking questions."

Janice asked, "Why would I have them confront you if I wanted things around here to be brought to light?"

"That is what is puzzling me," Trey answered.

Trey thought now was a good time to bring up her adopted brother, Jack. "We had talked to Martha Boudreaux about what she thought had been going on many years ago, but I don't think it was she who told them, what would she have to gain?" Trey said.

Janice spoke up, "The only other person that may have heard us was Jack."

Trey agreed, "You mentioned to me that Jack had made some bad decisions in the past. Maybe he is tied in some way with what is going on," Trey said.

"Yes, he has been in and out of trouble, but nothing that serious," Janice said. "The sheriff has talked to him, and I think he has learned to stay out of trouble. The last time he was in trouble was when the sheriff found some stolen property that Jack had taken and made him give it back. The owner got his property back, and no charges were pressed."

"Do you know what was stolen?" Trey asked.

"Jack only told me it was a briefcase and some cash from the center console of a car."

"Did the sheriff tell you anything more?"

"No. He said the owner was not pressing charges, and he had talked to Jack, and everything would be okay."

Trey looked at Janice. "You said there was a briefcase taken. Did you ever find out what was in it?"

"Yes, it was a briefcase, and no, I don't know what was in it."

Trey was putting things together in his head. "Jack stole a briefcase and cash from a car. Did anyone tell you anything about the car Jack stole the items from?"

"I never thought about asking," Janice answered.

Trey thought to himself for a moment, then told Janice, "If it was the black Lincoln or one of the vans that came to town, Jack may have found something in the briefcase that could expose the organization. They got with the sheriff, told him to get the briefcase back, and cut a deal with Jack to keep quiet about what he found. With this, they could use Jack in the future, and he might even get a nice sum of money for helping them." Trey thought maybe Jack tipped them off about the conversation he and Janice had, hoping to earn more cash. "I hope this isn't the case, but there seems to be no other answer."

Trey just finished telling Janice this possible scenario when Jack came through the front door. Trey was not going to confront Jack. Instead, he was going to leave that to Janice, which he did not have to wait long for. Janice told Jack to sit down because she had some questions to ask. Trey noticed the look on Jack's face. He had seen that look many times in the past when a suspect is told to sit down for some questions. There is this look of *I've been caught.*

"Jack, are you involved in things that you know are against the law?" Janice asked.

Like most people who are guilty, Jack answered, "What do you mean, what are you talking about?" Most guilty people answer a question with a question so as to find out what defense they have to take for what crime.

"Mr. Thompson was assaulted at his motel room last night. Do you know anything about that?"

"No," Jack snapped back. Janice and Trey both knew he was not telling the truth.

Janice said, "Okay, have you told anyone about what Trey and I have been discussing in the past few days?"

There was a long pause. Trey spoke, "Jack, Janice told me you took something from a car or van a while back, and you were not punished for it. Did you make some type of agreement to get you out of trouble?"

"I'm not upset with you. I just want the truth," Janice said.

Trey said, "Jack, if you are involved, I will do what I can to help you get out of any trouble you've gotten yourself in, but you have to tell us the truth."

Jack started to whimper; while looking at Janice, he said. "You have told me for a long time you thought there was something going on in town that concerned organized crime, and the person in the black car may have something to do with it, so I wanted to help you out. I watched, thinking maybe I would be able to find out something that could be of help. I saw the driver of the black Lincoln drop off a man at the bank, then he drove around the corner and parked the car. He got out and walked to the little coffee shop. The car was somewhat hidden from the shop's front window, so I crouched down as best I could and crawled to the driver's door. It was unlocked, and I slowly opened it. There was a small briefcase on the seat, so I grabbed it. I saw the center console was partially open, so I raised it and saw a roll of bills. I grabbed those as well. I guess the driver saw me walking away with the briefcase when he came out of the shop."

Trey asked Jack, "Did you open the briefcase?"

"Yes, after I got back here, I opened it. There were a few folders as well as a sheet of paper with a list of names. I did not open the folders."

Janice said, "Names. Do you remember any of them?"

"I did better than remember them. I made a copy of the list, then put it back in the briefcase with the folders and locked it."

Trey said, "Good thinking, to a point."

"Guess I shouldn't have taken the roll of bills."

Janice said sharply, "You should have known better than to do a stupid thing like that at all. You could have been shot."

"I just wanted to help you out," Jack said softly.

"And you did, with the list of names, but now we have to see how we can get you untangled from this," Trey said.

Trey asked Jack, "Did the sheriff come and get you, or did you turn yourself in?"

"A couple of hours after taking the briefcase and cash, the sheriff's deputy came here and told me to go to the sheriff's office and bring the briefcase, so I got it and the roll of cash and walked to his office. On the way there I was so worried about going to jail or maybe prison for stealing. The sheriff was sitting on his chair, and off to the side was a man I did not recognize. The sheriff pointed to the man in the chair and told me the briefcase belonged to him, as well as the roll of bills. The sheriff told me that since I had brought the briefcase back along with the roll of bills, and everything was still in the briefcase, the gentleman did not want to press charges. Young people make mistakes, and did I open the briefcase, and I told him no. I had been too scared to do that. The man told me if I would be willing to help him in the future and if he ever needed a favor, I could keep the roll of money, and he would not press any charges. I wondered what kind of help he might need but thought, hey, I'm not going to jail and have made a little cash as well, not bad."

"So, Jack," Trey asked, "did you do them favors after the briefcase incident?"

"Not really, they had already known a few people in town were concerned and asking questions about things that were going on, and since I worked for the newspaper, to let them know who and what was being said, and I told them I would."

Trey asked Jack, "Did you tell them about me, who I was, where I had come from, what your sister and I had been discussing?"

"Yes, and I'm sorry. Yesterday they stopped me and said they would make it hard on Janice if I didn't tell them what you were doing here." Jack was looking at the floor as he told them this.

Trey said, "I have one last question. Did you tell, or do you think they know, you made a copy of the list of names?"

Jack answered, "I did not say anything about the list. I told them I did not open the briefcase it was locked."

"Okay, good," Trey answered. "My flight out of Jacksonville is scheduled to leave the day after tomorrow but I am going to try and get it rescheduled for a later date so I can spend more time in Hardwood trying to figure out how to help you get out of this problem and I needed to gather more information before I contact my friend with the FBI."

CHAPTER 19

─── ❧ ───

Another Invitation and
a Puzzling Find

The rest of the morning, Trey, Janice, and Jack discussed what they might do to help Jack out of what he had gotten into. Trey suggested Jack continue to work with whoever his contact was so as not to arouse any suspicion. Trey told Jack to keep him informed as to what they want from him, which he can do through Janice. Trey was also sure he would probably be watched to make sure he leaves town, but while he stays in town, he will continue to do research on the murder of Luke Hampton to possibly divert any attention from the crime ring. They all agreed. Trey told Janice to lock up the list in her safe—if she had one, which she did—and go about business as usual at the newspaper. He was going back to his motel room to make some calls and give the information he had to his friend with the FBI.

As Trey was leaving, he asked Janice if she would be interested in having supper with him again that evening, she quickly agreed. He would pick her up at her house around six, and she gave him the address. Trey was pleased she had accepted and said he would be there right on time as he walked out the door.

On the drive to the motel, he watched each side street as he drove through the intersection and was continuously glancing in his rearview mirror. Pulling into the parking spot in front of his motel room, before getting out of his car, he made a thorough inspection of his surroundings, all of which looked normal. He slid the door card into the slot on the door, opened it, walked in while quickly shutting the door behind him. The room curtains were pulled shut, and the room was dark. He turned on the lights, and there sat a man in the desk chair with a gun pointed at him.

The man said, "I thought we invited you to leave, it doesn't look like you listen too well, does it?" Trey looked around the room; the bathroom door was open, and he did not see anyone else.

"I listen perfectly well. My flight is scheduled to leave the day after tomorrow, and I could not get it rescheduled any sooner," Trey responded, knowing it was a lie and hoping the man would accept his story.

"Well, that's a shame about your flight. Looks like you will have to drive back to LA now. Don't you think it would be a good idea if you checked out now and head down the road, it's gonna be a long drive?"

Trey's mind was working overtime, trying to figure out a way to overtake the man with a gun pointed at him.

"You're right. I need to get my things and head out," he told the man, who was still sitting on the chair. Trey pointed to the small travel suitcase that was on the floor next to where the man was seated, he walked over, reached down, grabbed the small suitcase and swung it, hitting the man and knocking the gun out of his hand while also knocking the man out of the chair. In an instant, Trey grabbed one of the man's arms and forced it upward behind his back as far as he could. The man let out a scream as Trey heard the man's arm or shoulder snap. Trey got off him and picked up the gun, stepped back checked it for shells, and told the man not to move. He did not figure the man was going to be doing any more wrestling around but did not want to take any chances.

"Now I have a few questions or suggestions for you since I have your attention," Trey said to the man as he rolled over and tried to sit up.

The man looked at Trey and said, "You know you're a dead man."

"I know I'm going to die someday, but you are going to have some pain before you die, so let's get started." The man's eyes widened with fear as Trey grabbed a small hand towel that was lying on the small table and told him to open his mouth. He jabbed the towel into the man's mouth. Trey then grabbed the man's hurt arm and started pulling him up. The man let out a scream, which was muffled by the towel as he got to his feet. Trey told him to sit down on the chair next to the table. The man did as he was told while cradling his arm.

"Okay, are you the strong arm for your boss, or are you just one of the errand boys to send messages?" Trey asked as he pulled the towel out of the man's mouth. The man did not answer. Trey grabbed the man's hurt arm, and when he started to scream again, Trey jammed the towel back into the man's mouth.

"One arm is out of commission, so let's see if we can work on the other one, what do you say, want to answer some questions?" There was a small towel on the bed, Trey grabbed it and wrapped it around the end of the gun muzzle to help muffle the gun shot. He then grabbed the man's working hand and held it on the table. He pointed the gun at the top of the man's hand, and he saw him shaking his head in a yes motion.

"So, we are going to have a nice quiet conversation, right?" The man shook his head in agreement.

"Now wasn't that easy?" Trey said, smiling and taking the towel from the man's mouth.

"What is your name?"

"Jake," the man said.

"Well, Jake, all I want from you are yes-and-no nods, got it?" Jake shook his head up and down.

"Are there only three of you here in town?" Yes, the man nodded.

"Are you from the northeast?" Another up-and-down nod.

"Are some of the townspeople involved in what you are doing here?" Again, an up-and-down nod for yes.

"Are you smuggling in illegal aliens using the vans?" Another nod, yes.

"You are doing such a great job, Jake. These next questions will require you to answer out loud." Trey took the rag out of Jake's mouth.

"How about running drugs or bootleg whiskey?"

"Both," Jake answered.

"Now hasn't this been a nice little chat. We both have learned a lot, haven't we?" Jake did not nod nor answer. Instead, he sat there holding his arm.

"I guess our friendly little talk is over, so you can leave now. I suggest you get to a doctor. I think your shoulder may be dislocated. I'm sure you can come up with some reason for it being hurt, and I'll keep the pistol," Trey said with a slight grin on his face while he opened the motel room door and made a gesture to the man to leave.

Trey sat down on the edge of the bed and took a couple of deep breaths to relax as best he could. He knew this would not be the last episode. He looked at the clock on the nightstand; it would be a couple of hours before he picked Janice up. After his chat with Jake, Trey needed to call his friend with the FBI and inform him about the information he had learned. He would shower, then find Janice's house in the small town but thought about whether he should even go after what had happened. He knew the crime crew would have to respond after what had happened, but did not think they would rush into another plan so quickly, seeing how this one had turned out. After speaking with the FBI, he showered, got out the piece of paper that had Janice's address, got some directions from the motel desk clerk, and headed into town. He pulled into her driveway right at 6:00 p.m. Janice was standing in her doorway.

She walked to the car, opened the door, and said, "Thought you would never make it."

"Why? Am I late?" Trey asked.

"Yes, about three minutes."

"It's the motel room clocks fault, and there was a little personal business to take care of. Let's go eat."

She guided him to another small restaurant he had not noticed before. It was a small place with not many cars out front.

Janice told him as they got out and walked to the front entrance, "Martha is meeting us here as well. She wants to talk to you."

"Do you know what it is about?"

"Not for sure, guess she'll tell us."

Trey was looking forward to their evening alone and was going to tell Janice about his room visitor, but that would have to wait.

They entered and saw Martha seated at a table off to one side. There were only three other couples in the little café, who were all on the other side of the room. Trey wondered if Martha had specifically asked for a table away from everyone else, and if so, that was good. He did not want any listening ears close by. Janice and Trey sat down, and he asked how she was doing. Martha told him she was fine and hungry, as the waitress handed them menus and asked what they would like to drink. The waitress came back, and they all placed their orders.

Martha spoke up, "Ever since I became a teacher, I have kept a diary, or maybe you could call it a journal, of things I wanted or needed to remember. I got it out the other night and found where I had written down comments about Luke Hampton, Matt Benson, and the murder trial. There are a few things I think both of you should hear."

"Any information, even the smallest amount, is always helpful. In detective work, the littlest things may help solve a crime."

Martha told them what she had written down. She brought her journal but did not read from it. She was going off of her memory, which seemed to be very good. There were a couple of kids in her classes that knew they could talk to her without the fear of her telling anyone. They trusted her. One of these students told her that he knew Luke and Matt were into things that were against the law but dared not to say anything to anyone or the sheriff. He knew the sheriff and dads of Luke and Matt were good friends.

Trey could see Martha was a little upset and asked her, "Did he tell you what they were doing?"

Martha said, "They were hauling whiskey to another county and getting paid to do so by some people up north."

"Do you think Luke and Matt's fathers knew?"

"I don't have any evidence, but I'm sure they did, by what Donnie told me."

"Luke and Matt Benson are deceased but Mark Benson, Matt's son is still alive and now runs the Hardwood National Bank, and I think he is still doing some kind of business that is against the law. Too many people talk quietly about what goes on at the Hampton Lumber Mill, the small camp just outside of town, and the bank," Martha said.

"Do you think the people Luke and Matt were hauling whiskey for had something to do with Luke's death?"

"I don't know, but I don't think young Billy killed Luke Hampton. I mentioned to the other jurors in our deliberation that I thought Luke was involved in hauling bootlegged whiskey, and maybe he double-crossed someone, and they murdered him. Most of the other jurors said I didn't know what I was talking about and had no proof that he was involved in anything like that because he was a fine young man. I knew he wasn't the good young man he wanted everyone to think he was." Martha paused and took a long drink of water, then began again.

"There were a couple of other students that also told me Luke, Matt, and Luke's younger brother, Danny Hampton, were always up to no good. They always had cash, and because their fathers were good friends with the sheriff, any time they were caught doing something wrong, the sheriff would simply say they're just kids, and nothing was ever done. I know firsthand most of the kids their age did not want anything to do with them, especially Danny Hampton. The kids that would talk to me said he was the worst. Somehow, it got out that Donnie had spoken to me about the things Luke and Matt were into. Danny almost beat Donnie to death with a stick."

Janice commented, "Well, that pretty much sums up what has been going on around here for years. Like father like sons."

Trey said, "It does sound like organized crime has been around here for a long time, and I would bet that instead of bootleg whiskey, it has changed to drugs, and with the camp out there, the importing of illegal aliens. They are probably doing the work to produce meth and other street drugs. Is there anything else you can remember?"

"No, not that I can remember or have written down. I sure hope you can help put an end to what has been going on for a long time, and I hope some of what I told you will help with your book."

"It will," Trey answered, giving Martha a smile as they finished their meal.

Their meal finished, Martha said she enjoyed the evening and needed to get home before it got too late and said good night.

Trey said to Janice, "I need to tell you what happened when I got to my room after leaving your office this afternoon."

"Another meeting with your friends?"

"Well, I guess you could call it that, but just one friend this time. We had a nice active conversation after I was told that I did not listen the first time and leave. After our pleasant, informative conversation, my friend had to leave suddenly to go to the doctor about a possible dislocated shoulder. I sure hope he is okay."

"I'm sure you do. Are you going to check on him?" Janice asked.

"Na, I think someone will tell me soon enough how he is doing."

Trey did not tell her all of the details of the fight and said he was still planning on leaving in a day or two. He told Janice he would be going back to the courthouse to see if they would let him look through an evidence box pertaining to Luke Hampton's murder if they had one.

"Do you think it is safe to stay?" Janice asked in a concerned voice.

"I think it will be okay after what happened today. I think they will come up with a new plan, maybe call in some heavy hitters."

"Unless they already have some here locally," Janice said.

Trey hadn't thought about that. They may have some locals on the payroll. Years ago, they had Luke and his friend Matt. They did recruit Jack, but for different reasons. He would have to be extra careful and watch his back since he was without a partner.

He took Janice home and got an even better kiss before leaving. He was looking forward to their next meeting. He drove through the motel parking lot in front of his room and waited to see if any headlights appeared coming down any of the surrounding streets or anyone walking around, he saw none. He placed his hand on the butt of the pistol he had tucked in his belt just before getting out of the car. He inserted the card into the slot to unlock the door, then pushed the door open while standing to one side. So far, so good, he thought as he flipped on a light. He slowly eased his head around the doorframe and saw that no one was in the room. He went in, shut the door, and laid the pistol on the bed and sat down, thankful that he didn't have another friend waiting to have a nice quiet conversation about travel.

He hadn't checked in with his grandparents back in Idaho in a couple of days and did not want them worrying about him. They should be just finishing their evening meal, so now would be a good time to call. He got his cell phone out and called. Grandma Jo answered on the first ring. He told them he had spoken with a couple of the locals, had met with Martha again, and learned a little more. He did not tell them anything about what had happened to him so they would not worry. He told them he was going back to the courthouse in the morning for one last look at the files and the evidence box if they had one. His Granddad Bill asked when he was coming home, and Trey told them that he would be back in a couple of days and that he would call them when he got back to his condo in LA. They were glad to hear he was okay and going home, they had been worrying about him and didn't care if he found out any information or not. His Grandma Jo told him that Bill had been resting more easily now, and she could see he did not seem to be as worried about being followed. Trey was glad but also sad that he had not found out more to ease his grandfather's worries. He said goodbye and told them that he would call them as soon as he got back to LA.

The next morning, Trey got his usual coffee, and this time, he tried the biscuits and gravy, after which he decided that he will stick with cereal or a roll. He topped off his coffee and drove to the courthouse. Anna was at the counter.

"I would like to do some last-minute research and would like to know if there was an evidence box concerning the murder, and if so, would it be possible for me to look through it?"

"I'm not sure. I will have to get a key and go downstairs to the vault and see. I think there is a small box labeled 'Evidence: Luke Hampton murder.' I'll be right back." Trey stood at the counter for a couple of minutes, and Anna came back to the counter.

"There is a box, but you will have to go to the vault to look at it. I will have to lock you in. Nothing can be taken out."

"That's fine. I understand the rules." She led him downstairs. Anna unlocked the vault door, much like the ones back in LA, with bars and a little trap door to slide items through to an officer who was appointed to guard the vault. There was no officer in this vault, and Trey walked in.

"The file box is down the center aisle. You will see the name Luke Hampton on the end of the box. Please put everything back after you're through looking at it, and put the box back on the shelf."

"I will."

Anna locked him in. Trey found the small file box and took it to a table, sat down, opened the lid, and pulled out the items list that was lying on top. He looked down the list of items, and there were not many. He pulled out a piece of fabric that was tagged "Sarah Bersha dress." It had some blood spots on it. Next, he pulled out a piece of wood with what looked like a bullet hole in it; it was labeled "door frame." Then he pulled out a pistol. It was a six-round .38 Colt revolver, tagged as "possible murder weapon." There was a small cloth bag tagged "bullets," and he opened it, there were two bullets in the bag.

This coincided with his grandfather telling the court he had fired only four times. The only item remaining in the little box was wrapped up in a faded white rag with a tag that read *weapon used to murder Luke Hampton.* Trey reached in, picked it up, untied the string, and unwrapped a knife and let it lay in his hand for some time. He held the knife up and looked it over. It looked like a standard fixed-blade hunting knife. Blades on hunting knives did not fold back into the handle like a pocketknife. The blade and handle were one piece. The blade was about six inches long and had rusted in a few places. Then Trey took a closer look at the handle. It appeared to be ivory with a carving on it that looked familiar. He knew he had seen that carving before. He studied the handle more closely and saw that the carving was of a deer with antlers standing in tall grass. He knew he had seen this same deer carving?

He sat there looking at the handle, searching his memory when he heard the elderly clerk call to him, "You about done down there?" she questioned. The older woman's voice brought the memory to him—the pocketknife that his Grandma Jo wanted him to have. It had the same type of carving on its handle.

"Just putting things back. Will be up there in a minute." Trey took out his cell phone and took a couple of pictures of the knife and several close-ups of the handle. He put everything back and put the file box on the shelf, went upstairs, and told the clerk he was finished.

Back at his motel room, he sat down and looked at the pictures on his cell phone. A lot of knives he had seen had carvings on the handle, and most of them were of a deer, but this one showed the male deer with huge antlers standing in the tall grass next to a tree. He tried to remember if the handle on the pocketknife his Grandma Jo wanted him to have, had the same scene in tall grass. He did remember the deer having antlers. He knew deer carvings on knife handles were fairly common. He turned off his cell phone and concentrated on the few notes he had written down while going through the evidence file. One stood out. Why was the pistol labeled a possible murder weapon? Was it a mistake or had someone done it on purpose? Perhaps to frame someone, he wondered. There was organized crime going on back then, and according to Martha Boudreaux, Luke was involved to some extent.

Trey lay in bed with his notepad, trying to think of anything he may have missed in his search for the truth about the murder of Luke Hampton. He could not get one thought out of his head. Had his Granddad Bill been framed for the murder of Luke Hampton?

He had one more day in Hardwood before driving to Jacksonville to catch his flight. His FBI friend was to call him back in the morning with ideas about how they could help Jack get untangled from the organization he had gotten involved with. Trey was hoping for one last meal with Janice, so he could tell her what plans the FBI had.

CHAPTER 20

Jack the Informer

While having his breakfast in the small motel breakfast room, Trey thought of several questions that he could not answer. Was his Granddad Bill framed? If so, then who killed Luke Hampton and what could he do to help Janice with the corruption around Hardwood?

There was a lot on his plate, and he felt that helping Janice was his first priority. He had to watch his back while he was in Hardwood for one more day.

It was almost 10:00 a.m. when he got to the newspaper office, and as usual, Janice was at her desk. He wished her good morning as he walked in.

"It's a little early for supper."

"I know. I would ask you about having breakfast but I see you have already eaten," Trey said as he looked at the half-eaten doughnut on the paper plate to the side of her desk.

"There is some coffee over there." Janice pointed across the room. "Help yourself." And he did. He filled a cup and sat down in front of her desk and stared at her.

"What's wrong?"

"I am leaving tomorrow, and I am not looking forward to saying goodbye."

"You sound like it is for good."

"I don't want it to be, I like having a companion for supper. Back home I usually eat alone."

"Is that so?" She chuckled. "I kind of figured you were hanging around just to have me show you another new and improved diner that serves exotic foods?"

"Well, that's one reason. So, would you honor me with one last supper this evening as a going-away gift?"

"You are making it sound like we will never see each other again," Janice said.

Trey replied, "I hope not, but I don't know when I will be able to make it back down here."

Janice said, "What makes you think you have to come back down here?"

"What are you getting at?"

"I have never been out of the state of Georgia, and now that I know someone in California, it's about time I see other parts of the country."

Trey's eyes lit up.

"I would love for you to come see California. I could be your personal guide around town."

"I have not taken any time off in several years, and Jack can handle things around here."

Trey felt like a young teenager getting yes to his first date.

"All you have to do is give me a day. I don't have anything planned for years," Trey said eagerly.

"It would not be years before I come out there. I was thinking in a couple of months," Janice said.

Trey felt butterflies in his stomach.

"That sounds great. Let me know when, and I will book a flight for you."

"I have your number, so I will call you," Janice said.

"Now since breakfast is out of the question, and my summer vacation is planned, what can I do for you?"

"I contacted an ex-partner who is now with the FBI and told him what I thought was going on around Hardwood and I had a list of names that might be of some help. He called me back and asked

list of names to the FBI and be there if they called back. He didn't mention it to her but he also wanted a little more time alone to think about the hunting knife with the carved handle.

Trey had been in his room for about two hours when his cell phone rang, it was Janice. She told him that Jack had been contacted shortly after leaving the café and was told to get to the regular meeting place at the camp as soon as possible for instructions. Jack had just returned from his meeting and needed ~~to him~~ to inform him as to what he had learned. Trey grabbed his briefcase and headed back to the newspaper office. Jack and Janice were both sitting around her desk when he walked in. He pulled up a chair, making sure he could not be seen from the front window.

"So, you had another meeting today?"

"Yes, I was handed a note informing me to get to the regular meeting place at the camp as soon as possible. When I arrived, there were a couple of others there along with Stan, the older man who was my contact. I knew Stan had lived in or around Hardwood most of his life and had worked for the organization for many years and he wanted to warn us about this new man whose name was Dan. He was not like the two previous men, Jake and Mickey who had worked for the organization for many years, Dan's methods were more brutal when it came to extracting information, convincing someone to cooperate, or when someone was caught skimming from the organization and an example needed to be made. Stan told us Dan was from Hardwood and fairly young when he began working for the organization. He was sent to the northeast to work with the enforcers that were used to keep their associates in line, protect their products and collect the cash made from the selling of their products, mostly moonshine back then. Word is that years ago just before Tom Hampton died, his youngest son Paul D. Hampton promised his dad, Tom Hampton that he would get revenge for the murder of his older brother Luke Hampton and he would find Billy Bersha and take care of them. Tom Hampton made an agreement with the organization to take his son Paul and teach him how the organization works and in return, Tom Hampton would supply the materials and labor at a discount to make moonshine back in those days, which now has changed to drugs, and Paul could also learn the tricks as how to find and get information ~~form~~ from people and this may help him in the search for Billy Bersha. While Paul Hampton was up north learning how the business operated and going along when it was time to pick up the cash or watching how to set an example of someone that took from the organization, Jake and Mickey were the go-to guys to do the enforcing down here. Stan told us that since Jake had a run in with the retired detective from LA and got his shoulder broken and Mickey had gotten killed in a shootout up north, the organization has called in Dan to take over down here."

Trey asked, "Do you know Dan's last name?"

"No, Stan did not tell us that."

Jack got a glass of water, looked at Trey and asked.

"Isn't Billy Bersha the person you are doing research on for the book?"

"Yes, it is, but I don't think they are coming after me for that, I think they are concerned I may be gathering information about the drugs or illegal aliens in and around Hardwood. Is there anything else I should be concerned about?"

Jack continued.

"Stan told us over the years several people had been assigned to find Billy Bersha with little success, but Mickey had been the most successful and found out that Sam Williamson was Billy Bersha's best friend. The Williamson's had moved to Hardwood from Ocoee, Tennessee and Mickey learned that Sam's little sister, Bobbie Jo had a good friend back in Ocoee named Tammy Low Watkins. After the Williamson's got here Bobbie Jo and Tammy wrote letters back and forth to each other. Every time Mickey came up with new information, he gave it to the higher ups in the organization so they could pass this information on to others who were also looking for Billy Bersha. Stan said Mickey found out that Bobbie Jo Williamson, Sam's little sister, had vanished with Billy's daughter, shortly after Billy's escape from prison, and he guessed she was with Billy Bersha, but no one knew for sure where they might have gone. Mickey probably gathered all the information he could from the Williamson's and the next thing you know, the Williamsons' house burnt down with everybody in it except Bobbie Jo Williamson, the daughter."

Trey remembered his Grandma Jo telling him about wanting to go back to Georgia because her family had died in a house fire. He now knew what probably happened.

Jack continued.

"Stan said Mickey continued inquiring around Hardwood and questioned anyone that might have information as to the whereabouts of Bobbie Jo. Mickey had told his boss he was getting close and the next step was to go to Ocoee and locate Bobbie Jo's friend, Tammy Lou Watkins, but he never got to follow up on that lead because he died in gunfight at a money drop. Stan told us since Mickey was out of the picture, Dan was taking over and would continue where Mickey has left off as to the hunt for Billy Bersha as well as all the other duties Jake and Mickey were requested to do around here.

"Dan must be reliable and good at what he does to be replacing two of the organizations heavy hitters," Trey said.

"Stan told all of us to always be straight with Dan, don't ever cross him, he is not one to mess with."

Trey ask, "And Dan is arriving tomorrow, correct?"

"Yes, he is coming here so we can all meet him and get our instructions as to how to work with him. Stan emphasized; do not get on his bad side you will regret it. Stan told us he was sent up north to help with some collections and he and Dan drove to a house where they were to pick up some protection money, but the bagman that was supposed to have the protection money had left town with most of it. His girlfriend told us she did not know where he had gone. Dan told her she needed to be very cooperative, or she would truly regret it. She insisted she did not know where he had gone. Dan slapped her to the floor. He started pulling out drawers, throwing furniture around, then he walked over to her, grabbed her by the hair, and pulled her up. Stan said he remembered seeing the frightened look in the girl's eyes when he pulled out a switchblade knife and said, you will lose a finger for every wrong answer, and he held her hand on the coffee table. He cut off three of her fingers before she passed out. She never told us where the guy ran off to, I truly don't think she knew.

Even though she had passed out, Dan cut off a finger on the other hand. He left a note and said he would be back in a week and hoped she would be more helpful or the other fingers would be removed."

Jack paused then said, "I sat there nauseated, listening as Stan told us about Dan."

"It takes a certain type of person to do that, but that is the type of people organized crime hire to get done what they need done to control people with fear," Trey said.

"There is one last thing," Jack said.

"What's that?" Trey asked.

"The organization is expanding and we need to keep our eyes and ears open for anyone we can trust to help them out."

"Have you learned what all they are into?"

"I know for sure they are using illegal aliens to make some of the drugs in the long building in the camp and they ship it out in the vans."

"So, that means they are dealing in the illegal drug trade as well as illegal aliens?" Trey asked.

"Yes, and they also use the vans to transport the aliens. But the main reason I wanted to speak with you as soon as possible is to let you know, I heard Stan tell one of the other men that Dan is coming here to question you about what you are doing here."

"I Appreciate what you have told me and will be on guard. Jack, you need to stick with the story of my being here to do research on the book. I'll handle Dan if we meet. If you find out they want to question you about me asking about their dealings around town, try to avoid the meeting as long as you can and tell Janice to get in touch with me."

CHAPTER 21

Piecing Together the Leads

Trey was back in his motel room, sitting at his small desk with his notepad, writing down the series of events that Jack had told him about. Luke's dad, wanting revenge, hiring Mickey, the enforcer, to try and find Billy Bersha, then Dan taking over after Mickey's death, and lastly, the burning down of the Williamsons' house with the family inside. He hoped they were killed before the fire, but he would not say this to his Grandma Jo. He planned on telling her who he thought had set the house on fire and for what reason; she needed to know that much, at least.

Trey was guessing Dan was probably in his sixties but sounded like he was still up to the job he was hired to do. Trey had one day left before his flight, and he pulled out a map to see if he had time to drive to Ocoee, Tennessee, and see if he could locate his Grandma Jo's friend, Tammy Lou Watkins. It was probably a six-hour drive, which meant that it would take him most of the morning to get there. He would not have time to find Tammy and drive back to Hardwood, or even to Jacksonville, in the remaining day before his flight.

He called the travel agent to see if he could reschedule his flight back to LA. She said all the flights out of Jacksonville were booked up for a week, but he could catch one out of Atlanta in three days. However, he would have to be on standby, and she could not guarantee his flight. Trey looked at the map and saw that Ocoee was not that far from Atlanta, so for a small extra fee, he booked his standby flight. If he left early in the morning, he could make it to Ocoee, and that would give him at least a day to see if he could locate Tammy Lou Watkins. He pulled out his cell phone and found Janice's number. He wanted to see her before he left and tell her his plans. Then he had a second thought. He would not tell her he was going to Ocoee to try and find Tammy Watkins, just in case someone started questioning her. He would tell her he was leaving as planned for Jacksonville first thing in the morning to catch his flight back to LA. He dialed her number.

"What's for supper?"

"I'm having leftover meatloaf with brown gravy and a baked potato."

"Boy, that sounds good."

"Well, if you want some, you better hurry or I will put what's left in the dog dish."

"Hey, I'm not too proud to eat out of a dog dish. I love meatloaf, so I'll be there shortly." His heart was beating a little faster than usual as he drove to Janice's house. He did not even have to ring the doorbell; Janice opened the door and gave him a big kiss.

"What will the neighbors think?"

"I don't know. I'll tell them you're a long-lost kissin cousin."

"Sounds good to me." He walked in and closed the door. She led him into the kitchen and handed him the dog bowl.

"Fill her up, food on the counter." Trey looked at her, puzzled, but she grinned and handed him a plate and took the dog bowl.

"Good. I hate eating after the dog."

"You won't have to. I don't have a dog anymore. He died a few months back; I just can't get rid of his bowl."

"My grandparents back in Idaho have two dogs that they think the world of, and my grandfather talks to them like they are human. He told me about a hunting dog he had for several years named Ole Red. My mother and that hound were inseparable. They are even buried side by side on a hillside. It was my mother's favorite place to sit on a stump overlooking the valley. My granddad says he owes his life to Ole Red."

Janice looked at Trey and said, "How's that?"

Trey almost started to tell her the real reason he was in Hardwood.

"It's a long story, and I promise I will tell you about it when you come to LA."

"Sounds interesting. I'm looking forward to it." They ate and talked about Janice coming to LA and about Jack's situation. Trey said as little as possible about his grandparents. He mostly talked about his mother and how much he missed her and a little about his job and living in LA. They finished supper, and Trey helped Janice clean up. She was not used to having help and was pleased to see Trey helping. She enjoyed his company. It was getting late, and Trey wanted to get an early start to Ocoee.

"I need to head back to the motel. I want to get an early start in the morning for Jacksonville and need to have some spare time in case I get lost." Janice looked at him, and he saw a look that said she wanted him to stay, and he wanted too as well.

"Janice, I need to get going," Trey said melancholically, and he walked to the front door. She followed him, and when he turned around, she grabbed him and pulled him close, giving him a long hard kiss,

"I want you to stay," she said to him.

"You don't know how much I would like to, but it isn't the right time. I do not want to rush what I think we have to go on, and I hope you understand." Janice gave him another hug and said that she understood and was looking forward to going to LA and spending more one-on-one time with him.

"I will call you as soon as I get back to LA, and you can give me the date, and I will book the flight."

"That sounds great to me." She gave him a peck on the cheek and wished him good night.

On his drive back to the motel, Trey regretted not staying but knew it was best to leave. Back in his room, he packed up most of his things and went to bed. It was early for him, but he knew he had a long drive ahead of him in the morning.

It took him some time to get to sleep, but it did finally come, and before he knew it, his alarm was going off. He looked at the small clock on the nightstand, which showed 6:00 a.m. He washed his face, got dressed, and went to the motel breakfast room, where they had limited choices. He knew not to get the biscuits and gravy, so he opted for a doughnut and coffee instead. He grabbed a local newspaper from an empty table and looked at the date. It was from three days earlier. He sat down and opened it up. The newspaper had only three pages, most of which included news that pertained to local events, while only one article was about national news. The rest of the paper was made up mostly of ads by the local merchants. On the back of the last page was a column titled, "*What Do You Think.*" This last page of the paper appeared to be where local people would write pieces voicing their comments, concerns, or opinions. He glanced down the page, and one particular piece caught his eye; it was written by Martha Boudreaux. She wrote about a retired detective being in town who had interviewed her about the murder trial of Luke Hampton back in the '30s. He was doing research for a book he was going to write on the questionable conviction of Billy Bersha for the murder of Luke Hampton.

Trey did not need that kind of publicity, but there was not much he could do about it since the paper had already been printed and sent out to the public. He felt a little betrayed by Janice not telling him she was going to place it in the paper. He thought at least it might have diverted attention away from him looking into the organized crime in the area. He finished his coffee, went to his room, loaded up his car, and headed out of town north to Ocoee, Tennessee.

On his way out of town, he drove by the Hardwood National Bank and noticed three men standing at the front of the bank. He thought he recognized one of the men, so he slowed down. One of the men resembled his Granddad Bill's friend Dan Moran. Trey slowed his car and looked as best he could while trying to drive. The man looked directly at him; even though the man was not wearing an animal hat, Trey was almost certain it was his granddad's friend Dan. As Trey was turning the corner onto the road that would take him out of town he took one last look at the man, and saw that the man looked straight back at him. If this was Dan, what was he doing here? Trey reached the highway, got up to the speed limit, set the cruise control and settled in for the drive to Ocoee. Watching the timberland pass by as he drove, he could not shake the thought of Dan being in Hardwood. Trey was sure it was him, but with no hat, he couldn't be certain and tried to forget about it as he drove on.

He had just gotten off the I-285 loop going around Atlanta and was headed north to Chattanooga when his phone rang. He picked it up and said hello.

"Can you talk?" It was Janice.

"Sure, I'm driving, but I'm on the interstate, and it doesn't have much traffic. What's up?"

"Jack just called me and said he needs to talk to you as soon as possible."

"I just saw a sign for a rest area five miles ahead. I need to stop anyway, so have him call me."

"Jack is on his way here, and I will have him call you as soon as he gets in."

"I should be at the rest area in about ten minutes." She sounded in a little bit of a panic, so he wondered what had gone wrong. He pulled into the rest area about the time his cell phone rang. Janice's name popped up on the caller ID.

"Trey, this is Jack, and I have some information that you should know about."

"Slow down, Jack, and tell me what's going on."

"I just got out of a meeting with a few of the others, and we were introduced to a man named Dan Moran, but I don't think that is his real name. He told us he will be taking over for Jake and Mickey, and if we need anything that needs special attention, he can take care of it."

"Does he have a beard?"

"Yes, how did you know?"

"I saw him on my way out of town," Trey told him, then asked, "why do you think Dan Moran is not his real name?"

"After the meeting, I was walking to my car, and two men from the meeting were walking in front of me, and I heard one of them say, that's Paul D. Hampton, guess he is back in town. When we got to our cars, one of the men said, 'we called him Danny Hampton when we were younger.' He then started telling us that he and a couple of other men watched as Dan tortured an illegal for stealing a bag of drugs. He was going to teach everyone a lesson, this is what happens when you steal from the family, and Dan began cutting off the illegal's fingers while two others held him down."

"Be careful. Do not do anything stupid, keep a low profile, and just do what you're told."

"Trey, before I hang up, there is one more thing, but you have probably already figured this out. Dan Moran, is Danny Hampton, and he is Luke Hampton's younger brother."

"I kind of figured that. Tell Janice I will call her later."

Trey pulled back onto I-75 and continued on. After a couple of hours, he exited off I-75 onto Highway 40 and headed to Ocoee, Tennessee. He knew Ocoee was not a large town; it was more of a tourist village for people to stay while they floated the Hiwassee/Ocoee Rivers or hiked on the local mountain trails. As he entered the small community, there was a sign that said "Population: 1,587," and a little further up the road, he saw a Quality Inn motel and decided to check in. After settling into his room, he pulled out the telephone book from the nightstand and looked for Tammy Lou Watkins but found no listing. He did find a Watkins and called, but they did not know anyone by the name of Tammy. He then found the number for the police department which was in Benton, a few miles to the north of Ocoee.

Ocoee did not have a police department it was too small. Benton was also the county seat for Polk County, Tennessee, which Ocoee was located in. He thought, when all else fails, ask the desk clerk. He walked to the front office and asked the young lady if she had ever heard of Tammy Lou Watkins, who lived around here thirty or forty years ago. The young lady said no, she had not, but there was a couple that owned the little café up the street that might know. She thought they had lived here most of their lives. Trey thanked her and headed for the small café. It was getting close to suppertime, and he was hungry anyway, so as the old saying goes, "kill two birds with one stone." Get a meal and maybe some information as well.

Trey sat down at a table for one and was looking at the menu when an elderly woman approached him and asked if he had decided on anything. Trey placed his order and asked for a glass of water. He watched her as she gave his order to an older man at the grill, then brought Trey his glass of water.

Trey asked, "I don't mean to be nosy, but have you lived in Ocoee long?"

She said, "I have lived here all my life as well as my husband." She pointed to the man at the grill.

Trey said, "I am looking for a Tammy Lou Watkins. She was an old friend of my grandmother from many years ago. Do you happen to know her?"

"Tammy Lou Watkins. That name rings a bell. At my age, I tend to forget. Let me ask my husband." No one else was in the small café, so Trey did not feel like he was taking her away from waiting on other patrons. The lady walked to the little window behind the counter, and the man handed her a plate. She brought Trey his ham sandwich.

"My husband remembers her, and since we are about to close for the evening, he will come and sit with you, if you don't mind, and maybe he can be of some help. The older man wearing a white apron got himself a cup of coffee, pulled a chair up to the table and sat down.

"I'm Thomas Jackson. So, you want to know about Tammy Lou Brown?" he asked Trey.

"I was looking for Tammy Lou Watkins."

"Tammy married Sam Brown. And after a couple of years, he had an accident and died. Tammy never remarried. She kept the name of Brown."

"Is she still around?"

"No, she was killed some time back, a bad death."

"What do you mean by bad death?" Trey asked inquisitively while leaning slightly forward.

"The police said it looked like she had been tortured before she was killed."

"Did the Ocoee police do an investigation?"

"No, we don't have police here, the county sheriff investigated that crime, and he is located in Benton, up the road that way."

Trey wrote down the information while finishing his sandwich, he and Thomas talked a little longer, then Trey paid his tab, thanked the Jacksons, and walked back to his room. He failed to ask Thomas if Tammy had any relatives but would inquire about that at the sheriff's office in Benton in the morning.

As usual, Trey was up early and on the road to the Polk County Sheriff's Office. It would take him about thirty minutes, and he was hoping the sheriff's office would let him review the file; if not, he would call on his old superior back in LA to see if he could help him out. At the Polk County Sheriff's Office, Trey told them who he was and if he could view the file on Tammy Watkins Brown. The desk clerk asked a couple of questions then called for the deputy sheriff. Trey was led into the deputy's office, and he told him he was trying to locate Tammy for his grandmother since she had not heard back from her in quite some time. He told the deputy that the owner of the café in Ocoee told him Tammy had been murdered and if possibly, he would like to review the file to see if there were any relatives he might speak with.

The deputy was reluctant to give him the file, and Trey told him he was a retired police detective from LA and was just trying to help out his grandmother. Trey gave the deputy his LA police ID card, and the deputy called LA to confirm what Trey had told him. The deputy told him to wait here while he went to get the file. A few minutes later, he handed Trey a folder and pointed to a small table and told Trey he could sit over there while he looked through the file.

Trey opened the file and started to read. It did look like she had been tortured before being shot in the head. As he read the type of torture she had endured, it was obvious that it was the same MO that Dan had used before. Trey knew why he had tortured Tammy. He scanned through the remaining pages and found that Tammy had a younger sister named Betty Smithwick who lived in Benton and he wrote down her address. Handing the folder back to the deputy, he thanked him and asked if he knew Tammy's sister, Betty. The deputy said he did not, and Trey left the deputy's office. But on the way out, he stopped at the front desk and asked the clerk if she had a local phone book, she did, which she handed to him. There were two Smithwick's listed, and Trey wrote down the number of the one that matched the address he had written down. He got to his car and placed a call.

The phone range twice then Trey heard "Hello."

"Is this Betty?"

"Yes, it is."

Trey told her who he was, about his grandmother, and if she had time to talk with him. Betty agreed, so he told her that he would be there shortly.

Trey found the house, Betty invited him in. Trey told her how sorry he was about her older sister and that it was going to be hard telling his Grandma Jo about what had happened. Trey asked Betty if she remembered his grandmother Bobbie Jo Williamson.

She did but was very young when Tammy and Bobbie Jo played together but did remember the Williamsons moving to Hardwood and how her sister missed Bobbie Jo. Trey finally got around to asking Betty why she thought her sister had been tortured.

Betty said, "I think whoever did it was looking for something or someone. After they finally let me go into the house, I saw that all the drawers had been pulled out and tossed around. The sheriff said they had found a shoebox on the kitchen table that still had some letters, pictures, and other stuff in it but it appeared to have been rummaged through. All the envelopes had been opened, and some still had letters in them, while others did not."

"Did they give you the shoebox back?"

"Yes, they did. I will get it."

Betty set the shoebox on the table, and Trey started to look through the envelopes. He picked out the ones with no return address on them but had an Idaho postmark. He laid them all on the table. One stack of open envelopes had no letters in them, while the other stack of envelopes was opened with a letter in it. It appeared as though whoever was rifling through them had kept the letters that told the person more about who or what they were looking for. Trey asked if he could read some of the letters. Betty said she did not mind. Trey unfolded a few of the letters that had been left in the open envelopes to see if his grandmother had signed them. She had. In one of the letters, she had mentioned a nearby town. Trey was guessing there was more information about his grandparents' whereabouts in the letters that were missing from the opened envelopes.

Trey had told Betty when he first arrived that he was a retired detective from LA but had no idea why Tammy had been murdered.

"I may have an idea who did this and will return to the sheriff's office and tell them what I think," Trey said. He told Betty how much he appreciated her letting him see the letters and was sorry to bring up old memories. He stood up, thanked her, and told her he would keep her posted of any new information that might come up. He would also tell the sheriff to do the same. She hugged him and said she enjoyed the visit, even though it brought back heartaches. Betty gave Trey the shoebox of letters and told him to give it to Bobbie Jo next time he saw her.

Back at the motel, Trey got out his pad and started writing down the events and connected dots. From what Jack had told him about Dan Moran, a.k.a. Danny Hampton, to get information from someone or to make a point, cutting off his fingers was his method. He was glad he did not bring this up to Betty because it was hard enough for her to look through the shoebox of letters. Trey was becoming more and more worried about his grandparents. If the man who was in front of the bank when he drove out of Hardwood the day before was Dan Moran, and he recognized Trey as Bill's grandson, he may be convinced that the man known as Bill Perkins is really Billy Bersha. Trey was convinced that his Granddad Bill was right; someone was looking for him. Trey wondered if he should call his granddad and tell him that he is fairly certain that Dan Moran is Danny Hampton, Luke's younger brother. Trey did not want to alarm his granddad, but he needed to tell him that he saw someone in Hardwood that resembled Dan, the mountain man. Trey made the call, and his Granddad Bill answered.

"Hello, Trey. When are you coming back?"

"I will be at your place in three or four days. But before I get there, I need to tell you something, and you need to follow my instructions."

"Are you okay, is something wrong?"

"I'm okay, but I want you to avoid Dan Moran. I have learned that Dan Moran is probably Luke Hampton's younger brother, Danny Hampton, and he has been looking for Billy Bersha for several years. He is following some leads that have led him to Hillside and you."

"Are you sure?"

"I don't know if Dan knows for sure you are Billy Bersha, but when I was leaving Hardwood, I saw a man that looked like Dan, the mountain man, and he saw me. So, if he had any doubts about you being Billy Bersha, all of those doubts are gone, and I'm sure he will be coming for you, so you need to stay close to home and away from the woods and river."

"How did you find out all of this?"

"I will explain all of it to you when I get there. For now, please, just do as I say, and tell Grandma Jo to not leave the cabin."

"I will tell her, and we will stay close to home. I'll keep my rifle loaded and close."

"Good, I'll see you in a few days." And with that, Trey said goodbye and hung up the phone.

CHAPTER 22

Back to the Grandparents' Cabin

Early the next morning, Trey packed his things and headed to Atlanta to catch his flight back to LA. After being on the road for an hour or so, he called Janice and told her about his trip to Ocoee and had found the sister of one of his grandmother's old friends, Tammy Lou. He told her that Tammy had passed, but he had a nice visit with her sister. He did not mention anything about how she died nor about Dan Hampton. He thought it best for now to wait. Janice told him nothing new was going on with Jack, he had not met with anyone since his last meeting. Janice told Trey to be careful, enjoy his flight home, and that she looked forward to flying out to see him. Trey told her that he would be going to his grandparents as soon as he got back and would call her after returning from visiting them. Tammy's sister had given him a shoebox with letters and other things that she wanted him to give to his Grandma Jo.

Back in his LA condo, Trey sat down and phoned his grandparents. His Grandma Jo answered after the second ring.

"I have learned to carry the phone with me so I don't miss any calls, as though I get that many."

"Yeah, you can become attached to these cell phones, but unfortunately, they are a necessity nowadays. I just wanted to let you know I am back at my condo and plan on coming up to see you and Grandpa Bill tomorrow. I should be there late afternoon. I am flying into Spokane and will rent a car to drive the rest of the way to your place."

"Call us when you get to Spokane and let us know about what time to expect you, and I will have a nice supper waiting."

"I definitely will. I don't want to miss any of your meals. Can I talk to Grandpa Bill? Jo handed Bill the phone. "I hope you have not been looking for Dan."

"No, we have not even left this place since you told us not to, have stayed mostly in the house."

"That's good. We can talk about what I found out when I get there tomorrow evening."

"Did you get any leads on who might have killed Luke Hampton?"

"Possibly. I will go over a couple of things that might help shed some light on the issue when I get there."

After landing in Spokane, Trey phoned his grandparents and told them he was getting his rental car and would be at their place around five or six in the evening. Bill asked if he remembered how to get there, and Trey said yes but would call if he got lost. Trey made his way out of the airport rental lot and headed to Hillside. In the past, when his mom or dad drove to Hillside, it took at least two days from California, and they would spend the night somewhere along the way. He also remembered after they got out of California and Nevada and into Idaho, the scenery became more mountainous, especially the closer they got to his grandparents' place. He also remembered his mom and dad fighting because of the long trip, which took a lot of the joy out of the drive. He knew his dad did not care that much for his grandparents, so the last few times Trey visited his grandparents, it was just him and his mom. To be able to spend more time with them they flew to Spokane and did as he was doing now—rented a car and drove the rest of the way. Trey did not like to remember the bad times when his mom and dad argued. When these thoughts came to mind, he shook his head and forced his focus on only the good memories of his mother the short time he was with her.

Enjoying the passing scenery, listening to the radio, and thinking of the good times, before he knew it, he was coming into Hillside,

Idaho. The little town sat in a valley with the Purcell and Kootenay mountain ranges to the west and the Kootenay River to the east. On the road leading out town, he slowed to watch for the gravel road leading his grandparents' cabin. After driving on the blacktop for a few miles, he approached the turnoff that he thought led to the cabin and made the turn, hoping it was the correct one. After driving on the gravel road, it made a sharp curve, and as he rounded it, he saw the cabin, with his grandfather sitting on the porch in his rocker with the two hounds at his feet.

Trey pulled up the drive and stopped in front of the little workshop. He grabbed his small suitcase and headed to the porch where his grandfather and now his grandmother both met him with hugs and smiles.

"We are so glad you are back." She took his overnight suitcase.

"Me too," Trey said, smiling warmly.

"Sit down there with Bill, I will bring out something to drink for the both of you," Grandma Jo said.

"And I will bring some water for the ladies," she said before heading inside.

"They can go to the end of the porch where their bowl is. I filled it this morning." As if on command, one of the dogs got up and went to the water bowl. Trey wondered; can they really understand?

"Well, Trey, how was your trip to Hardwood?"

"It was long but interesting, and I met the nicest lady. She owns and runs the newspaper there."

"The *Hardwood Review*?" Bill asked. "

"Yes, it was owned by Henry Weston, he is deceased now, and his granddaughter and her adopted brother own it now. They actually were a great help. As you and I talked before I left, I told them I was there researching information on a book I wanted to write about the death of Luke Hampton, and as far as they know, that was all I was looking for."

Trey lowered his voice and said to Bill, "I am almost certain the man you know as Dan Moran is Luke Hampton's younger brother, Danny Hampton. Other men, as well as Dan the mountain man, have been searching for you for quite some time. Dan is seeking for the revenge that his father, Tom Hampton, never got before he died."

"I have always had a feeling someone was still tracking me."

Grandma Jo yelled from the kitchen, "Supper is on the table. Get it while it's hot or out the door to the pups it goes." Both dogs raised their heads as if waiting for the food to come flying out the door but lowered them disappointingly when the food did not fly out. Trey and his Granddad Bill both sat down at the table. As usual, Jo had fixed way more food than they could eat, but Trey would eat all he could; her meals were never disappointing.

"When I stepped out to fill your glasses, I heard you mention that you met a lady in Hardwood?"

"Yes, for no longer than I was there. I think she and I became attracted to each other."

"Do you think it is serious?" Jo asked.

"I don't know. We are making plans for her to come and visit me in LA sometime next month. Depending on how much time she has, I may bring her here to get a taste of real home cooking."

"That would be wonderful." As they ate, Trey told them about the people he had spoken to and about the organized crime that appeared to have been going on even when his grandparents lived back there. They were not too shocked to hear about the crime. Even at their young age back then, they both had heard stories about the making and transporting of moonshine out of Hardwood. They just didn't think it would still be going on. Trey told them it was mostly drugs nowadays and he had given one of his friends with the FBI all the information he had, and his friend was looking into it.

They finished their evening meal, and Jo had gotten each of them a cup of coffee and sat back down at the table.

"You mentioned you had found something that you wanted to talk to us about." Trey opened his small briefcase.

"Yes, but first, can I have a look at the pocketknife your brother Sam gave you to give to grandpa Bill?"

Puzzled, Bill and Jo both looked at him, and Jo said, "I will get it."

She came back to the room and laid the small box on the table. Trey opened it and took a long look at the handle. He took out his phone and tapped on the photos he had taken of the hunting knife that was in the evidence box at the Hardwood courthouse and compared them. The carvings on the handle appeared to be exactly the same. He then opened the pocketknife so that the blade was out, and where the blade was attached to the handle, there was a stamped number; it read "73415B." Trey then looked at the close-up photo he had taken of the fixed-bladed hunting knife; it read "73415A," both blades had "W. R. Case Co." stamped on them.

Trey told them, "Fingerprinting started around 1892, but for small towns like Hardwood back then, they simply did not have the expertise or a big data base to compare with, so prints were not taken from the knife nor the pistol." Bill sat there and said nothing. When Trey glanced at his grandma Jo, she had a look of shock on her face.

"What do you think the numbers mean?" Bill asked.

"The numbers on the knives are in sequence, so it would appear Sam's dad bought them as a set and gave them to Sam."

Trey looked at his Grandma Jo and said, "You told me before you left Hardwood years ago that your brother gave you this pocketknife to give to Grandpa Bill to remember him by, right?" Jo said nothing. "Do you know if Sam kept the hunting knife?" Trey questioned his grandmother.

Bill asked Trey, "Do you think Sam killed Luke Hampton?"

Trey shook his head, no. "I don't know what to think. You told me Sam dropped you off, and then he drove home. According to the trial transcript, Sam told the court he was back home in thirty minutes after dropping you off, and his father and a store clerk confirmed that. I don't think Sam would have had time."

Nothing was said for several minutes, then Trey saw that his Grandma Jo had tears running down her face. He knew something was wrong.

"Do you know something that will help us figure this out?" Trey asked.

"Yes." Through her sobbing she said, "I killed Luke Hampton." Putting a hand towel to her face she began to cry uncontrollably.

After a bit, Bill said, "I don't believe it. You are covering for your brother."

"No!" Then in a very determined voice she repeated, "I killed Luke."

Trey did not know what to say, except, "Do you want to tell us about it?"

After a minute or two, Jo's crying slowed enough so that she could talk.

"I am so sorry. I have held this in for all these years, knowing that someday, somehow, it would come out. I'll tell you what happened"

She was looking at Bill.

"I wanted so much to tell you. I just did not have the nerve. I wanted the truth out before either of us died. I'm so thankful our grandson is the one that has helped me with this."

"You should have told me a long time ago!" Bill exclaimed.

Trey spoke up, "What is done is done. It's in the past now and cannot be changed. All we can do is forgive and go on with life with forgiveness."

Trey could tell his grandfather was getting upset, and he was trying to think of some way to calm the tension that seemed to be building.

"Can you want to tell us what happened?"

Jo said between the sobs, "I will as best as I can remember.

I was in town and overheard Luke and Matt talking about Luke going to the cabin in the afternoon and he was going to take Sarah one way or another while you were at work. Matt said he would drop Luke off at the cabin, then go back to the sawmill to make sure you and my brother did not leave until late in the day so Luke could be with Sarah. I did not know what to do, so I went home and got Sam's hunting knife and walked to your cabin and waited in the back. I heard Matt's truck stop and watched from the bushes as Luke got out and Matt drove off. I heard Luke and Sarah arguing then I heard Sarah scream so I crawled to a window and looked in. I saw Luke on top of Sarah then he got up and started getting dressed. I started to go into the house when Sam pulled up, and you got out. I crouched down as best I could and ran into the bushes along the trail behind your house. The next thing I heard were gunshots. I ran further down the trail into the woods and hid. I saw Luke running down the trail toward me. I saw you further back up the trail running after Luke, you shot just as he was coming around the curve in the trail straight toward me. He was right on me when I jumped up and stabbed him with the knife. Then I ran off into the woods and hid."

Jo started to cry again, and through her sobbing, she said, "Even though you were married to Sarah, I still loved you. I killed Luke for what he had done to Sarah and you."

Bill was stunned beyond being able to speak.

Trey asked, "Did you intend on killing Luke?"

"No, he just stopped right in front of me with a startled look. I thought he was going to kill me, so I jumped up, and before he knew it, I stabbed him."

She looked at her husband. "I don't think he knew what I had just done. He just looked at me, then fell to his knees. I heard you running toward us, so I ran into the woods, hid, and waited until you had left, then I ran home."

"Why didn't you tell this to the sheriff, that you thought Luke would kill you?" Bill asked.

"Do you think the sheriff would have believed me if I had told him Luke knew what I saw and heard and would have killed me if I hadn't killed him first?"

"Did Sam know what you did?"

"No. If they found you guilty and sentenced you to death, I was going to tell the sheriff what I did. When the jury found you guilty and you got a life sentence, Sam and I started planning a way to get you out."

"So, after I had told Sam I was training the prison tracking hounds, that was when you and Sam came up with a plan to help me escape using Ole Red."

"That's right. I only came to visit a couple of times because I felt so guilty about you being in there for a crime you did not commit. I am so sorry that you spent those terrible couple of years in there."

Bill got up and walked over to her.

"All these years, you have held this inside. I watched you raise my daughter like she was your own. I have been blessed to have had you by my side all these years. There is nothing for you to be sorry about, you did what you did out of love, and I love you for that."

Bill helped Jo up, and they held each other for a long time. Trey looked at his grandparents holding each other and thought, *this is true love.* He had rarely seen his parents hug like that and hoped someday, he too, could find that kind of love.

They all dried their eyes, and Jo filled their cups with fresh coffee.

"Now that the mystery has been solved, we need to think about Dan Moran, or Hampton and what to do about him."

"You said you saw him in Hardwood, do you think he is back here now?" Bill asked.

"I'm not sure. I will call Janice and have her brother Jack check and let me know. Jack is the one who told me Dan Moran was really Danny Hampton. It is getting too late to call, I will call her in the morning, and we can work on a plan on how to get Dan behind bars."

They said their good nights, and Jo said, "There will be a good breakfast in the morning."

CHAPTER 23

⁓

Tracking Down Dan Moran

The next morning Trey settled in his room and called Janice. She was so glad to hear from him and that he was with his grandparents. Bill asked her to check with Jack to see if Dan Hampton was still in town and get back with him as soon as she could. Janice told Trey that his FBI friend, along with several other agents, had come to town two days earlier and had arrested several people, including Mark Benson, the president of the Hardwood National Bank, and Henry Hampton, the manager of the Hampton Lumber and Sawmill Company. There were a few other local businessmen that were also arrested. Janice said it looked like the FBI was cleaning up the town. She had not heard if Dan Hampton had been arrested but was guessing he had not.

"After the FBI gathered up all the people and put them on buses, your friend with the FBI stopped by and wanted me to tell you hello and thanks for the information. It was all they needed to stop this organization in its tracks and to keep it from expanding. They knew something was going on in this part of the country and wanted to put an end to it, and now they had." She and Trey spoke a little more about her trip to LA. She would have Jack call him as soon as he could to let him know if Dan Hampton was still around. Trey told her how he missed spending time with her and would see her soon.

Trey hung up the phone and got a smell of breakfast coming from the kitchen. He got dressed and hurried into the kitchen where Grandma Jo was cooking.

"As always, it smells great," he said as he got a cup of coffee and sat down at the table. Bill walked into the room from outside, sat down at the table, and told them that he had been on the porch rocking, drinking coffee, and talking to the pups, thinking about what to do about Dan Hampton.

"Did the pups have any good ideas?" Jo asked.

"No, they aren't fully awake yet. Maybe after their breakfast, they will have some good ideas."

"I just got off the phone with Janice and she said the FBI had rounded up most of the people involved in the crime around Hardwood, and they were being bussed to Atlanta."

"That's good to hear. What about Dan?" Bill asked.

"She did not know if he had been caught. She would have her brother Jack check around and call me if he finds out anything." With breakfast finished, Bill and Trey filled their coffee cups, went to the porch and took their positions in the rockers and began the all-important rhythmic rocking so they could think and talk. Trey's cell phone rang, it was Janice.

"Jack told me Dan had not been caught in the raids, and no one has seen him for several days." Trey's first thought was that Dan has probably come back to Hillside; this made him nervous.

Trey said to his granddad, "Dan is not around Hardwood. I would guess he recognized me when we saw each other the morning I was leaving town, and he probably has made it back to here."

"Do you think we should look for him or let him find us?"

"I think we need to be vigilant and watch for him. I will call my FBI friend and tell him where I am and that Dan Moran or Hampton is probably around here. I will also tell him that I think Dan killed Grandma Jo's friend Tammy Lou Watkins Brown in Ocoee, Tennessee."

"What makes you think Dan killed Tammy?"

"When I went to Ocoee, I found out from the county sheriff's deputy that Tammy had been killed. He told me some of her fingers had been cut off before she died. Back in Hardwood, I learned this was the tactic Dan used to extract information from someone or to set an example. Last night, I did not want to say anything about

Grandma Jo's friend Tammy being dead or how she died. There was enough going on with her telling us she killed Luke. While in Ocoee, I asked around and found Tammy's younger sister. I went to her house and spoke with her." Trey stopped talking and took a sip of coffee. He needed to think about how he was going to tell Bill about the letters that Jo had sent to her friend Tammy. He did not want his grandfather getting angry with his grandmother about sending letters when he had asked her not to. After a sip or two and a few more rocks, Trey began talking again.

"I also need to tell you about what Tammy's sister showed me, and I do not want you getting angry with Grandma Jo. She is remorseful enough after telling us about killing Luke."

"I won't. I don't want her feeling any worse than she does." Trey started telling his Grandpa Bill about Tammy's younger sister, Betty.

"Betty knew about Bobbie Jo, but she was young when Grandma Jo and Tammy were friends back in Ocoee. She knew that her sister missed Bobbie Jo very much, and they wrote back and forth often. Over the years, Tammy had kept the letters from Grandma Jo in a shoebox. When the police finally let Betty go into her sister's house after the crime scene had been gone over, Betty saw the house had been torn apart, as if someone was looking for something. Betty told me that Tammy kept the letters from Grandma Jo in a shoebox and it was on the table with envelopes and letters scattered all over. All the envelopes were open, most of them still having letters in them, but a few envelopes were empty. Betty had collected everything and put them back in the shoebox and gave it to me to give to Grandma Jo. I have the shoebox and will give it to Grandma Jo and tell her about Tammy after things settle down." Trey continued telling his granddad that Dan tortured her until she finally told him that she had been writing to Bobbie Jo and about the shoebox. Then Dan killed her and started looking through the shoebox for more information as to where you were.

Trey took another sip of coffee.

"When I got back to LA, I pulled out the envelopes and sorted them by the postmark date. I read some of the letters from the envelopes with the oldest postmark first. Nothing in them mentioned anything about where you and Grandma lived, just how you and she were doing and how the two of you had settled in and that my mother, Sally Ann, was growing and enjoying the country life. In one letter, Grandma wrote about the cabin the two of you had built on the side of Lookout Mountain and how my mother enjoyed running around playing with Ole Red. I read through a few more letters, and in one, Grandma Jo wrote that my mother, Sally Ann, had died, and her funeral was here at the cabin, and a few people from Hillside attended. Grandma Jo wrote that it was the saddest day of your lives. I suspect Dan looked at the postmark on the envelopes and saw they were from Idaho and looked through the letters trying to find out more information as to where you were exactly. He took some of the letters with him because some of the envelopes were empty. I suspect the letters mentioned Hillside or some other reference as to where you two lived, and Dan came here, got a place, and started tracking you down by asking questions around town. I don't think he knew for sure that you were Billy Bersha from Hardwood until he saw me in Hardwood last week."

"You're some kind of detective. Wish I had had you back in Hardwood on my murder case."

Just as Bill finished saying this, they heard a gunshot, and the glass in the window shattered just behind Bill's head. Trey yelled, "Get down on the floor!" Bill and Trey fell out of the rockers onto the porch floor. Trey listened for another shot; there was none. He yelled to his Grandma Jo and told her to stay in the kitchen and away from the windows. Trey told Bill to stay down while he crawled back into the cabin to get his pistol.

"A pistol is no good at a distance. My rifle is in the closet behind the kitchen door, it is loaded and there are shells on the shelf." Trey crawled in, found the rifle and shells, and peeked outside from the lower corner of the broken kitchen window; he saw nothing. Hearing the glass break, the pups jumped from the porch and hid under it. They were not afraid of gunshots but were not used to glass breaking above them.

"Bill, can you see anything?"

"No, I have a good view of the woods from here and I see no one." The porch was on the east side of the cabin where Bill was.

Trey crawled to the other kitchen window that faced the north and looked out.

Trey whispered, hoping Bill could hear him, "I saw someone running back into the woods on the north side of the cabin. Stay as low as you can and try to crawl back into the kitchen." Bill did as he was told and shut the kitchen door behind him after he got inside. They pulled the kitchen curtains closed, and all three sat on the floor, breathing harder than usual.

"How long do you think we should stay down here?" Jo asked. Trey did not want to answer but knew they could not stay on the floor forever.

"I think with the curtains pulled together, it will be hard for anyone to see in. It should be okay to stand up." All three got up and sat at the table.

"Well, guess we all know where Dan is now," Bill said.

"I would like to think so, but it is possible he has sent someone to do his dirty work for him, while he stays low since the FBI is now involved back in Hardwood."

"I remember Danny Hampton back in Hardwood. He was about ten or twelve years younger than me, and he was a mean kid. He was always picking on the other kids, sometimes even using sticks or tool handles to beat them. His older brother, Luke, would urge him on to hit harder, so I don't think Dan is going to have anyone try to take care of this other than himself."

"You're probably right, Grandpa."

"I am going to call my friend with the FBI and tell him what is going on here. I am sure he will want to know where Dan is."

After their breathing slowed and things seemed to settle down, Trey pulled out his phone and called his FBI friend and told him where he was at, what had happened, and that he was fairly certain it had been Danny Hampton. Trey's friend told him that he would get in touch with the FBI office in Spokane because it was the closest and would have people in Hillside first thing in the morning. Trey thanked him for his help and told his grandparents that the FBI would be in Hillside in the morning.

"Do you think Dan will still be around, he might try later today or in the morning what he did not get done this morning?" Bill asked.

Trey thought about this and the safety of his grandparents and himself.

"I don't know, but it is very possible Dan heard what the FBI did in Hardwood, so he probably knows I have contacted them and told them about his shooting at us here."

"I'm not one to sit around and wait to be shot at," Bill said. Trey saw the determination in his grandfather's eyes.

"You trained tracking dogs most of your life. How are Hunter and Tracker at tracking down a human?"

"They have never tracked a human before, but I have confidence they can do it. They are American Fox Hounds that are known for their excellent sense of smell. I have a sack in the shed that Dan gave me a few weeks back that should still have his scent on it. Let's see if the pups can pick up Dan's scent where he ran into the woods north of the cabin. It's only been a little while since you saw him running into the woods, so let's get going."

Jo spoke up, "I think it is better to wait for the FBI."

"Dan is on a revenge mission for the death of his brother, and I will not let him keep us in fear any longer. He thinks I killed his brother, Luke, for what he did to Sarah Lou, so now it's my turn for revenge." Trey did not want to go tracking down a man with an attitude of revenge; it clouds your thinking, but he was not going to argue with his granddad.

Bill got the sack from the shed and called Hunter and Tracker; they came out from under the porch with their tails wagging. Bill waved the sack in front of the dogs. They all walked to the edge of the woods where Dan had gone in. Bill held the sack down so the dogs could get another good sniff and lock in on Dan's scent. "Track 'em, girls," he said. The dogs put their heads down, and off they went into the woods. It appeared as if Dan was running along a narrow trail that Bill and the dogs took to go hunting in the woods, which made it easy going for them.

Bill said to Trey as they were jogging along. "Just ahead was a small clearing where the trail splits. Looks like Dan is doing the same thing his brother Luke did years ago, Dan took the trail that leads deeper into the forest instead of the one that leads to the river, it will be harder for him to run."

The dogs did not hesitate a bit, as they kept their heads down and stayed on the trail leading into the forest. They had not been howling as much as they ran, but now they started to bark and howl in a different manner.

Trey asked Bill as they were slowly running, "What does that mean?"

Bill, a little out of breath, answered, "They are getting a fresher scent. They are closing in on him, and we need to get to the dogs before they catch up to him."

"I don't want Dan shooting the dogs if they corner him," Trey said.

Bill, too, was a little worried that Dan would stop and try to shoot them, then they both heard a gunshot. They did not hear any type of howl as if one of the dogs may have been hit but heard louder barks, howls, and growling.

Bill said, "They have him." Bill and Trey picked up their pace, and when they rounded a bend in the trail, they saw Dan trying to climb a small tree with the dogs grabbing and pulling on his pants leg. Dan had dropped his rifle while trying to climb the tree. He saw Trey and Bill and knew he had been caught.

Bill called off the dogs. "Climb down. You're under arrest," Trey said with as much authority as he could muster.

"You don't have the authority to arrest me, and if so, on what charge?" Trey responded by pulling out his private investigator badge, "Sorry, but I do have the authority, and you are under arrest for the murder of Tammy Lou Brown and attempted murder of Bill Bersha." Dan climbed down without answering. Trey knew he did not have the authority to arrest, but Dan did not know that. Trey had put a couple of zip ties in his pocket just in case they found Dan and needed to handcuff him. He told Dan to hold out his hands while Bill kept the rifle pointed at him.

"If he tries to resist, shoot him."

"Gladly," and Bill remembered a comment in one of the old movies he and Jo had watched which said, "Go ahead, make my day." Trey looked at his grandpa and grinned. They turned and started back to the cabin, Dan leading the way with the dogs close behind him.

At the cabin, Trey called his friend with the FBI and told them he had caught Dan Hampton and was taking him to the Hillside Police Department to lock him up. They could pick him up tomorrow. Trey put Dan in the back seat, secured his feet with another zip tie, and told his grandparents he would be back shortly. He then reached down and gave Hunter and Tracker each a pat on the head, who were both still watching Dan in the back seat.

"Good job, pups. You're a chip off Ole Red." Trey arrived at the Hillside Police Station and told them who he was and what had happened. They would keep Dan until the FBI picked him up in the morning.

When Trey got back to his grandparents' cabin, Jo had lunch prepared and waiting. Trey was glad because he was hungry and ready to eat. They all sat down at the table, and Jo said a prayer thanking God for watching over Bill, Trey, and the pups and keeping them safe.

After finishing lunch, Trey broke the silence. He said, "After dropping Dan off at the jail, I called my friend with the FBI and told him about some other crimes I thought Dan Moran or Danny Hampton had a hand in, and he would definitely look into it using the information I gave him."

"What other crimes?" Jo asked.

Trey stood up and said he had something to give Jo. He went to his room and came back with an old shoebox and gave it to Jo.

"I went to Ocoee to try and find your friend Tammy but found out that she had died. I spoke with her sister, Betty, and she gave me this shoebox of letters from you and wanted me to give them to you since you were Tammy's best friend."

"Tammy is deceased?"

"Yes, she was murdered. I think Dan did it. I am sure with the information I gave the FBI; they will have enough to prove he did it. I also think he or his partner set fire to your house back in Hardwood that killed your family. And he may have had something to do with the car wreck that killed Mr. and Mrs. Smith. Although he would have been fairly young when that happened, which is why I'm not sure."

Jo was clutching the shoebox while listening to Trey.

"Do you think he used the letters to track us down?"

"I am not sure." He saw that she was squeezing the box, tears running down her cheeks.

He changed the subject. "I have never seen such good tracking dogs. You trained them well," Trey said.

"They are good. I didn't know how good until today. It will take a special hound to beat Ole Red, though, he was the best. Hunter and Tracker are in his league. I sure miss that old dog and am so grateful that he saved my life, as I am grateful for you two as well," Bill said as he looked at the screen door where the pups were looking in.

Trey saw that his granddad was getting emotional.

"I didn't mean to bring up old sad memories."

"That's okay. It is sad that he is gone but good to remember him." They continued to visit a while longer, and Trey told them about the Smiths car accident and that he would be heading back to Spokane in the morning to catch his flight back to LA and to make plans for Janice to come to visit him. He told them he had become very fond of her and could not wait for her to come to LA.

"If she has time, you need to bring her here. We would love to meet her," Jo said.

"I would love for her to meet you, Grandpa Bill, and the pups." He did not know how his grandparents would react to him wanting them to meet Janice. Now he knew. He was glad Jo had suggested it.

CHAPTER 24

Janice's Visit; Romance in the Air

Back in LA and rested up, Trey called Janice. He told her he and his grandparents were fine and he said they were anxious to meet her. She was glad he was safe, and they decided on a day for her to fly to LA for a visit. Trey said he would take care of the flight, and she would be flying out of Jacksonville. She had never flown but was looking forward to it. She would have Jack take her to the airport since he was familiar with Jacksonville. Trey told her if she had time and wouldn't mind, he would like for her to meet his grandparents. She said she would be happy to meet them and she could see more of the country. He decided to wait and tell her in person his real reason for being in Hardwood and all that had happened in his grandparents' younger years. That would give them something to talk about if things got awkward and he ran out of things to say. He was not used to being with a woman for longer than a few hours on a date, so he was nervous about keeping her entertained the entire time she was there.

Trey made the flight reservation the next morning, then went around his condo picking up things and rearranging some items that he thought looked out of place. He decided to have someone come in and do a deep cleaning to be on the safe side; he simply wanted to impress Janice. He called his grandparents and told them when she was coming and what day they would be coming up for a visit. Bill and Jo were pleased that Trey felt at ease enough to bring her for a visit and were looking forward to it. Trey decided to contact his dad and update him on what had been going on in his life. It took a few tries to finally reach him, due to his job and traveling. He said with his job now there was more travel and he had just gotten back in town. Trey wanted to see him, but every time he suggested a time and place to meet, his father seemed to always have other plans. Trey told him a short version about Bill and his past along with a few of the things that had happened, and his father seemed unconcerned and only said he always knew Bill was hiding or running from something, and he cut their conversation short. Trey decided if his father wanted to keep in touch in the future, he would let his father contact him. It troubled him to realize his father wasn't that interested, but he would make do with or without his father's blessings.

The day finally came when he picked Janice up at the airport. She looked better than he had remembered. She gave him a kiss and a big hug. As he drove to his condo, Janice was taking in all she could.

Trey asked, "How was your flight?"

"It was a little scary, being my first time. I think I held onto and squeezed the armrests for most of the flight. Other than being afraid of getting lost when I changed planes in Atlanta and my hands being tried, watching the ground go by was amazing. You can see for miles up that high. This town is so big."

"It is easy to get lost if you do not pay attention." Trey drove several miles with Janice, continually asking questions until they finally reached the exit off the freeway that would take them into the area where his condo was. He pulled to a stop.

Janice looked at the condo. "This is nice."

He asked her, "Are you sure you want to stay here? I can take you to a motel if you would feel more comfortable?"

"No, I'm okay staying here if you are."

"Great." Trey said, taking her luggage from the car. He unlocked the front door and invited her in. Janice looked pleased.

"This is better than a motel room. I'll stay here for sure." Trey took her bags to the guest bedroom and showed her around the condo so she would know where everything was. The flight had taken most of the day, and Trey could see she was tired. "Would you like me to order Chinese for supper?"

"Sure, sound good, I have only had it a couple of times when Jack has taken me to Jacksonville to do some shopping." Trey realized that Hardwood did not have a Chinese restaurant, and she probably had not had that many chances to try it.

"I will order some dishes that you might like and have them delivered."

Janice, with a puzzled expression looked at him.

"It is fairly common out here for people to have food brought to their homes instead of going out. I promise, I will take you out to a good seafood place just off the beach, it is one of my favorites."

The food arrived, Janice tasted everything he had ordered and finally said, "I'm filled up, it was great." They talked while Trey did what little cleaning up there was to do. He told her it had been a long day for her and that there were fresh towels in the guest bathroom, and she should make herself at home. She thanked him for the meal and for inviting her to LA to spend some time with him. She walked over to him and gave him a kiss.

"You are the sweetest man I have ever met," she said and then turned and headed to her room. Trey got a beer out of the fridge, sat down at the kitchen table, and thought about where this relationship was headed. He had never felt this way about a woman. He wondered if she was the one. He finished his beer and went to his room to read if he could.

The next day, Trey drove Janice around to see some of the sights, and by the evening, he had ended up at his favorite seafood restaurant, where they enjoyed a nice evening meal, talked about their lives and the people in them. It was still early in the evening.

"Let's take a walk along the beach," Trey suggested, and she agreed. He bought two bottles of beer, and off they went. They sat down at a wooden park table at the water's edge. Trey began telling her the real reason he was in Hardwood. He told her about his grand-dad Billy Bersha from Hardwood, about him being in prison, his escape using Ole Red and about how he and his granddad found out from his Grandma Jo that she was the one who killed Luke Hampton and how they felt as if someone was still looking for them. He told her about Danny Hampton, his capture, and that he had murdered Jo's best friend, Tammy, in Ocoee, Tennessee, and more than likely had set the fire that burnt down the Williamson house several years ago. Janice took it all in, very seldom interrupting. She was totally captivated by him and his story. With the beers finished and the night getting late, he drove back to his condo. Trey asked if she needed anything, and she answered no.

She walked over to him, took his hands, looked into his eyes, and asked, "Are you feeling the same thing I am?"

Trey responded, "Yes, I am, it would be nice. I don't want you to be offended, but I think we should spend a little more time together getting to know one another."

Janice said, "I was thinking the same thing. Let's give this a little more time." He kissed her; she turned and headed for her room. Trey went to his bedroom, a little disappointed but for some reason not angry, but pleasantly happy.

Janice was taking ten days off. They had several days before her flight back to Georgia. The next morning, Trey fixed breakfast, and he asked her if she still would like to meet his grandparents, and if so, then they could fly to Spokane, then drive the rest of the way. She said it sounds fine and by flying, they will have more time with them. Trey was pleased and excited for her to meet them. After breakfast, he called and was able to book a flight to Spokane, which left early the next morning. This gave them the rest of the day. He took her to see downtown LA then out to see the famous Hollywood billboard sign. He did not think she was that impressed with the sign, but she did seem amazed at the buildings downtown. He drove them to a winery outside of LA where they had lunch, then drove back to his condo. He ordered a pizza and had it delivered for the evening meal while watching a movie that Trey thought she would like, which she did. After the movie they drank a couple of glasses of wine and they both seemed to be totally relaxed just talking about anything and everything. Trey told her about trying to meet with his dad, who seemed uninterested in what was going on in his life. Janice told Trey he was lucky. At least he did know his father. Trey remembered her telling him back in Hardwood about her father leaving her mother and he felt a little embarrassed and changed the subject.

"I shouldn't ask this, but do you ever think about getting married and having children?"

"Sometimes. But there are not a lot of choices in Hardwood and I am getting a little old for children. How about you?"

"Not really. I dated a few women, mostly from around the office at work. All we had in common was law enforcement, and after being around it all day, the last thing I wanted to talk about was detective work, and I too am probably getting too old for children."

"Sounds like we both may be meant to be loners."

"Maybe so, but I hope not." Trey wanted to end this conversation, so he suggested they head to bed since it was going to be an early flight in the morning. He started cleaning up the kitchen, and Janice helped.

"Looks like that is it. I will see you bright and early in the morning." As she walked to her bedroom, Trey wondered if he had offended her in some way since she did not give him a good night kiss. Had he scared her off by talking about marriage and children? He would have to make his conversational topics a little less personal for the time being.

While waiting for their flight, Janice seemed a little anxious.

"You, okay?"

"Yeah, just a little nervous about flying again."

"We can cancel, and I can drive us."

"No, you have already paid for it, and I want to spend more time with your grandparents."

"What about me?"

"Oh, I can probably fit you into my schedule."

"That would be nice."

As the plane took off, Janice grabbed Trey's wrist and started to squeeze it. Her nails were digging into his skin, but he seemed to enjoy the pain for some reason. He thought to himself, *she is trusting and depending on me*, which felt good to him. She was sitting in the window seat and taking in all she could. Trey did not want to bother

her with a conversation. He was glad she had relaxed somewhat and was enjoying the view, and had stopped squeezing his arm.

After a couple of hours, they landed, and Trey rented a car. Before leaving the parking lot, Trey called and told Jo that they would be there in a few hours.

Trey turned onto the gravel road leading to his grandparents' cabin. When he rounded the curve, and the cabin came into sight, Janice said, "This looks like a postcard picture of a country cabin. It's lovely."

"I thought the same thing when I first saw it."

"I think I see your grandparents in the rockers on the porch."

"Yeah, that's their favorite place."

"I can see why. It is so beautiful and peaceful."

Trey introduced Janice to his grandparents, and Jo gave her a big hug and invited them in as supper was waiting.

"This place is gorgeous, and I could smell your cooking a mile down the road."

"Hope you enjoy it. Trey seems to."

"It looks delicious."

They ate while Janice told them about how Hardwood had changed over the years. Bill and Jo were full of questions about their old hometown. Janice was delighted to answer every question about what had happened to the people they knew when they lived back there. The evening flew by, and Jo finally suggested that they turn in. Trey was a little nervous about him and Janice sleeping in the same room and bed. He wondered, what would his grandparents think. Trey knew his grandparents knew he and Janice were adults and that they would never purposefully make them feel uncomfortable so Trey guessed that was why they had set up a small extra bed in the room.

Jo had breakfast ready and was waiting when Trey came into the kitchen.

"Grandpa Bill is on the porch, as usual, talking to those pups about the capture of Dan and bragging about how good trackers they are."

"I figured as much since I did not see him here. I'll join him so I can listen in on the conversation."

"Good morning," Janice said to Jo as she walked in and got herself a cup of coffee. Jo was glad that Janice felt at home enough to help herself.

"Did you sleep well?"

"Yes, it was one of the best night's sleep I have had in a long time. And to wake up to these wonderful smells is something I will never forget."

"Trey says the same thing, and we are so glad you two are here together to enjoy it. I know it is none of my business, and I don't want to pry into your personal life, but it seems to me that there is more than just you and Trey being friends."

"We haven't known each other very long, but I hope he feels the same way as I do and that it is more than just a casual friendship. I think I have fallen in love with your grandson."

Janice turned to sit down at the table and saw Trey standing in the doorway after she had just told Jo how she felt. A smile appeared on Trey's face. He walked over to Janice, leaned down, and kissed her.

"I fell in love with you the first day we met."

"Well, I guess that's settled," Jo said, "let's eat." She yelled at Bill to come in. "Pups, stay outside."

Bill sat down at the table.

"I told them they could eat in the kitchen for doing such a good job tracking down old Dan."

"Well, after you get through eating, you can take some scraps out and explain to them, even though they are the best trackers in the country, they are still dogs. They eat outside."

Bill looked at Janice and said, "Guess Trey told you all about us, and how the love of a woman got me put in prison and how the love from one wonderful woman and one dog name Ole Red, got me out?"

"Yes, he did. It was some story. Since he told everyone back in Hardwood, he was doing research for a book he was thinking about writing, I think he should write the book. It would be an interesting read."

They finished breakfast, and Bill put some scraps on a plate and saw the pups looking through the screen door.

"I sure hope they will understand why they can't eat in the kitchen. I will have to explain to them how *love got me in* and *love got me out,* but they still have to eat outside."

Bill and Jo looked at each other, grinned, and both shook their heads yes.

Bill had put two extra chairs on the porch so all four could sit on the porch. With two of them rocking, they discussed, with some tears and laughter, all that had taken place over the last few weeks. Around midmorning, Trey and Janice said their goodbyes and drove off, headed for Spokane to catch their flight back to LA.

On their drive, Janice and Trey talked about their future together. Janice asked Trey if he was going to tell the authorities about his Grandmother Jo being the person that killed Luke Hampton. Trey had decided not to say anything. He thought his grandparents had suffered enough over the years, and as the old saying goes, "let a sleeping dog lie." Janice agreed.

She then said to Trey. "Even though there was danger, it seems as though you enjoyed solving the mystery as to who murdered Luke Hampton."

"That I did. I have always loved solving a crime, guess that is why I enjoyed being a detective. Solving this one was especially enjoyable, being it was so old and helping my grandparents."

"Maybe you should think about looking into other old unsolved murders or crimes?"

"I will have to think about that; besides I don't know of any old unsolved case."

"Well maybe if you come back to Hardwood in a couple of months for a short visit, I can give you a couple of old files my grandfather was working on that he never got to finish, they might pique your interest. You may be able to solve them like you solved this one and help people easy their minds and suffering."

"Sounds good to me, and I may find my future bride there as well."